T0196076

Other novels by the same author:

The Embracer

Shaya

Alternating Worlds

Workshop of the Second Self

THE KICKER OF
ST. JOHN'S WOOD

Gary Wolf

iUniverse, Inc.
New York   Bloomington

The Kicker of St. John's Wood

iUniverse books may be ordered through booksellers or by contacting:

iUniverse
1663 Liberty Drive
Bloomington, IN 47403
www.iuniverse.com
1-800-Authors (1-800-288-4677)

Because of the dynamic nature of the Internet, any Web addresses or links contained in this book may have changed since publication and may no longer be valid. The views expressed in this work are solely those of the author and do not necessarily reflect the views of the publisher, and the publisher hereby disclaims any responsibility for them.

ISBN: 978-1-4401-2509-6 (pbk)
ISBN: 978-1-4401-2510-2 (ebk)

Printed in the United States of America

iUniverse rev. date: 05/08/2009

Acknowledgment

▼

The author would like to thank his parents, Don and Riva Wolf, for their unwavering support during the writing of this book. It was critical to the completion of the project.

I have often noticed that there are good and honest citizens in Athens, who are as old gold is to new money. The ancient coins are excellent in point of standard; they are assuredly the best of all moneys; they alone are well struck and give a pure ring; everywhere they obtain currency, both in Greece and in foreign lands; yet we make no use of them and prefer those bad copper pieces quite recently issued and so wretchedly struck. Exactly the same way do we deal with our citizens...

Madmen, do change your ways at last; employ the honest men afresh; if you are fortunate through doing this, 'twill be but right, and if Fate betrays you, the wise will at least praise you for having fallen honorably.

—Aristophanes

CHAPTER ONE

▼

What was simply extraordinary about that field goal with two seconds left on the clock was not the distance, as one might have expected. I had kicked several shots that season from over fifty yards, clearing the uprights with room to spare. No, it was rather a mental image, clear as the light of day. It was my grandfather's face; his kind, serene countenance, almost as vivid as if he were there in person. "Jayesh, my boy," I recalled him saying, "to accomplish anything in life, you must realize that success depends greatly on relaxation and concentration, and the two go hand in hand." Years of similar enlightenment from his lips had prepared me for that stressful moment, enabling me to maintain total calm despite the roar of seventy thousand fans and the fact that the outcome of the game now depended on the angle and thrust of five toes connecting with a piece of leather.

My arms dangling loosely at my sides, my back arched forward, I awaited the snap of the ball. Gonzales the holder barked the count, enunciating several decoy words before uttering the decisive *hut* that brought the pigskin flying toward him. I launched myself into the two-step that resulted in my right leg pounding away with full force, lifting me briefly off the ground. It was not necessary to see the ball's flight, for my eyes merely confirmed an inner sense that the kick was perfect, gloriously splitting the uprights from fifty-six yards out.

What happened next came so fast that all I remember is seeing the tight end Barton shrieking from behind his face mask as he leaped in the air, and then it seemed that in the same moment I was on the ground covered by a pile of bodies, writhing every which way like worms released from a can. It would be egotistical of me to claim that such an outburst of joy could result from my having broken the record for most consecutive field goals. It certainly boosted the celebratory energy, but the primary cause was that we had just won the last game of the regular season and had clinched the division.

Much as I shared the common sentiment of the moment, I was soon having trouble breathing, which somewhat dampened my enthusiasm. Luckily, Hubbard, one of our big offensive tackles, sensed the danger and began pulling bodies from the pile. The second I saw the sky, I was being hoisted in the air, and found myself perched on Hubbard's huge shoulders. I'm no midget, six foot one, a hundred and ninety pounds, but next to this man-mountain I always felt like a toddler accidentally running into someone's leg. I inclined forward and said thank you, though I doubt if he heard it, what with the noise of the crowd, compounded by fireworks and electronic explosions emanating from the stadium loudspeakers.

A pulsating human throng, with me at its center, gravitated toward the tunnel at the corner of the end zone. Prominent in my memory is one woman, with green and orange war paint on her face, leaning over the railing just above us, hollering to the point of pain, her upper lip curled back to her nose. Maybe I just imagined it that way, but maybe not; the excitement of the occasion produced some remarkable contortions. It makes more sense when you consider that this was the first time that our team, the New Mexico Coyotes, had made it into the playoffs. After five long and miserable years, the young NFL franchise finally pulled itself together. During that season, 2019, everything functioned like clockwork.

Not that we didn't have some quality players from the outset. When the team was established, agents scoured the country looking for talent. They brought in some good material, including several players who were still with the Coyotes: the starting quarterback, Burt Stanwell; Thomas Hubbard, whom you already met; wide receiver Bill Harrison; and Thelonius Brown, the strong safety.

Brown had many laudable character traits, but he was drastically extroverted, at times quite over the top. He was proving it once again in the showers after the game. "Hey, Ja-*hesh*," he said, deliberately mispronouncing my name. "What's your secret? Do you pour curry oil all over your foot before you go out on the field?"

What good would it do to explain to him one more time that my only connection to India, aside from my first name, is that it happens to be my mother's native land. I never lived there, I don't speak any of the dialects, I'm not a Hindu, and we never ate curry at my house while I was growing up (my father hated it). But Brown was on a roll, his bravado exacerbated by the interception he returned for a touchdown in the third quarter.

Hubbard stepped into the shower between Brown and myself, effectively shielding me from further aggravation. This was a typical move on his part. From that very first season we played together six years previously, he had appointed himself my guardian angel. For all his three hundred and forty pounds, he was one of the gentlest human beings I have ever known. On the field, he hurled himself into the opposing players with a force that could damage a pickup truck. On the street, he would feel remorse for accidentally stepping on an ant.

I soaped and rinsed with great haste, grabbed a towel, and dried myself en route to my locker. This was one of my least favorite moments of football life. The sight of enormous, sweaty naked men, together with a stench that defies description, left me with a morose, sinking feeling, a sort of emotional claustrophobia. I hurriedly dressed myself and flew out of that malodorous swamp.

Upon exiting the locker room my path was blocked by the special teams coach, Joe Gramercy, who had an attractive young lady at his side. "Jayesh," he said, "I'd like you to meet Marcy Huddlewell, senior correspondent for the women's sports magazine *Breast of Iron*. Marcy, this is Jayesh Blackstone, our champion field-goal kicker."

"Nice to meet you."

"Nice to meet you."

"Could you spend a couple of minutes with Marcy in the press lounge?" asked Gramercy, knowing that I could hardly refuse.

Long experience had taught me that a couple of minutes with a reporter means at least half an hour. Well, I thought, at least it might save me from the crowd of autograph-seekers that inevitably congregated around the players' exit after a game. Gramercy escorted the two of us up to the lounge, located on the middle level of the stadium, next to the press boxes. We took the elevator, which deposited us a few steps from our destination. The coach opened the door and led us inside. The place was empty, aside from the bartender and two or three cleaning personnel.

I marveled at the swanky decor, so out of tune with the rest of the rather threadbare facility. Above our heads were huge, crystal-laden chandeliers; spread across the floor was a plush carpet. The seats in the booths were covered with a soft, luxurious leather, and the table-tops were a highly shellacked, golden-colored oak in which the rings of the tree were visible. Huddlewell and I parked ourselves in one of those booths. Gramercy went to the bar to order drinks for myself and the lady, and then quietly slipped out the door.

I was all alone with the *Breast of Iron* writer. She had fluffy blond hair, about shoulder length, and a nicely shaped figure. Despite the cool temperature, she was wearing a tank top, exposing her thin but muscular arms. Her left bicep featured a tattoo of a woman curling a barbell. As Huddlewell spread her papers and recording equipment on the table, she flashed a devious smile. I braced myself, knowing full well that there were only two types of journalist in the world: the sympathetic and the hostile. In the former case, they bend the story to make you look good; in the latter, they bend it to make you look bad.

"So, Jayesh," said Huddlewell, lifting her chin and sniffling quite audibly, "how does it feel to break the all-time consecutive field-goal record?"

"It feels good," I said, "and I could do it only because of the great players on the team, who clear the way for me, and of course our special teams coach, Joe Gramercy." I finally said it just the way our director of public relations had instructed me.

The sportswriter displayed an acerbic little pout. "That's really nice, Jayesh. Tell us a bit about yourself. Not the usual stuff that everyone knows. Something different."

The bartender arrived with our drinks. "I'm not sure what you're looking for," I said, taking a sip of my soda. "Could you be more specific?"

"Okay then, Mr. Blackstone, let's start with your life stats, and then we'll dig out something juicy. When exactly did you come here from India?"

"Uhh…I didn't come from India. I came from England, in the year 2000."

She looked perplexed. Her reaction was nothing I hadn't seen before. It's understandable, because I so look the part. I rectified the misunderstanding by reciting my standard biographical speech: "I was born and raised in London. My father is American, he was on assignment there for an American company when he met my mother, who comes from India. I am named after my mother's brother, who died just before I was born. I lived in the St. John's Wood section, I went to the American School, and then did my bachelor's degree in philosophy and English literature at Yale. I am now, and have always been, an American citizen."

"You never lived in India?"

"No. In fact, I visited only once, for about a week. My relatives there are quite distant. Most of my mother's family lives in Europe or the U.S."

"I see," said Huddlewell, looking disappointed. She shuffled some papers. "How does it feel to be the first star Indian player in American football?"

I felt blood rush to my head, and I almost took the bait. But, drawing upon my grandfather's priceless lessons, I imposed a state of relaxation on my body. "I wouldn't know," I answered, without displaying emotion.

"Okay," she said, in a tone of voice laced with impatience. "Now a question that will especially interest our readers. What would you say is your sexiest body part?"

"My toenail," I declared, surprising myself with the speed and alacrity of the response, something that doesn't occur with great regularity.

She sniffled, eyeing me up and down. "Would you agree that you have a cute little butt?"

I responded with an icy silence. Huddlewell's face settled into a smirk. I looked at my watch. She asked a few more football-related questions, trying to demonstrate technical knowledge. I answered with the necessary level of detail. We parted coldly but in a civil manner.

I found my way downstairs to the exit, and hurried across the players' parking lot. Dusk had begun to descend. A cool wind was blowing, bringing with it the refreshing scent of New Mexico's desert terrain. I breathed in deeply, feeling my overall level of tension decline a notch. As I was about to open the door of my car, I heard "Jayesh," and turned around to see our PR director, Hank Hannibal, half-run half-stumble his way toward me. His collar was soiled by the band of sweat and grit around his neck.

"Jayesh, I had to see you before you go," he said.

"Sure, Hank, what is it?"

"What did Marcy Huddlewell have to say?"

"How did you find out about that?"

"How long have you been playing on this team?" he countered. "You know that nothing happens with the media that I'm not aware of. So how was it?"

I was distracted by Hannibal's chin and forehead, which both protruded noticeably, giving his head a half-moon shape. "The interview was okay," I said. "I gave her your line about being indebted to the team and the coach. Things got a little tense, though, when she asked me about body parts."

"What do you expect?" said Hannibal, wearing a wry grin. "She's writing for her audience. Anyway, that's not what I came to discuss. Big things are happening for you, kiddo. I mean *big* things."

"How big?" I asked in a sarcastic manner, my mind wandering to the hot tub that awaited me at home.

"The White House," said Hannibal, dropping his grin and retracting the entire half-moon down into his collarbone. "That's how big."

"The White House?"

"Oh, now we're impressed," he said, taking a step back and waving his finger. "Nothing less than being a personal guest of President Vesica Malpomme."

"President Malpomme?" I said, not believing my ears. "I didn't think she was such a big football fan."

"What difference does it make? They're having a reception for Asian people...for Asian...oh what the hell is it..." Hannibal extracted a sheet of paper from the inside pocket of his jacket. "Oh yeah, here it is. *Disadvantaged Asians in Sports and Entertainment*. I had to pull a few strings to get you in there, Jayesh, don't think it was easy."

"But I'm not disadvantaged and I'm not Asian," I protested.

"Oh, come on," he moaned, giving me a pat on the shoulder. "Play along. *Be* Asian. What do you care? For God's sake, Jayesh, you look like Mahatma Gandhi on steroids. Anyway, the reception's not until late March. With you breaking that field goal record, and who knows what'll happen in the playoffs, you might be front and center in this event. The exposure is tremendous. Are you aware what this is worth in TV commercials alone? You can write your own ticket."

Hannibal looked so enthusiastic, so genuinely pleased on my behalf, that I didn't have the heart to tell him what I really felt. "Okay, thanks Hank," I said. "We'll talk more about it later, I'm sure." We shook hands, and I stepped into my car.

I needed to decompress. Fortunately, my fully-loaded 2015 Salzburger sedan had a mood panel. I set it to "mellow evening" as I rolled toward the gate. Quite promptly the appropriate mix of smell, temperature, humidity, light, and music were combined for a relaxing cruise. I left the stadium grounds, and was soon heading south on the freeway toward the city.

The stadium was located in the far northern reaches of the Albuquerque metropolitan area, on land that had been purchased from an Indian tribe. On my right stretched the valley that led down to the Rio Grande. On the horizon was a crisp and fiery sky, typical of a winter dusk in New Mexico. On my left were the Sandia Mountains, rising majestically to a height of over ten thousand feet. The light of the setting sun bathed them in a deep orange glow, an effect I always savored, knowing that it was inevitably short-lived. I exited the freeway onto a secondary road that took me into the Far Northeast Heights, arriving within minutes at my residence. It was located within a gated, heavily-secured compound that was one of the most desirable addresses in Albuquerque.

I quite liked my house. It was, to quote a former girlfriend, an "adobe palace." Palace was a stretch, but I certainly did spend a lot of money on it. The most alluring feature was the indoor/outdoor spa. There was a sauna, a Jacuzzi, a swimming pool, and a training room.

The furnishings and decorative objects were all of the Southwestern/ Native American style—with the exception of a painting by Pissarro.

Although Pissarro is my favorite painter, I am ashamed to admit that I spent half my annual salary on a single work of art. It was at an auction in Monte Carlo in the spring of 2015. That purchase marked the culmination of a week-long shopping spree in which I acted the part of jet-set celebrity. It's a week that I would gladly expunge from my memory. I threw money around, buying my Salzburger sedan, the Pissarro, designer clothes, Rolex watches, women, you name it. It was one of the most sickening displays of arrogance that has ever befallen me. The only beneficial aspect of the experience is that it alerted me to the dangers of sudden wealth. When you earn more in one year than most men earn in a lifetime, it has its side effects. I still can't get over the fact that I'm paid obscene amounts of money to kick a ball between two poles. It makes me dizzy.

What's more, I'm not overly athletic. Sure, I always played sports, and did well. But what really matters is that from a tender age, I had an uncanny ability to place-kick a football, in perfect end-over-end fashion, to any spot I chose. I clearly remember my awakening: In London, when I was eleven years old, I went to Regent's Park to play football with some of my classmates from the American School. It was fourth down. We couldn't decide, first if it were even possible to kick a field goal without goal posts, and then whether anyone could attempt it. We stretched an imaginary line, starting from the branch of a tree, across the "end zone" of our little field. For some reason, I volunteered for this job that nobody wanted. I shuddered when I gauged the distance, probably no more than twenty yards, though it appeared to me then as a chasm. Something possessed me as the ball was snapped and held. My foot seemed to lift into the air of its own accord, hitting the ball at the perfect spot and the perfect angle. It gracefully sailed away, arriving at exactly the destination I intended. From that time on, I was able to out-perform any other field-goal kicker of my age group.

It wasn't long after arriving at the adobe palace that I settled my weary bones into the Jacuzzi. I desperately needed that therapeutic bath. As always, it turned me into a sloth, and I had to dig deeply for energy with which to drag my poor body to bed. I certainly don't want to overstate the case, as if I were a "real" football player, bruised and battered from the gridiron; that would be pretentious. I'm one of those people on the field whose uniform is usually as clean at the end of a game as it is at the beginning. But I will say this: The tension I feel is enormous, and it can be deadly. Some players fall ill from it, without ever being called off the bench. In some ways the really physical guys have it better. At least they have an outlet for their nervous energy.

The next day was Monday, our precious post-game day off. A more appropriate venue for the occasion could hardly be found than the home of my friend and holder, Steve Gonzales. Nestled in the foothills of the Sandia range, it was a sprawling twenty-acre wooded retreat. Everything about it was relaxing: the patios, the stables, the wood-burning fireplaces, the massive leather couches into which one sagged like a sack of potatoes. I headed there for lunch, as Steve and I had planned while chatting on the sidelines during the game.

I should tell you a bit about Steve before I recount the visit. In addition to being my holder, he was the second-string quarterback of the Coyotes. Back in college days, as star quarterback at the University of New Mexico, Steve was the closest thing to God. Handsome, from a wealthy and prominent family, a fine athlete, he lacked nothing. When you saw him, with that dignified, dark Spanish look, he took your breath away. And he was six-four, two hundred and thirty-five pounds, without an ounce of fat. He didn't need to open his mouth. Just a glance from his piercing black eyes was enough to confound anyone.

But there's a sad side to the story. Steve never made it big in the pros. Sure, he had some impressive plays to his credit, but it was clear from the beginning that he would never be the starting quarterback. Over the years, he spent most of the time warming the bench. The most reliable employment he had was to set the ball on the ground and hold it, awaiting the swing of my leg. Steve could still draw attention whenever he set foot in an Albuquerque restaurant, but it was that respectful, somewhat reserved admiration for past achievements, and not the spontaneous eruption of excitement for an individual who is breaking new ground.

He was married to the lovely Rebecca, a girl he had known since high school. She was his female counterpart, matching him in beauty and heritage. They had a little boy, Mario, barely a year old.

Steve and I took a stroll through the woods. It was a crisp day under the cloudless New Mexico sky, chilly but not too cold. Steve was dressed casually, in what I call his "mountain attire": cowboy boots, a checkered flannel shirt, and blue jeans adorned with a turquoise-studded belt buckle. Something was bugging him, I could tell. For most people, and for myself at first, Steve was hard to read. He always maintained that *sang froid* suited to his station in life, a quality inculcated in him since childhood. But when you work with a man as a team, a duo, as closely as we did, you learn to decipher the subtleties. It was somewhat akin in this respect to a pair of policemen in their patrol car.

After talking for a few minutes about the game, I changed the subject. "Is everything okay with you, Steve?" I asked.

"Well, not really, Jayesh," he replied. He bent over to pick up a small branch, which he proceeded to fiddle with absent-mindedly. "I can't discuss it with you, I'm afraid. It's a personal matter."

"All right," I said. "If that changes, let me know."

"I certainly will," he said, with his understated smile. "By the way, I saw you go off with the lovely Miss Huddlewell."

I chuckled. "It's true, I did. So you've tangled with her?"

"Oh, yes."

"You never mentioned it."

Steve snapped a twig from the branch. "It was a couple of years ago. She interviewed me in a pub down on Central Avenue. The whole time she only wanted to know about my Mexican roots and what I thought about the *Separatista* movement. I told her five times that I have nothing to do with any such organization. I also tried to explain that my ancestors are from Spain. We're not Mexican. It was just like that guy from the TV station, the one I told you about last week. It happens all the time."

We returned to the house. Rebecca called us to the dining room, where the Guatemalan maid was just beginning to serve lunch. That room always fascinated me. There was a long table made from a ponderous old slab of exotic dark wood, supported by equally imposing posts that rested on lion's feet. On the wall behind the head of the table was a coat of arms. Against the adjoining wall was a huge breakfront, made of the same wood as the table. Its shelves held numerous utensils, including a set of antique pewter plates and mugs. Whenever I entered that room, I expected the Knights of the Round Table to join us for some eating, drinking, and merriment.

Lunch was pleasant. Rebecca did most of the talking, giving me an update on Mario and on assorted domestic goings-on. This was fine by me, since I was never quite sure what to say at the Gonzales home. Aside from the football connection, we really don't have much in common.

After the meal, Steve accompanied me to the Salzburger. I repeated my willingness to listen to any problems he wished to share. He smiled and thanked me, assuring me that everything would work out just fine.

The next day, Tuesday, the team resumed its practice sessions. The practice complex, which also housed the executive offices of the Coyotes, was located about a quarter of a mile from the edge of the stadium compound. The original plan was to build everything together in a cluster, but agreement could not be secured from the association that managed the buffalo herds, which grazed on an eighty-acre strip of land that ran through the center of the parcel. In the end, the buffalo remained, and the practice complex was split off from the stadium.

Our field conjured up images of gladiators in ancient Rome, preparing themselves for combat. Scattered about were machines of the most ingenious design. One of my favorites was the Charger, half a dozen vertical pads, seven feet high and three feet apart, meant to simulate a wall of linemen. Each pad was held in place by a shaft that protruded from an engine about fifteen feet to the rear. The machine could be programmed so that the pads resisted with a given amount of force, and at variable rates. The pads also moved in different directions. It was quite a spectacle to watch six human rhinoceroses hurl themselves into the pads, which more often than not outsmarted and outpushed the players, thrusting them onto their backsides.

The equipment that Steve and I used for kicking practice was more refined. There was a hiking machine that snapped the ball at a preset rate or by voice command. We also had cameras and sensory devices that generated films and diagrams of the ball's trajectory. This provided us with all sorts of information that enabled us to adjust and hone our routine.

In practice that day, Steve looked distracted. Several times I had to repeat myself when he failed to absorb my words on the first go. Then, something happened that was unprecedented: He dropped the ball twice in a row as it was fired at him from the hiking machine. After the second drop, he excused himself for a short break and ran over to the main building.

After watching Steve recede from view, I put a tee on the grass, intending to practice kickoffs until his return. After the first kick, I had a vague perception of eyes at my back, and turned around to see Ramirez, the groundskeeper, leaning against the post that held one of our cameras. A cigarette was hanging out of his unshaven face. "Hey, Jayesh," he said, with his thick Mexican accent. "What do you think about your amigo?"

"Something's bothering him," I said, not sure how to state the obvious.

"Yeah, I know."

"*You* know?"

Ramirez detached himself from the post and waddled over. He took a deep drag on the cigarette, flicked it onto the ground, and stomped it out. "Your friend Gonzales, he has, well…maybe someone else gonna hold for you."

"Someone else?" I blurted. "What are you talking about?"

He was shaking his head. "I'm not telling you anything, okay?"

I was familiar with this standard disclaimer of his, recited before spilling a morsel of gossip. "Okay, then" I said. "You're not telling me anything."

Ramirez looked to each side before speaking. "Listen, he still gonna be the regular holder. But they want a special thing, someone come in once or twice, for the newspapers."

I looked at him in disbelief. The frightening thing was that he was quite reliable, always a purveyor of solid information. Something was most certainly transpiring, but getting to the bottom of it was no simple matter. "When is this going to happen? Who's going to replace him?" I asked.

"That's all I know, Jayesh," he said, shrugging his shoulders. He started to walk away, leaving me alone with the hiking machine.

Steve returned, and we continued our kicking exercises. His concentration was still not a hundred percent, but it was adequate. Several times I was about to say something, but each time I desisted, not sure how to compose my words. It did not seem reasonable that he would be so upset by the prospect of being temporarily replaced as my holder. After all, there was no glory in it, except for the fake field-goal play we ran once per season (and which had rarely been successful).

Steve went to join a group of players, as quarterback, for some "real" football, while I continued to practice my kicking. A bit later, I had a general workout: running, weight lifting, and calisthenics. Then I went to Moe, our masseur, for a rubdown of my legs. I did this every day to prevent cramps in those crucial muscles that constitute the Jayesh Blackstone field-goal machine.

I cornered Steve as he was getting dressed in the locker room. This time I didn't pause to formulate my speech. "I heard they want to bring in someone else to hold for me."

He was buttoning his shirt. "Yes," he said, remaining calm.

"When is this supposed to happen?" I asked. "And why?"

"It's only for the Super Bowl, in case we get there. And just for one field goal or extra point. One kick, that's all." Steve sat down to put on his shoes.

"I don't get it."

He looked up at me with his piercing black eyes. "You'll get it when you see her."

"*Her?*" I exclaimed.

"Yes, her. A woman. If we win the conference, she'll come to practice with us."

"What if we don't get to the Super Bowl?"

Steve finished tying his laces and stood up to his full height. "Then she'll play on one of the competing teams. The thing is, they prefer that she hold for *you.*"

"Me? Is this a joke?" My blood was boiling, and my grandfather's face was nowhere in sight. "A woman holding for me? What's this all about? Let's go see Coach Gramercy."

Steve shut his locker. "Jayesh, calm down. Let's take a little walk to the parking lot." We left the locker room, walked down a short hallway, and emerged from the building. Steve resumed his recitation of the story. "No one is supposed to know about this, it's not public yet. So we have to keep a lid on it."

"Okay," I said. "How did you find out?"

"Some people I know in the back office. The main idea is to have the first woman ever to play in a professional football game, and do it in a big way. We both know that the pressure on the league has been tremendous."

"Who's the woman?"

"That I don't know."

We paused at the spot where we needed to go separate ways to our cars. "This is crazy," I said. "A woman in pro football? And I might be the one the whole world sees, etched forever into the record books? No way, I won't do it."

"I feel exactly as you do, Jayesh, but it's not so simple. Would you toss away a Super Bowl victory? Could you do that to everyone on the team?"

I took a deep breath. Steve had framed all too well the dilemma looming on the horizon.

"Anyway," he continued, "let's see what happens when we play the wild card team, Nebraska, on Sunday. You remember how they beat us in the regular season. We're not very likely to win."

"Yeah, I guess so," I said, trying to swallow the bitter pill. "Now I know why you were upset."

He smiled. "We'll pull through this together. Let's take a couple of days to think about it, okay?"

I nodded, and said goodbye.

This time around, in my Salzburger, I forgot to set the mood panel, and paid no attention to the setting sun. My mind was elsewhere. I felt indignant that the team's coaching staff would undertake such a move without consulting me, or at least notifying me of their decision. After all, an historic moment was about to occur, and it would forever mark my career.

At home that evening, I was still agitated by the events of the day. I had a fleeting impulse to run away, to a place where I would not be aggravated by the dilemmas that faced me. This of course was not practical, so I turned my thoughts to a possible trip in mid February, safely beyond post-season play. I parked myself at the computer, and began to check destinations and packages.

High on the list was London. I didn't relish the thought of visiting the city in winter, but the trip was long overdue. My parents had been living in the U.S. for some time (in Houston, where my father's company was located), but there were still many people dear to me in London: my sister Julie, my grandfather, various relatives, and some friends with whom I kept in contact.

My mind wandered to childhood days. I pictured myself strolling along the high street in St. John's Wood, peering into the windows of its shops and specialty boutiques. Then there was the family house on Hamilton Terrace, nestled among stately apartment buildings and grand old mansions. In those days, there were still quite a few streets that preserved the traditional English charm. It was a backdrop that could never be replaced. I enjoyed living in America, including New Mexico, but from time to time I would sink into a melancholy mood as nostalgia for Old London overtook me.

I snapped out of my torpor. Refocusing my attention on the computer, I accessed the online version of *Breast of Iron*, to see whether Marcy Huddlewell had managed to cobble together a story from our disjointed interview. "Cobble" is an understatement. She wrote of "the arrogant Jayesh Blackstone, an Asian who fancies himself as an upper-class British snob, a classic white-male wannabe rejecting his Third World roots. He came to America to show the natives how to kick a ball. When complimented on his good looks, he unleashed a torrent of insults that demonstrates exactly how much class he really has."

Chapter Two

In the divisional playoff game against the Nebraska Prairie Dogs, I kicked two short field goals and three extra points in our 27-14 win, played in Albuquerque. Our starting quarterback Burt Stanwell was knocked unconscious in the middle of the fourth quarter. Although sustaining no real injury, he had to sit out the rest of the game. We were ahead by six points, but were backed up near our own end zone, at the four yard line. Steve stepped in to replace Stanwell. He engineered a seven-minute drive that was a textbook example of how to eat up the clock and wear down the defense. It sealed the outcome of the game. The last play of the drive was an eighteen-yard toss into the end zone, to the tight end Barton. When I came on for the extra point, Steve was beaming with satisfaction. It was gratifying to see him recapture some of the glory of college days.

New Mexico Governor Bettina Salazar threw a victory bash that evening in Santa Fe. I traveled there together with most of the team in a luxury coach, equipped with a full-service bar. A couple of players had organized the joyride. Most of the participants were fairly well inebriated by the time we arrived.

We parked in front of the spanking-new governor's mansion, a pyramid-shaped steel and glass structure that was almost entirely transparent. It provided a stark contrast to the surrounding architecture, which was of the adobe and Spanish colonial style. The visual clash did not seem to interest most of the players, who emerged from the bus in rather disorderly fashion, accompanied by the ruckus one would expect when so much tension is being released. Hank Hannibal herded us into the building, where a celebration was already in full swing.

The crowd at the party was a hodgepodge of media people, politicians, lawyers, business leaders, and miscellaneous publicity-seekers who attach themselves to high-profile events like barnacles to the hull of a ship. I tried my best to stay protected within a ring of players, avoiding journalists like the plague.

At one point, Governor Salazar joined a group composed of Steve, myself, Hubbard, Offensive Coordinator Williams, and Mike Launderhaven, the team's accountant.

"Hello there, governor," said Coach Williams, raising his champagne glass. "We appreciate your hospitality."

"The pleasure is all mine, coach," responded Salazar. As she engaged in the obligatory round of congratulations, I studied this interesting politician, then in her second term as governor. She was tall and thin, in her early sixties, wearing a closely-cropped business suit that kept her body upright at all times, a sort of replacement for the corset of yesteryear. The skin of her face was artificially smooth, probably the result of a face lift. Her mouth was constantly moving in a motion of cogitation, as if she were gnashing some chewing tobacco with her teeth.

"Coach Williams," she said, "what's the next step in your march to the Super Bowl?"

"We play the Utah Salts next Sunday, for the conference championship. It'll be a real challenge, they're an excellent team. But I think we can pull it off."

The governor looked at Steve. "Mr. Gonzales, you were fabulous out there on the field. You're a tribute to the entire Hispanic community of New Mexico."

"Thank you," said Steve, lowering his glance.

Salazar then turned her attention to Hubbard, who had turned in a stellar performance on the offensive line, immobilizing Nebraska's All-Pro defensive end. "Mr. Hubbard," she said, chin extended, "I enjoyed watching you play."

"Thank you," said Hubbard. One could tell from his embarrassed smile that he was feeling self-conscious at the attention. He began shifting his substantial frame to and fro, as if trying to walk away but finding his feet stuck to the floor.

"You know," continued the governor, "we're looking for a speaker at the special university graduation ceremony for African-Americans. Would you consider doing it? It doesn't have to be long, just talk about eliminating the racism that plagues our society, that sort of thing."

Hubbard hardly had time to respond because at that moment, Thelonius Brown, who had been creeping up behind him, stepped into the circle and opened his mouth. "What if he doesn't want to talk about racism," said Brown, looking around to gauge the reaction to his remark. It was met by several stunned faces.

"Well," said the governor, clearing her throat, "we could discuss the agenda in more detail later."

Brown was wearing wide, gaudy sunglasses, the rims of which touched the lower edge of his voluminous afro. His fingers were adorned with fat gold and emerald rings; his neck with a heavy gold chain. He was wearing a black and white body suit that looked straight out of the 1970s disco scene. His mouth expanded into a mischievous smile. "I mean, what if Hubbard wants to talk about football. Just football. Or how to be good at what you're doing. And what if he wants to speak to the white grads? Or do y'all need a nigger to talk to the niggers?"

Hubbard couldn't restrain a snicker, and I exchanged a subdued smile with Steve.

"That's enough," interjected Coach Williams. "Governor, I think he's had a bit too much to drink."

"I didn't have anything to drink," said Brown.

The two men stared each other down for a long moment. Brown let loose a fiendish laugh, turned around, and moved away from us with a demonstrative swagger. Steve excused himself to go to the men's room, and the group promptly dispersed.

I wandered toward the hors d'oeuvres. It was at that moment that I first saw Ashley. She was leaning against the doorpost of the dining room, drink in hand, conversing with Bill Harrison, the wide receiver. I stopped dead in my tracks at the sight of her: Tall and thin, with pale white skin, silky brown hair, and long, luscious legs. It was like manna from heaven. Harrison, describing one of his catches, was gesticulating every which way. Ashley was standing still, listening to the tale, nodding politely at regular intervals. When she saw me, her eyes widened for a split second, a gesture that sent a shiver up my spine. She pulled her hair back from her face and smiled in my direction. Harrison continued his flamboyant storytelling, seemingly oblivious to her change in demeanor.

I continued walking toward the food. As I passed through the doorway and alongside Ashley, she moved her arm so that I could not help but brush against it. I circled around the table, pretending to be viewing the appetizers. As I leaned over a plate of cheese, a woman's hand reached under my nose to grab a morsel. I looked up to see Ashley pop the piece of cheese into her mouth, which had adopted a playful smirk. I stood there, paralyzed, staring directly at her. She wiggled and pranced her way from plate to plate, occasionally glancing at a point in space just above my head. It was a voluptuous display of female movement, and I fell completely under her spell. I was so disoriented at that moment that I can't even recall who spoke first. I will thus recite our conversation from the first sentence for whose accuracy I can vouch. It was outside, in the garden. I apologize for not being able to recount how we got there.

"So what brings you to this event?" I asked, noting the fine curvature of her figure.

"I teach social anthropology for the Wellsburg Institute—you know, the big online university—while I finish my dissertation on the contribution of Christian fundamentalism to sexist attitudes in professional sports. I asked the governor's office if I could attend a social event with a significant population of male athletes, and they approved. The governor's assistant for human rights was kind enough to call me this afternoon, and I popped over." She looked at me from the corner of her eye, evidently expecting a reaction of some kind to her statement.

"I see," I said in my most scholarly tone, wondering whether my picturing her naked could be used as data in her research. "What's your name, by the way?"

"Ashley."

"That's a nice name. Do you live in Santa Fe?"

"Yes, just a few blocks from here."

"I suppose you know who I am," I said. She nodded as we exchanged smiles. "So going back to your dissertation, have you any findings to report thus far?"

Ashley giggled like a schoolgirl.

"What makes you laugh?" I inquired.

"Oh, nothing. It's just that it's so cute, you being a super-jock and all, with that posh English accent. The parts don't fit together, but it's so cute."

I confess that at that moment I preferred being cute and incongruous to being bland yet consistent. Ashley sniffed a flower, and then started to stroll across the garden. I followed her like a loyal dog.

I honestly cannot account for the fact that Ashley ended up in my bed that night. How we came to leave the event together, in her car no less, is rather vague in my mind. I do remember, however, that for most of the hour-long drive back to Albuquerque, she expounded upon her dissertation, which went something like this: Christian fundamentalists, spreading out from their original cells in Texas, gradually took over the educational institutions in the American heartland (and seriously threatened to take over the rest). The central pillar of their influence was the entrenched patriarchy, which was fueled by violent sports, such as football and ice hockey; merciless economic exploitation of the weak members of society; war; racism; homophobia; and the relegation of women to the most menial and accursed existence they have ever experienced on the face of the earth. The men indoctrinated in this way become addicted to a steady diet of sports, guns, porn, and cut-throat business practices. If they are not stopped soon, they may very well attempt a violent takeover of the U.S. government, depose President Malpomme, and institute a regime of martial law.

I tried to steer the conversation onto a less contentious track. "Where did you grow up?" I asked.

"In Westchester County, just north of New York City."

"Did you like it there?"

"No, it's too fast-paced for me. I like it out here in the West, where people are friendly and laid back."

"Me too," I said, noticing that Ashley was driving well over the speed limit. "Of course, I didn't grow up in America, but I lived back East for four years, in Connecticut, where I went to college. When I was drafted by the New Mexico Coyotes, I dreaded coming out here to what I thought was the middle of nowhere. But it turned out to be quite pleasant."

Ashley was silent for a moment, concentrating intensely. "You know, Jayesh, women playing in professional football is only a matter of time."

"It won't work," I said.

"And why not?"

"Football is a great sport, but it is brutal and violent. Gigantic men, mountains of muscle, are carted off the field with injuries. You want women to be subjected to that?"

"They have the right to choose. And women can be muscular, too."

"Not like that. And it would change the entire nature of the game. The men would let up, not throwing themselves into the fray with abandon, as they do now. They would be hesitant with women, not wanting to hurt them. Similarly, they would devote too much effort to guarding their own female players. And that's not to speak of life off the field, where the building of camaraderie is so crucial. It's almost military, and it can exist only among men."

"Oh, right," said Ashley, with a thick layer of sarcasm. "You sexists are all the same. Protecting women? Hah! You just love that violence, and want to develop and strengthen it, so that the patriarchy can be continued for another generation. We know all about it."

I had a fleeting urge to get out of the car right then and there, on the highway. But I stifled my natural reaction. The truth is, I hadn't had intimacy with a woman in quite some time, and Ashley was exquisitely attractive. I avoided taking any action that could spoil the evening.

The chain of events from the moment we pulled into my garage to our fully naked embrace is worthy of some remarks. I had never before met a woman quite like Ashley. The initial dialogue upon entering the house shall serve as evidence for the old adage that truth is stranger than fiction.

"This is a beautiful house," she said, viewing the rooms that were visible from the foyer. "Those beams are gorgeous."

"Thank you," I said. "I'm glad you like everything."

She suddenly straightened her back, as if standing at attention, and faced me. "Jayesh," she said, "do you have any particular requirements in the area of sexual relations that stem from your Indian heritage?" This, mind you, was said with the same tone in which a nurse asks her patient whether he is allergic to any medications.

I restrained a chuckle, so as not to disturb the flow of events. "No," I said softly, "but thank you for asking. And do you have any…well… ethnic requirements?"

"No," she said. "I was raised in the standard Eurocentric patriarchal family dictatorship. Thus my only requirement is to escape its clutches, and to embark upon meaningful relationships that are based on equality of function, equality of time, and equality of initiative."

After a minute or two of listening to her instruct me on this topic, I proposed that we have a drink. We moved into the kitchen, where I placed two fine crystal glasses on the marble counter. I proceeded to uncork a bottle of outrageously expensive French wine, hoping that this *tour de force* would put an end to Ashley's lectures. As I poured the wine, she proposed a toast to the emergence of American women, men, and transgendered individuals into a new era of fully ethical and fair sexual relationships. I cooperated, hoping once again that this would be the end of the story. After taking a couple of sips, I took her by the hand, and led her into the study, where the Pissarro was hanging. Ashley was immediately drawn to it, and stood transfixed for a long moment. She gingerly approached the picture, taking baby steps, eventually placing her nose not a foot away.

"Oh, a Pissarro," she exclaimed, as if seeing an old friend after a long absence. "This is a great copy. Where did you get it?"

"At the flea market," I said, playing along with her faulty assumption.

"Wow…You must have gotten it for very little."

"I think I paid about twenty dollars."

"Nice."

I again took her hand, this time bringing her to the living room, where I sat her down on the couch. Without delay, I kissed her lightly on the lips. She did not resist, but was a bit stiff.

"Wait, Jayesh…Before we start, please allow me to explain the way I would like to proceed."

"Okay," I said, fighting off my desire for just a bit longer.

"Please be patient. I'm not a cruel person, it's just that I'd rather do things right. The next time we're together, it will flow more smoothly. Just a little work up front will pay off down the road. Anyway, this is how it works: we basically take turns making the moves. You started already, now it will be my turn. We have to finish each step before moving on to the next. Please give it a chance, and you'll see how wonderful and fulfilling it is."

I nodded my assent, curious to see the next step she had in mind. I didn't have long to wait. Ashley placed her wine glass on the coffee table and removed her blouse and bra. She instructed me to perform the equivalent, which I did. I then proposed that we remove the garments from the lower part of our bodies. She agreed, and we implemented my suggestion.

There were still several rounds of this give and take, the last one taking place in my bed, before we arrived at the act itself. I must say, to Ashley's credit, that when we finally launched ourselves into the step that has no more steps following it, she proved to be a most passionate lover. Perhaps I've gone mad, but the whole thing actually *was* wonderful and fulfilling, in a bizarre sort of way.

My euphoria was short-lived. After a brief while in which we exchanged the gentle caresses of pleasantly fatigued lovers, she sat up and began to lecture me, right there in my bed. "So you see Jayesh, what this new approach can do for you. You do feel well, don't you?"

"Yes, I feel quite well." I gave her a series of kisses around the eyes and forehead, hoping to distract her.

"As I predicted. So you see, these are the kinds of countervailing influences you must bring into your life. You have been brainwashed by the fundamentalist minions, probably without being aware of it. Do you know that they own and run your team?"

"Don't you think that's a pretty broad statement?"

"Broad but accurate," said Ashley, her index finger pointing upward for emphasis. "It's leading the country to disaster. One important way to reverse the tide is to bring women into major league sports, particularly professional football."

"That's crazy," I said, as an image of Steve's suffering face flew across my mind. I peeled back the sheets and sat up at the edge of the bed.

"No, it's quite *sane*," said Ashley, still in her professorial voice. "What's crazy is the continued oppression of women and minorities throughout the world. This is what we've got to stop. The core problem is the male-dominated sports institutions that feed the sexist and militaristic tendencies of the ruling class."

It took about five more minutes before the discussion degenerated into a shouting match. Ashley dressed herself as quickly as possible, grabbed her keys, and literally ran to her car. I gladly opened the garage door and watched her car screech away. Good riddance, I thought. I headed for the living room, where I slumped onto the couch, turned on the TV, and watched a tape of our team's best plays of the year. Every hit and every tackle filled me with immense satisfaction.

The next day, the scene with Ashley faded from memory as the coaches drove us harder than any time in recent memory. They ran us into the ground, and took no pity. Head Coach Petersen, a former captain in the Marines, led us that night on a military-style march through the Sandia Mountains. With the men moaning from exhaustion, the coach sat us down in a clearing and gave us the pep talk that came to be known as the "mountain speech." He said he loved us like his own children, and wanted us to win the Super Bowl so that he could see the joy on our faces, which he knew would be unbounded. There was no question in his mind that we were capable, and he would squeeze the last drop of sweat out of us to achieve victory.

These words were not said in jest. Over the next couple of days, the tempo accelerated. All of us wondered when the torture would cease. Men in the finest physical condition, athletes of the first rank, wore grimaces of exertion that I had never seen in my life. I was feeling a bit less guilty about making so much money kicking a ball between two poles.

We ran and ran and ran. Everywhere. No place in the practice facility was safe from our stampeding feet. We ran up and down stairs, across the field, through the bleachers. We ran in single file, we ran bunched together, and we ran stretched out in a line, holding hands. We carried each other on our backs and in our arms. We performed rugby-style scrums, and had tugs of war with twenty men on each side—and then a tug of war lying on the ground.

It was an immaculate workout. With each new and unprecedented exercise, we looked at each other in disbelief. The coaching staff refused to tell us when we would start playing football. We did not leave the practice facility; we slept on cots in the dormitory. It was not until Friday that we resumed our football drills. And it was clear that the grind had paid off: We were primed for combat, hungry for action. It was almost with bloodthirstiness that we awaited the opening kickoff that Sunday in Salt Lake City.

One night, I think it was the Friday before the game, as I laid my bruised and aching body down to sleep, my cell phone rang. It was Ashley. She started to recite an apology before breaking down in sobs. She felt terrible about the whole evening, particularly her insensitive behavior. I was entitled to my views, and if she wanted me to think like her, it was incumbent upon her to win me over by logical argument, not provocative statements about the parts of my life that I most cherish.

I could not think clearly, and simply felt sorry for her. I told her that I wouldn't have a free moment until the game, and if we won, the pace would continue for another two weeks thereafter. She meekly asked if she could contact me again at the end of the football season, and I consented, eager to end the conversation and get to sleep.

That Sunday, the match against Utah became bogged down in a conservatively-played defensive battle, with few penalties and no turnovers. Each team scored only seven points in the first half. This thrilled us no end, being that everyone had expected Utah, favored by ten points, to run away with the game.

As the slugging match inched forward, Steve and I had the chance to talk on the bench. The air was cold and dry, but we were wearing warm jackets, and the seats beneath us were heated. It wasn't long before the topic of the female holder entered our discussion.

"I found out a bit more about the whole thing," he said. "They want to make it into a big, high-profile event. She'll come onto the field only once, during the Super Bowl."

"Who's 'they'?" I inquired.

"A coalition of human rights and other advocacy groups. They've involved the U.N., which is expected to pass a resolution calling for the abolition of all-male professional sports teams."

There was a roar and then a collective sigh from the crowd as a Utah receiver caught a long pass, but out of bounds.

"Where are you getting this information?" I asked, skeptical of the conspiratorial aspect.

"From very reliable sources," said Steve, "including Sam Kapulski of *Football Icon*. What's more, Jayesh, someone is backing them with a huge amount of money, some of it going to pay off, in one way or another, the owners of the possible Super Bowl teams."

"I don't like it, I don't like it at all. Are we still supposed to keep our mouths shut?"

"Yes, but not for long. With the Super Bowl fast approaching, the teams have to be informed and prepared. Then they have to practice with her, at least a little. It's all going to be public very soon. Listen, Jayesh, tonight, after we fly back to Albuquerque, I'm going to meet with Sam Kapulski. You're welcome to come along."

"Sure," I said, not fully concentrating. I was imagining a replay of my record-breaking field goal, but with Ashley holding. She was wearing a full uniform, minus the shirt, so that her breasts were visible from below the shoulder pads. I was frozen in place as the play began, and we were both overrun by the charging defense.

As I snapped out of the reverie, my thoughts turned to practical matters. How would I handle the entire issue, should it come to pass? Several times now, whether on the practice field, with Ashley, or with Steve, the prospect of a female player had elicited from me an angry, emotional response. This was counter-productive, as my grandfather used to say. I took a deep breath and tried to analyze the problem. If I made it known that I would refuse to do it, would they fire me for breach of contract? Would the league find a way to humiliate me in public, like they did last year to Coach Barnes of the Sentinels when he refused to accept a referee in a motorized wheelchair? Or to the quarterback Leroy Hagarty when he walked off the field on National Peace and Reconciliation Day because the national anthem was sung by one of the men who blew up the aircraft carrier last summer? It was hard to predict. Would the New Mexico Coyotes go to the Super Bowl without their star kicker? Perhaps the people providing the money would spend an extra million to entice another top kicker to fill in for the occasion.

The game continued its snail's pace. The score was still tied at seven with just over a minute and a half to go. Utah had the ball on our twenty-nine yard line; it was third and ten. The quarterback rolled out, and then lobbed the ball to the far side of the field, aiming for the goal line. At the last possible moment, Thelonius Brown stepped in front of the receiver, intercepted the pass, and ran it back a hundred yards for a touchdown. The entire New Mexico bench emptied onto the field in a spontaneous eruption of glee. The celebration was so wild and prolonged that the officials had to threaten penalties and fines to get the players off the field. After the extra point and the kickoff, our defense held the Utah offense like a stone wall. We took possession on downs, and the game was over. We were champions of the conference, on our way to the Super Bowl in two weeks time. There we would meet the team from Hawaii, universally acknowledged as the reigning powerhouse of professional football.

The short flight to Albuquerque was boisterous, to say the least. A parade of smiling faces fills my memory of the trip. No liquor was allowed this time, but the natural euphoria was more than adequate.

After landing, Steve and I grabbed our luggage, found our cars, and drove to the Eagle One hotel, located just a few blocks from the airport. It was one of those standard business-class establishments, like so many others across the country. We made our way to the rooftop bar, where Sam Kapulski was waiting. He was seated at a window table along the north side of the room. Steve and I joined him and ordered a round of drinks. For several minutes, we discussed Sam's trip, the game against Utah, and the huge growth of Albuquerque in recent years. This last topic was stimulated by the commanding view we enjoyed of the city, the mesa, and the Sandia Mountains.

Sam was one of the great stalwarts of sports journalism. He began his career in 1981 as a writer for a newspaper in Iowa. He spent time in radio, with network TV, and on cable sports channels before being named editor of the prestigious *Football Icon* in 2016. He was a no-nonsense kind of guy. Near the end of my first season, he did a short segment on me for one of the cable channels. He never once mentioned my ethnicity, and only referred in passing to the fact that I grew up in London. The only thing that interested him was me as a football player: my experience, my methods, my accomplishments. Nothing else.

Sam looked to me like a character in a film noir from the 1940s. His hair, graying a bit and thin around the top, was slicked back with a light gel. He wore thick-rimmed black glasses that sat atop his rather prominent nose. His impeccably shaven face was a good match for the dark blue business suit and tie, which were quite plain but perfectly pressed and arranged. Sam was one of those people who are so inconspicuous and unassuming that they stand out.

"Gentlemen," he said, "we've got a big problem on our hands. The announcement of the female holder will be in all the papers tomorrow. Expect to see enthusiastic endorsements by the NFL commissioner, the coaches' association, the governors of the contestants' states, the U.N., the European Union, and the president of the United States. Unless something very dramatic occurs somewhere on the planet, this story will dominate the press for at least a couple of days." He sat back and took a sip of his martini.

"Is there any opposition?" asked Steve.

"Yes, but only from people who don't really matter. Like myself, for instance." Sam smiled as he smoothed back the hair on one side of his head. "And a few others, here and there. Tom Hubert at Cable5, Mel Axelrod in Boston. I could probably count them on one hand, the ones who would really take a stand, I mean."

"Who's the holder?" I asked.

"That we don't know. I'm afraid that with all my connections, I couldn't find out. It's the biggest secret in the sports world, that I can remember. But the whole country will know the answer tomorrow or the next day."

"So what can we do?" asked Steve.

"Nothing," said Sam, downing the rest of his martini.

"What if we refuse to go along with it?" I said. "And get a few other players to do the same."

Sam laughed and shook his head. "You want to be a martyr? Go ahead. You'll lose a ton of money and they'll roast you alive in the press. Then you'll be sued by everybody and their grandmother. To top it off, your career will be over. You'll be blacklisted across the board: no commercials, no speaking engagements, no interviews, no endorsements, nothing. Nobody will touch you with a ten-foot pole. Tell me, do you own any property in South America?"

"No."

"Then I suggest you get some. If you're lucky, you can go hide there."

I lowered my head, taken aback by the verbal barrage.

"Hey," said Sam, opening his arms in a gesture of conciliation. "I didn't mean to jump all over you, Jayesh. I admire your guts, but I'm just trying to be realistic, to warn you. That's all."

"So," said Steve, "are you saying that we should all do nothing? Surely you didn't fly out here to tell us that."

Sam peered out the window for a long moment. "All right, here's what I think. Leave it to me. Let me take the flak. You two are young, you have long lives ahead of you. I'm close to retirement. It'll be my last hurrah. Me and my old buddies, the few that are left. Of course I can still interview you later this week, and you can criticize the league's decision. You'll get attacked plenty, but that'll blow over in the off-season. As long as you don't take any action to sabotage the event, you'll be okay."

Steve and I exchanged a glance of frustration. I kept turning the matter over in my mind, but was unable to sort through the web of contradictions. Sam was swishing the ice around in his glass, looking pensive. A couple of times his lips twitched, but no words were audible. Finally he sat up straight. "If you *are* going to do something, however, don't announce it beforehand. Don't utter even the slightest complaint. If you do, they'll be ready with a backup plan. That means they'll wreck your career and they'll go on with the show. You will have accomplished nothing. If you keep your mouth shut until the very end, there's a chance for some impact. Okay?"

"Okay," we said in unison.

Sam excused himself, saying that he needed to grab a quick dinner before returning to the airport. We said our goodbyes, and I watched this gutsy, unassuming man in the plain dark suit disappear from view.

Steve and I remained in our seats for a while. It did not take us long to reach a decision: we would carry out an act of protest at the Super Bowl. We had no idea what such an act would entail, or whether anyone else would be invited to join us, but we could figure all that out later. The key issue at that moment was to keep a low profile and not arouse any suspicions. I knew that this would not be an easy task, especially for myself. I felt in my bones that someone, at some point, would discern that I was upset by the prospect of being the first professional football player assisted on the field by a woman.

We toasted our new resolve, and headed out to the parking lot. Our path was blocked by a group of autograph seekers, a couple of whom I had seen stalking us in the rooftop bar. We patiently performed the signing ritual, and departed.

My new holder arrived the very next day. The young lady was brought to the kicking station by an entourage consisting of Joe Gramercy, Hank Hannibal, and four photographers. She was on the short side, a bit plump but not overweight, with a light bronze skin color. Something about her looked familiar. After combing my memory, I realized that she was none other than Mahinta Zagumbi, the Miss America of 2016.

Coach Gramercy conducted the introductions, and then proceeded to show her the various pieces of equipment she would be using. Meanwhile, Hank Hannibal took me aside. "Smile, Jayesh," he said, beaming with joy. "This is a big day for you. Put this together with the White House reception, my friend, and you can write your own ticket. This is one of the greatest moments in American sports, and *you* are there. When little kids learn history, they'll see pictures of the Marines on Iwo Jima, Neil Armstrong on the moon, and Jayesh Blackstone kicking a field goal with Miss America."

Up until that point I had been calm, but at hearing Hannibal's little speech, I had a sudden urge to kick a field goal straight into his gut. It was with difficulty that I held it all in. I recalled Sam Kapulski's advice, and realized that it was for a greater good that I needed to maintain a poker face.

Coach Gramercy informed me that Ms. Zagumbi would get suited up that afternoon so that we could start practicing. I would of course show her how to hold the ball at the angle I preferred. I indicated my assent with a nod, and tried to make eye contact with the young lady. She cast her glance downward.

The delegation headed back to the main building. I went to the gym for my daily round of weight lifting, followed by a leg massage. Later, after some more kicking, I joined a group of players for running and calisthenics. We were no longer in the "military" regimen of the previous week, but the coaches were still pushing us hard.

My first time alone with Ms. Zagumbi that afternoon was a rather odd experience. I tried to be civil and even friendly. Her mind, however, was elsewhere. I showed her the angle at which it was necessary to hold the ball, but the result was unsatisfactory. She managed to catch the ball as it was ejected from the hiking machine, and was fairly quick about it. But it ended up in the strangest positions when she placed it on the ground. It wasn't out of stupidity or ineptitude, I'm sure of that. She looked sad, distracted, and hopelessly out of place in her football uniform, like a dressed-up circus bear. Somehow, after numerous attempts, we managed to work out a reasonably effective kicking routine.

Hannibal came to fetch her. We said goodbye, never having discussed anything but the task at hand. Watching her walk away with the chattering PR man, I felt pity. Here was a feminine, gentle creature encased in shoulder pads, hip pads, and a helmet. It was a truly pathetic sight.

Soon it was time for supper in the cafeteria. I sat at my usual table, with Steve, Hubbard, Harrison, and, inevitably, Thelonius Brown. He was always attaching himself to me, perhaps because, in a strange sort of way, I accepted him for who he was. He teased me no end, but it was never mean-spirited, and it always ended with a warm smile. It was as if he were saying, "Jayesh, I want to be your friend, I want to get to know you better, but I just don't know how." He possessed a superior intelligence that found expression only with difficulty. It was the barrier experienced by people with sharp minds who emerge from social environments that are inimical to intellect and creativity.

Brown's popularity among the team was not particularly high. Some of this could be attributed to his outlandish style of dress, and to his habit of saying exactly what he thought at all times. Everyone, however, respected him as a football player. He was a five-time All-Pro strong safety out of the University of Oklahoma, where he broke a number of NCAA records, including most interceptions in a game and most punt-return yards in a season. His open-field tackling was legend, and his patented safety blitz was the scourge of quarterbacks across the league. In general, he was a lightning rod that fired up the defense. But off the field, he was a social leper.

At the dinner table, it didn't take long for him to swing into action. No sooner was everyone seated than he launched his first salvo. "Hey Jayesh, I saw you doing some kicking with your lady friend. You two make just the couple. One big bowl of brown sugar."

"Listen, Thelonius," said Steve, trying to sound nonchalant, "it's no big deal. Just one play, and it might not even be with us. She's also training with Hawaii. It's a publicity stunt, that's all, like they often have during the halftime show."

The waiters arrived with our meal, lamb chops with baked potato and green beans. Everyone spent several quiet moments cutting and chewing.

"That's a pretty controversial publicity stunt," said Harrison. "Anybody catch some TV this morning? That's all they were talking about."

"An interesting concept," said Thelonius, gesturing with his fork. "A player who can play with either team. Maybe I'll try that myself." He leaned back and stroked his chin in a feigned gesture of introspection. "If we're getting our butts kicked halfway through the fourth quarter, I'll go play for Hawaii. You guys don't mind, do you?"

I barely held back a laugh, and avoided eye contact so as to prevent myself from divulging my true allegiance.

"They had a poll," said Harrison. "Based on a random sample, sixty-two percent of the American people support the woman playing."

"That would be a random sample of brainwashing," said Thelonius.

"I wonder if she has to wear a jock strap," said Hubbard.

The table erupted in laughter, Steve and myself included. It was a much-appreciated release from the tension to which I had been subjecting myself.

After the meal, Coach Gramercy assembled the special-team squad to discuss Mahinta Zagumbi. He downplayed the importance of her participation, saying it was just a little thing we had to do to mollify some people in the league administration. None of us were thrilled, but that's life, we can't always get what we want. As he spoke, I glanced at the faces of my teammates. They looked passive and uninterested. There were no questions and no challenges.

The coach released us, allowing us to go home if we so wished. The only conditions were that we "behave ourselves" and show up for breakfast at 7:30 am. It was not a wildly enticing proposition, being that it was nearly nine o'clock.

I knew that calling Ashley was not a particularly wise course of action. I needed to avoid all stress and get a good night's sleep. But my desire overcame me. I didn't need to suggest that she come over; she suggested it herself, about twenty seconds into the call. She would leave Santa Fe immediately, expecting to arrive at my place in an hour.

During my drive home from the practice facility, I wondered how much information I could safely divulge to Ashley. I had a desire to spill the beans, to share my secret plan of staging a protest at the Super Bowl. Could she be trusted? On the one hand, she seemed honest. Her sudden apology following our heated argument was undoubtedly the work of a solid conscience. On the other hand, she was possessed by the demon of ideology, and there was no telling what she might do "for the cause." In any case, too much depended on the success of my disinformation campaign. It overrode the momentary inconvenience of pretending that everything was normal.

The whole debate turned out to be moot. Not long after Ashley's arrival, she began to mock football players, imputing to them less than honorable intentions. She claimed that as early as high school, they are indoctrinated to use their elevated status to seduce innocent girls, who are then thrown away like a paper bag from the supermarket. She explained to me, in the tone one uses with a small child, that placekickers have particularly delicate egos, being that they already feel inferior to the players who engage in violent contact. Thus she could well understand my reticence to embrace the truth, despite my evidently more refined nature. It was only with great difficulty that I restrained myself. As in our first evening together, I channeled my energy toward the physical aspect of our relationship. This provided an escape hatch from the looming blowup.

Ashley responded well to my advances, and abandoned her lecture. This was accompanied by another favorable turn of events: She announced that when we make love, we would still follow the

Alternating Reciprocity method, as she called it, but only up to a certain point. We agreed that after two rounds each, I would have the right to revert to the procedures followed "during the era of male oppression of the female gender." I thanked Ashley for being so patient with me, giving me time to internalize these pearls of societal progress that conflicted with my deep-seated, retrograde male instincts. As it turned out, I lasted *three* rounds of alternating reciprocity. When it was over, Ashley rewarded me with a special kiss, and the promise of good things that would flow from my sincere efforts.

Our earlier argument faded from memory as we settled into a peaceful sleep.

CHAPTER THREE

▼

From the moment we began our second practice session, Mahinta seemed to be restraining her tears. At first I ignored it, continuing my instruction in the proper placement and angle of the ball. But after twenty minutes of waiting for the dam to burst, I decided to inquire as to the cause of her misery.

"Ms. Zagumbi, forgive me if it's none of my business, but is something bothering you?"

There was no response. She rubbed her eyes, experiencing some difficulty sliding her hands over the face mask.

"You can take your helmet off for a few minutes," I said. "You don't even have to wear it, actually."

Mahinta did as I suggested. Her face was moist from the mixture of sweat and tears. She muttered something that was inaudible.

"What was that?" I said.

She tilted her head to one side and smiled. "You're very nice, for a football player."

I winced from the bittersweet compliment.

"Oh, I'm sorry, I didn't mean it that way. It's just that they told me to expect the players to be crude and nasty."

"Who told you that?"

"The women at the International Sisterhood for the Reinstitution of the Matriarchy."

"Reinstitution?" I said.

"Yes. They say that three thousand years ago, the whole world lived in peace. That's when women were the leaders of humanity."

Overlooking the dubious historical footnote, I suggested that we rest for a minute on a nearby bench. As soon as we took our places, she promptly slumped forward, as if weighed down by equipment and emotion alike.

"I was upset, Mr. Blackstone, because I really don't want to do this."

I looked at Mahinta in disbelief. I had expected an Ashley-style lecture on one aspect or another of male depravity.

"I have no choice," she continued. "Oh, you probably don't want to hear this."

"Actually, I do. We're a team, you and I. Go ahead, tell me the rest."

She smiled her soft smile. Once again, I was irked by the contrast between her feminine features and the inherent brutality of the shoulder pads that surrounded her neck. "You see, I need the money. Not me personally, that is. When I won Miss America, I promised my sister…well, you see she's a dancer, and I promised to send her to the best school in New York, but then I had to spend the prize money on something else. This business with the Super Bowl seemed an easy way to make it up to her. But now…"

"Yes?"

"I feel terrible. This isn't right. I don't want to break down the last…what did the women at the International Sisterhood call it… the last vestiges of the macho rape culture. It's ridiculous, this is just a football team. I don't want to break anything down, I just want to go live on a farm in Peru."

"Why do you want to live in Peru?"

"It's so beautiful, and I love the culture. My mother is from Peru. So it's my heritage…well, most of it. One of her grandparents was Swedish. My father is half Sioux and half black, well, if you don't count his great-grandfather who was French—you know, from Louisiana."

"That's quite interesting," I said. "Do you still have a lot of family in Peru?"

"Not really. My uncles and cousins tried to stop the Shining Path from taking over the village. That was back in the 1980s. Most of them

were killed, but a few escaped and came to America with my mother."
She paused, and tried to arrange her hair. "I'm sorry you have to see me
like this. I must look awful."

"Oh no, not at all. It's rather charming. Of course, if we were going
out to dinner, I don't think I would object if you wanted to take that
thing off and put on a dress."

Mahinta burst out laughing. I joined in, and we shared a moment
of joviality.

"And what about you?" she asked. "Aren't you from England?"

"Yes, I am. From London, actually."

"That must be a wonderful city."

"It was, yes."

Mahinta smiled, and ran her hand repeatedly over a particular
strand of hair while twisting it, as if she intended to braid it. After a
minute, she stopped playing with her hair, and stared dreamily into the
distance. We sat in silence for several moments.

"So," I said, "shall we continue kicking?"

"Okay."

We resumed our routine. She was much more focused, and was
reasonably successful, on most of the snaps, in her placement of the
ball. There were no more tears and no additional bouts of melancholy.
I would say that she (and myself as well) passed the remainder of the
session in good spirits.

I escorted Mahinta back to the main building, dropping her off
at one of the offices. I then went to Moe for a massage. When I left
the massage room, Steve was waiting for me. He asked whether we
could have a word. We left the building and walked toward the kicking
station. He seemed quite tense; I had a premonition that something
weighty was about to follow.

"Jayesh," he said, "I cannot participate with you in any kind of
protest at the Super Bowl." He pursed his lips. "It has to do with my
family and their business connections. I won't bore you with the details,
but someone who is, shall we say, well-placed in the hierarchy, has a
significant interest in the successful conclusion of this event. I can't
ruin it. The result would be catastrophic for people very close to me."

I didn't argue with him. I was well aware of Steve's background,
and the structure of the Gonzales family, whose roots went deep into

the social fabric of the Southwest. I was tempted to ask whether he could launch an intrafamilial lobbying effort. But I desisted, assuming that if it were possible, then surely he would have attempted it.

"By the way," I said, "what did you tell Sam Kapulski?"

"Sam? I haven't heard from him. What did *you* tell him?"

"I haven't heard from him either."

"That's odd," said Steve, now with a look of concern. "The interview he promised is way past due. It's not like him. When he says he's going to do something, he does it." Steve pulled out his cell phone, dialed a number, and waited. A few moments later, he left a message for Sam.

The next day is one I would rather forget. The news of my grandfather's death reached me just after the first practice session of the morning. I became distraught and confused, unable to take any action. Fortunately, the players and coaches stepped in to help, and in a big way. Head Coach Petersen arranged for a private jet to take me to New York, where I would connect with a regular commercial flight to London. This would be just fast enough to arrive in time for the funeral. He asked me to be back in New Mexico within seventy-two hours. Steve drove me to the airport, and before I knew it, I found myself at 35,000 feet, just hours away from a tearful reunion with family and friends.

I was racked with guilt. During the previous year, I had repeatedly put off a trip to London to see my grandfather. Something always seemed to come up at the last minute. I upbraided myself for not having made more of an effort. In the end, he had to die so that his grandson would come visit him. I bit my lip, thinking that this is the way I paid him back for all that he had given me as a child, and beyond.

When the plane pulled up to the gate at Heathrow Airport, I had to force myself to move. Few things are more depressing than being compelled to return to one's home town under tragic circumstances. The feeling only intensified when I got in the taxi, and began the ride to my sister Julie's house. As we drove through the city streets, I viewed the passing scenery with trepidation. Every inch of London conjured up memories of my grandfather.

Hyde Park, for instance, where he used to take me boating. We would row to a relatively secluded spot on the pond, where he trained me in the art of meditation. Back in India, he said, it was easier. In

Europe, there is too much background noise, too much striving and nervosity. Nevertheless, if one masters the methods, one should be able to surmount the obstacles. He told me to close my eyes, and then guided me through the steps. I must admit, it was almost never entirely successful. I often exaggerated and said that it was. Once, however, I really did reach a state of "complete nothingness," as he called it. It was uplifting, to say the least.

I will not burden you with the details of the funeral and the mourning. We are all familiar with this unpleasant business. Also, I do not wish at this juncture to describe my parents, my sister Julie, her husband, or any of the other people with whom I was in contact during that brief and lamentable sojourn. It would not be proper for me to portray them to you—for the first time—in such a state. Allow me, therefore, to defer that narrative to a later point in the story.

It is important, however, that I describe a most unusual meeting that was entirely unforeseen. The fateful phone call came about three and a half hours before my return flight. I was lying on a day bed at Julie's house, just awakening from a nap and not quite fully lucid. The caller, a man with a friendly voice and a foreign accent, said that Sam Kapulski had asked him to call me. Would it be possible for me to meet him and another gentleman, on my way to the airport, to discuss a very important and confidential matter related to the Super Bowl?

I probably should have asked him to call back in a few minutes, so that I could have time to think. But in my fuzzy state, I simply agreed to the proposition. His tone was compelling without being aggressive. It was like an agile salesman who latches onto an aspect of your personality, gently trapping you into doing his bidding.

I packed my bag with great haste, and made my way through the hugging and kissing. Julie accompanied me out to the taxi, giving me a final embrace before my departure. I instructed the driver to take me to the upscale restaurant in Marble Arch at which the meeting was to take place. Upon arrival, I told him to wait outside, and to come and fetch me should there be a risk of missing my flight.

The man who greeted me in the lobby of the restaurant was named Peter Larsen. His accent was distinctly Scandinavian. He had strikingly blond hair, bony features, and a frequent twitching of the nose and upper lip. He was dressed in a classic business suit whose conservative aura was ruptured by a garish yellow tie.

Larsen led me to a booth in the recesses of the cold and somber establishment. There he introduced me to another man: Joseph Hoomty Azala, chairman of UNSAINE, the United Nations Special Advisory Institute on National Expropriation. Azala looked at first glance to be from the Indian subcontinent, a supposition that turned out to be correct.

It was early afternoon, so we ordered drinks and hors d'oeuvres. After the obligatory small talk about the nasty London weather, I floated the question of how they knew Sam Kapulski, and whether they could apprise me of his whereabouts.

Larsen's nose twitched as he looked me over. Azala, meanwhile, took a sip of his cognac. He was smiling, though his mouth remained tense, giving the smile an equivocal air. "It is very difficult to explain what Sam is doing right now," he said, in a somewhat high-pitched voice. "He wants only the best for you, that is sure. Which is why I think you should listen carefully to our proposition. Oh, and by the way, we are sorry to hear about your grandfather."

"Thank you," I said, wondering how they knew about it. "But why all the mystery? If I recall our phone conversation correctly, Sam had asked you to call me."

Azala cleared his throat and displayed his distinctive smile. "Please, Mr. Blackstone, listen to what we have to say. Give us five minutes and *everything* will be clear."

"You will have the chance to perform a great service for world peace," said Larsen.

I was starting to feel annoyed, but was curious to get to the bottom of it. I folded my arms and leaned back. "Okay. What is this great service I am to perform?"

My two interlocutors exchanged a look of satisfaction. Larsen spoke first. "Mr. Blackstone, it appears that you will most likely be a key player in the Super Bowl. And the Super Bowl is the most important annual celebration for Americans, surpassing even Christmas or New Year's Eve. Sports is their religion, and football is the most important sport." He paused, adjusting his yellow tie.

"Yes, it certainly is," I said, playing along for the moment.

"And you," said Azala, "being descended from a Third World people, I am sure that you feel in a similar way to us, that the Americans show off their arrogance at this contest like at no other. It is the peak of their materialistic culture. And it is viewed by more people at once than perhaps any other event in the world. You, Mr. Blackstone, *you* have an amazing opportunity to do something about it. Imagine, just once, *just once*, somebody playing in the game had the courage to get up in the middle of that giant extravaganza of imperialism, and tell everyone the truth."

"What is the truth?" I asked.

"The truth?" thundered Larsen, pounding the table and startling both myself and his colleague. "You want to know the truth? Let me tell you then. That country of yours exploits half the world and drags the other half down in its orgy of overconsumption. And then it has a big festival once a year to rub it in our faces." His eyes were bulging and bloodshot.

"Just a minute, Peter," said Azala, placing his arm on Larsen's shoulder while casting a friendly glance in my direction. "Look at Jayesh. I can call you that, right?"

"Yes, of course," I said. At this point I was starting to feel anxious.

"Look at Jayesh. Is he not one of us, one of the oppressed? Time is short, we should be discussing strategy, not stating the problem, which everyone knows. Right, Jayesh?"

"Right."

"Very good," said Azala, nodding his satisfaction slowly and deliberately. "So let us talk the turkey, as the Americans say…"

"Wait," I interrupted. "Before we do that, I would like to hear the rest of what Mr. Larsen wanted to tell me."

Azala frowned but remained silent.

"Look what has happened to my beautiful country, Sweden," said Larsen, now in a calmer tone. "We have riots, people at each other's throats. The nation is protesting against the terrible oppression. It has suffered greatly at the hands of the Washington oil machine."

Azala had a grim face. "I didn't want to say anything, Jayesh, but Peter is right. I think now of my own village, a typical case of life in a less developed country. Everything is owned by greedy chieftains who are paid off by American corporations."

"Even now?" I asked, in a matter-of-fact tone. "What about President Malpomme's requirement that all corporations have sixty percent people of color on their board of directors, instead of the previous thirty percent? Or her new repatriation program, allowing the Third World bloc of countries to select, every year, ten million of their most oppressed people to come live in the U.S.?"

"These are good things, Jayesh," said Azala in a conciliatory but condescending voice. "Yet they are merely a sprinkle in the bucket compared to the billions of souls who continue to be exploited right now, as we speak."

"We must punish the imperialists in Washington," exclaimed Larsen, his face turning red. Azala again calmed him with a hand to the shoulder.

"Okay," I said. "What about your proposition?"

"It is very simple," said Azala. "At the halftime break of the Super Bowl, when your team goes to the lockups, you will remain on the field. As soon as I give you the signal…"

"What—you're going to be there?"

"Yes, I am giving a speech on behalf of UNSAINE. So, when I give the signal, you come up to the podium, raise your fist, and shout 'America is guilty'. That is all; we'll take care of the rest."

"Your act of protest will be the perfect climax for the halftime show," said Larsen.

"Yes," said Azala, "and the perfect prelude to the flag ceremony."

"What flag ceremony?"

"Didn't Sam tell you about it?"

"Where is Sam, anyway?" I blurted.

"He's taking a holiday," said Larsen, looking down into his drink.

"A holiday? What kind of holiday?"

Azala glanced at Larsen, shaking his head. "I am sorry, Jayesh. Peter sometimes speaks like a cryptic. Don't worry, Sam has gone away for a while—completely of his own accord—until after the Super Bowl. He made it known to everyone before he left. He is in no danger." Azala paused, looking at me for approval.

"How do you know Sam?" I asked.

"We've had a number of dealings over the years. Anyway, I was telling you about the flag ceremony. After some music, which will be brief, the American flag will be lowered to half-size; no, how do you say it…"

"Half-mast?"

"Yes, half-mast. This is in honor of the people of color who have been ruthlessly exploited by America. Then, to symbolize the start of the new era, large balloons, each with the flag of a Third World country, will be released into the air. President Malpomme will appear on the scoreboard monitor in a satellite hookup, and will formally apologize to the world for America's crimes."

"Where do you know this from? Did Sam tell you?"

Larsen twitched his nose and smiled. "You've been out of touch for a couple of days, Mr. Blackstone. It was on the front page of yesterday's *New York Times*."

I glanced at my watch. I probably could have remained for another ten minutes or so, but my patience was wearing thin. "Gentlemen, I'm very sorry, but I absolutely must leave, or I'll miss my flight. Let me think about it for a couple of days, your proposition, that is."

"Certainly," said Azala. "I will contact you."

We shook hands, and I hurried to the taxi. The driver set off for Heathrow. I leaned back in my seat and made an attempt to calm my nerves. I was rattled by the conversation that had taken place at the restaurant. Never in my life had I been exposed to such nefarious plotting. What is worse, I felt like a dupe.

After a relatively quick ride, we pulled up to the curb outside the airline terminal. There was not a moment to spare as I hurried through check-in and customs, almost running to the gate. The plane departed on time. Every stage of the long voyage was smooth, but it was anything but pleasant. In fact, it was miserable. I alternated between torturing myself about my grandfather, worrying about the Super Bowl, and wondering how I would tell Steve about the meeting with Azala and Larsen. How does one go about describing such a meeting?

We arrived in New York slightly ahead of schedule. I felt relieved to be on American soil. After passing customs and getting my luggage, I took a taxi to the terminal housing the private jet that would take me back to New Mexico.

It was almost 9:00 pm when I stepped off the plane in Albuquerque. The last person I expected to see at that moment was Thelonius Brown.

He greeted me warmly, and then escorted me to his car, which was parked outside the private-jet terminal. I learned that Steve Gonzales had been detained at the practice complex, so Thelonius decided to come in his stead. I can't say I was disappointed by the switch. Steve, unfortunately, was a reminder of my helplessness in the face of the gathering storm.

When we arrived at the curb, a chauffeur was waiting alongside a long, black limousine. He took my suitcase and placed it in the trunk, and then opened the rear door, motioning for the passengers to step inside. Thelonius and I entered the spacious cabin, which featured a bar and an elaborate entertainment center. The driver took his spot behind the wheel, turned around to check that we were ready, and then pulled away.

"How's it going, Jayesh?" asked Thelonius. His voice was subdued, and he pronounced my name correctly.

"Tired," I said, not sure whether to launch into anything other than small talk.

Thelonius not only sounded different, he looked different as well. His fingers were lacking the usual rings, and the gold necklace was absent. He wore plain sweatpants, some old sneakers, and a black leather jacket that was unzipped, exposing the football jersey underneath.

"Sorry to hear about your grandfather," he said, patting me on the forearm.

"Thank you."

"And welcome back to the fight." Thelonius looked more serious than I had ever seen him. "You heard about the flag thing—the ceremony and the speeches."

"Yes," I said, glancing out the window at a plane about to land.

"Over my dead body they'll lower that flag."

"I didn't realize you were so patriotic," I said, instantly regretting the silly remark.

Thelonius gave me a piercing glance as he folded his arms. "Not letting someone insult my flag and my country, you call that patriotic? I call it a minimum of self-respect."

"Yes, now that you put it that way, I see your point."

"And that woman coming in to hold for you. Don't tell me you're thrilled about it, Jayesh."

I took a deep breath and sighed a little louder than was necessary. What's the sense holding back, I thought. I looked straight at him. "No, there is no thrill to be had. It has caused me great anxiety. I don't know what I'm going to do."

Thelonius let loose a torrent of laughter that exposed his large teeth. He smoothed his afro, and then slapped me on the thigh. "Jayesh, my man, you're okay. You're the only one on this team with a backbone. The rest of them can smash you to pieces on the field, but threaten them with a little bad press, a little unpopularity, and they come crawling on their hands and knees. I talked about what's going on with just about everyone. And nobody cares."

"What, not even…" I stopped my mouth from its imminent incrimination.

"…Steve Gonzales?"

"Yes, Steve," I said, too exhausted to pretend.

"He made believe it didn't bother him."

I was amazed at the acuity of Thelonius's perception of events. He had the entire situation figured out. I felt encouraged having this new ally at my side.

He proceeded to give me a rundown of goings-on at the practice field during my absence. I made an effort to stay focused, but my mind kept wandering back to the meeting with Azala and the rest of the trip to London.

We arrived at my house. The driver opened the door for me, and removed my suitcase from the trunk. I thanked Thelonius for all his trouble, and watched him roll away in the limousine.

I stood in the driveway, facing the house. The air was cold, but I remained in place for several moments. I was overcome by fatigue. I walked slowly to the front door and opened it. A light was on, shining from the living room. I took a couple of steps, put down my suitcase, and looked around. Ashley was sitting on the couch, smiling coyly.

It took me a second or two to collect my wits. "How did you get in here?" I asked.

"You gave me the key, don't you remember?"

"Oh yes, I did."

"I'm sorry about your grandfather," she said.

"Thanks. How did you find out?"

"It was on some website I was looking at. Sports trivia and gossip. I wanted to see what you were up to."

Before I could respond, my cell phone rang.

"Hello?"

"Hello, Mr. Blackstone. This is Joseph Hoomty Azala."

"Oh yes, of course," I said, with weariness in my voice. I asked Ashley to excuse me, and went into the study.

"Have you had the chance to consider our proposal?" said Azala.

"Yes, but I'm afraid I'll have to decline."

"Are you sure?"

"Yes."

"Very well. Good day, then." He hung up.

I returned to the living room and took a seat on the couch next to Ashley. I gave her a kiss, leaned my head back on the cushions, and stared at the ceiling.

"Who was that?" asked Ashley.

"Just a salesman, badgering me to buy some life insurance. But I told him it's a definite no."

"Oh, I see," she said.

I rolled my head to the side to look at her. She was wearing one of my football jerseys—and nothing else. It came down to just above her knees. My mind was aware of how sexy she looked but my body was exceptionally tired.

"Jayesh," she said, lifting her bare feet up to the edge of the couch and tucking her knees under the jersey. "Would you like me to make you something to eat?"

"Yes, something light would be nice, but I don't know what I have in the kitchen."

"I brought over a few things, don't worry." She stood up. "But don't think I'm *always* going to do this. You also have to do it for me." Her index finger was pointed upward, a gesture I had grown to despise. It ruffled me at that moment, more than I could tolerate.

"Forget it," I said sternly. "I'm not interested in any deals. Make it or don't make it."

She looked stunned.

"I'm tired, Ashley. My grandfather passed away, I just got back from another continent, and I'm playing in the Super Bowl in four days. The last thing I need is some spoiled brat telling me what to do." I looked right at her, my teeth clenched. "You can storm out the door right now and save us both some time, okay? I'm sick of that political stuff and I don't want to hear about patriarchies and conspiracies. Your gorgeous body only works up to a point. Somewhere along the line, you have to be *kind* as well." I stopped as abruptly as I began, and surveyed the recipient of my verbal barrage.

Ashley's mouth was quivering. One hand was gripping the side of her face while the other tugged on the hem of the jersey, as if to indicate that she felt naked without a bottom to her outfit. The tears began to fall. "I'm sorry," she said. "I didn't mean to hurt your feelings."

"Come here," I said tenderly, extending my arms fully in her direction. She fell into a heap on my lap, letting loose a fit of sobbing. I could distinguish several repetitions of "I *am* kind." When the sobbing subsided, she withdrew her head from my belly. "Jayesh, I don't want to storm out. No more politics, I promise." She proceeded to apply the most gentle caresses and kisses to my neck and the side of my head. It was a wonderfully tender display of affection, and it began to arouse me, notwithstanding my frazzled state. We soon found ourselves in bed, crowning the evening with blissful union. There were indeed no politics, no diatribes, not even any alternating reciprocity—just good old-fashioned lovemaking.

The next day was devoted to grueling sessions on the practice field. A major effort on my part was needed to perform adequately. My body was heavy and unresponsive. My kicking leg felt like it was filled with sand. But the worst obstacle was my state of mind. Distracted doesn't begin to describe it. Every few minutes, my grandfather drifted into my consciousness. Efforts to banish it proved futile. Every corner of my soul was filled with sorrow. I wished to high heaven that I could reverse the clock, just enough to see him one last time.

A funny thing about life's problems: Whatever level they are at, we tend to sink into them with our entire spirit. Then when additional hardship arrives at our doorstep, we look back, wondering how it could be that we were so disturbed by the relatively light burden of yesterday. So it was when I received another phone call from Joseph Hoomty Azala. I don't recall the details of the conversation, probably because of the emotional disarray it caused. But the gist of it was simple enough:

Do what he demands, or people will die. In case I had any doubts, I could go watch his videotaped statement, waiting for me in a package dropped off five minutes earlier at the team's front office.

And to the front office I ran, as fast as my legs could carry me. There was no sand in them now; I raced faster than a punt returner. Just as I entered the back of the main building, and passed the doorway of the medical clinic, I literally slammed into a teammate. It was Thelonius, who was on his way out.

"Sweet Jesus!" he exclaimed. "Are you trying out for running back? Good thing I got all my pads on."

I stood there, dumbfounded, panting, pointing to a vague spot down the hall.

"Jayesh, what the hell's the matter with you, man?"

"They're going to murder people!"

"What are you talking about?"

"I have to get to the front office. There's a package there, with a film. I have to see it."

I bolted, he followed, and in short order we had obtained the package, found an empty office, and began playing the disc.

It was a statement from Azala. He was seated at a simple desk; there were no other furnishings and no decorations, other than the seal of the United Nations on the wall behind him. "Mr. Blackstone," he said, in a calm and monotone voice, "you have ignored our call for help. This was your chance to make history. The Super Bowl is an institution whose time has come and gone. It is a relic of an era that must be forgotten, wiped out, erased from our collective memory. We are liberating our own people from the yoke of American imperialism, and at the same time helping America progress into the new era. But you have turned your back on us."

Thelonius and I exchanged a look of consternation.

"You have decided to betray your people in the Third World. But it is not too late to change your mind and help us. Don't think the game is over, Mr. Blackstone. Let us say that we are at the warning of the two minutes, but you have no time-outs left. Please do not disappoint us. If you persist in your obstinate course, we will be standing by at the Super Bowl itself, and we will create our own little disruption. It is too bad that people will have to suffer whereas if you help us, no one will suffer. It is up to you. Finally, we advise you not to contact the police. I would prefer not to give you new condolences the next time we meet in London." The screen went dark.

I sat frozen in place. Thelonius had the presence of mind to remove the disc from the machine, put it back in its envelope, and place it in my hands. "Let's go to the locker room and put that away," he said.

We walked to the other building as fast as possible without looking conspicuous. I put the package in my locker and bolted the door. I leaned my head against the cold steel and shut my eyes.

"Do you have someone in London you can really trust?" asked Thelonius, almost in a whisper.

"Of course. Why?"

He looked at me with his head tilted at a strange angle. "Jayesh, I mean someone you can *really* trust."

"Well, I suppose, yes."

"Call whoever it is and tell him to get bodyguards for everyone. Right now. And for your folks here, too."

"Yes, of course, an excellent idea," I said, a bit embarrassed that I hadn't thought of it myself. "Thanks."

Thelonius put his hand on my padded shoulder. "Do it now. I'm going back to the field. Come back, too, as soon as you finish the calls. Let's not make people suspicious. Act natural, okay?"

"Okay," I said, amazed by his calm supervision of my fate. "Should we call the police?"

"We'll think about that later," said Thelonius. "After practice today, go straight home. I'll drive around for a while and then I'll come to your house." He turned and left the locker room.

I called Prescott, my brother-in-law, Julie's husband, in London. It was necessary to wake him from a deep slumber. It took some time for him to attain a state of sufficient clarity to grasp what I was saying. I refused to provide any details, despite his insistence. I simply demanded that he assign bodyguards to everyone, promising to reimburse any expenses. Being a barrister, he surely had some experience with such matters. I assured him that the controversy would be resolved very soon after the Super Bowl. The conversation ended with a commitment from Prescott to implement my wishes first thing in the morning.

The next call was to my father. He laughed at my request, saying that I was watching too many spy movies. After a couple of rounds of pleading, he agreed to hire a bodyguard, but only temporarily.

Fortunately, these nerve-racking exchanges were followed by some strenuous physical training in the brisk, cold air. I did not have the leisure to immerse myself in doubt and worry. I left for home that evening thoroughly drained. It was not clear how I could muster sufficient energy for the upcoming meeting with Thelonius.

Prior to that time, I had never dreamt that Thelonius Brown would one day be sitting on the couch in my living room. Then again, I never expected any of the bizarre events that were rapidly and rudely overtaking my life.

I recounted to him the conversations with Prescott and my father. I also described the meeting with Azala in London. He patiently absorbed the flow of information.

"Should we call the police?" I asked.

"What would you tell them?"

"Well…about Azala and his plans, that the fans at the Super Bowl are in danger, and that my family has become a target, for starters."

"Let's talk about it," said Thelonius. "You have to be clever with criminals. And the police don't always do such a fantastic job."

"You sound like you know something about it."

Thelonius ran his hand through his hair. "Where I come from, you can't help knowing about it. Crime was everywhere. My older brother was shot by drug dealers. In the hospital, before he died, he made me promise that I would never give in to them. And I never did. My dream was to become a narcotics officer and wipe them out. To survive, I got in with the football team in high school. Football wasn't really my thing, but I learned all about it, and worked out constantly. I made the team. They protected me. There were a couple of other players in the housing project where I lived. We stuck together.

"So," he continued, "if we call the cops right now, what happens? Azala and his guys go completely underground, hidden and protected by their people. He's a U.N. guy, right?

"Right…of course—diplomatic immunity," I said.

"You got it, my man. Who knows what kind of people might get involved. The Feds, everything. Azala could say he's being threatened by us, and then things might get worse. Jayesh, I think you should play along until the end. Tell them you'll cooperate. We can call the cops a few hours before the game, and the place will be flooded with security. Doing it this way will be better for your family, too."

"Sounds like a good plan," I said, impressed by my guest's dissection of the situation. "But should I call off the bodyguards, then, after I speak to Azala?"

"No," said Thelonius, without hesitation. "If you do that, they'll think you're stupid, and they'll be tempted to take shortcuts."

I nodded. "By the way, what do you think happened to Sam Kapulski?"

"Blackmail. Plain, old-fashioned blackmail."

"Are you sure?"

"Pretty much. He's near retirement. Always honest, loves the game of football more than anything else. Normally, he'd just speak his mind. So your buddy Azala is probably telling the truth: Sam decided to take a little vacation where no one can find him. He'll be back after the Super Bowl."

With Thelonius at my side, I made the call to Azala. I did my best to convince him that I really did sympathize all along, I was just concerned about the fallout that would occur after my "declaration of American guilt." Thinking about it more clearly, I could see that I would be making history, and it would very much be to my advantage. Numerous opportunities would follow as a result of my bold action, which will have been witnessed by tens, maybe hundreds of millions of people. Azala was thrilled to "have me on board."

It was getting late. I invited Thelonius to sleep over, sparing him the extra trip to his downtown penthouse. He dispatched his driver, who had been waiting outside in the limo. We continued our discussion a bit longer.

"What would happen," I said, "if, in the Super Bowl, at the last minute, I simply refuse to kick the ball with Mahinta Zagumbi as holder?"

Thelonius was shaking his head. "We have to come up with something better than that. You don't think they'd be ready for it? You'd be serving yourself up on a silver platter. They would call a long time-out, you know, the kind the officials call for no apparent reason. Then our coaches would huddle with the officials, the media would be told that you're injured, they'd escort you to the locker room, and the team would go for it on fourth down. You'd be fired and fined, and as soon as the game was over, they'd tell the press the real story. I can see the headlines now"—he motioned with his arm across the space above his head—"Jayesh Blackstone snubs Miss America."

"Well then, what do you suggest?"

"I don't know, Jayesh, I really don't know," he said, stretching his legs, yawning, and leaning his head back on the reddish Aztec-motif cushions. "We have a few days to think about it. And who knows—something might happen, someone might give us the answer. So stay cool, my man. And remember that while you have to deal with Miss America, the whole team has to deal with the flag thing."

I set up the guest bedroom for Thelonius and said goodnight, thanking him for all his help. I then showered and went to bed, falling asleep immediately. When I awoke in the morning, Thelonius was already gone. I got dressed, had some breakfast, and drove to the practice complex.

That day, Steve Gonzales did not hold for me. He said he had to drill a few new trick plays that were introduced for the big game. I trotted off to the kicking station to start exercising my game-winning foot. Not long thereafter, Mahinta arrived, accompanied by Head Coach Petersen. We said hello, and then Mahinta sat down on the bench and started reading the rule book.

Coach Petersen led me out of earshot. "Miss Zagumbi tells me that you've been very, very nice to her, Jayesh."

I smiled.

"We appreciate that. For today, make sure she can handle that snap. Take as much time as you need. Joe Gramercy said that she was doing well, but we can't be too confident." As Petersen spoke, I saw in his rugged face the features of an individual who had led men, in the Marines, through the most extreme trials. His facial muscles moved as a block; if he smiled, every muscle participated. Likewise for anger and disappointment. There was never a raised eyebrow or other rogue movement that might convey a mixed message. At all times, you knew exactly what you were getting.

"How do you feel about kicking with Miss Zagumbi?" he asked.

I swallowed hard. When I glanced at him, his concentration was complete. When Coach Petersen listened to you, you felt as if a giant radar dish were pointed in your direction. In a way, it was flattering, but it could also be intimidating.

"Well, yes…" I mumbled. "It's fine."

The coach put his arm around my shoulder and led me a few steps further away from Mahinta. "Sometimes, Jayesh, we have to do something unpleasant to achieve a greater good. Right now, the league has made a decision. Should I fight it, knowing full well that one way or another, they would implement it? Should I jeopardize the standing of our team by bringing on a tidal wave of bad press just before the Super Bowl? We have to choose our battles, Jayesh, and this is one we can't win."

I looked at him and nodded. There was indeed a certain logic in his remarks. We both looked at Mahinta for a moment. She was hunched over the rule book.

"What about the flag desecration?" I asked.

Coach Petersen looked away from me and bit his lip, something I had never seen him do. "We're working on that, Jayesh. I'm talking with other coaches and League officials, and with people I know in the Pentagon. I'm hoping that something will develop in our favor. At the very least, when the president delivers her message—we can't very well stop her from doing that—they can leave our flag alone, and keep it as the only flag in the stadium. This is the compromise I'm hoping for."

"Good luck, coach," I said.

He gave me a pat on the back and left me alone with Mahinta. We spent an hour or so practicing our routine, particularly the taking of the snap. I was quite impressed with her progress, and had no doubt that she could perform the task.

After lunch, Steve and I left the cafeteria together. He explained the new trick plays they were practicing, as a backup to the normal game plan. If things got desperate, our team could try the razzle-dazzle.

"By the way," he said, "I tried again to contact Sam Kapulski. No luck. At *Football Icon*, they said he went on vacation for health reasons, and that he had asked not to be contacted until he returns. Then I spoke to Sam's old buddy, Tom Hubert from Cable5, and he gave me the same line."

I was startled by a football flying into Steve's hands. He threw it back to one of the receivers, yelling that he would be with them in five minutes.

"Oh, I forgot to say that Hubert gave me some other information. It is almost certain that the day before the Super Bowl, the U.N. will pass a resolution condemning all-male sports teams."

"We knew that was coming," I said, becoming exasperated.

"Yes, we did. Hubert also told me that during halftime, the U.N. representative will deliver a full-blown speech, not just some brief greetings. It might last ten, fifteen minutes. He and his people will be standing on a giant stage constructed for the occasion. There's going to be a lot of pomp and circumstance. Then of course they'll release balloons with the flags of all the Third World countries, and President Malpomme will make her speech via satellite hookup. It's a complete extravaganza."

I pictured Azala and Larsen addressing the crowd, fists in the air, balloons rising around them. I experienced a lapse of strength, stopped in my tracks, and fixed my eyes on the towering ridge of the Sandia Mountains.

"What is it, Jayesh?"

"Nothing really," I said, as I placed my hands on my hips, stretched my back, and groaned. "Just feeling a bit overwhelmed. I'm not sure what to do, to tell you the truth."

"Well, hang in there," he said. "I'm not so sure myself. I told you that I was out of the picture, and said the same to Thelonius Brown. But all that was based on the issue of the female holder. Now things are getting a lot more complicated."

"You can say that again."

"We'll talk later," said Steve. "See you." He ran to another area of the practice field.

I returned to the kicking station, and completed a full battery of exercises. Later, I joined the special-team squad to rehearse our onside kick. By the time I made it home, well after supper, I was more than ready for the Jacuzzi.

That evening was my last with Ashley before the team's trip to Vermont, site of the fifty-fourth Super Bowl. We were scheduled to depart early the next morning.

The entire visit could not have been scripted any better. Ashley demonstrated that in addition to being highly attractive, she had a good heart as well. I received nothing but tender affection, kind words, and encouragement for the stressful task that awaited me. And this was apparent even before I presented her with a ticket to the Super Bowl, a voucher for five-star hotel accommodations, and a plane ticket.

It is no surprise that at the end of the evening, I fell into a sweet, peaceful slumber. If ever in my life there was a calm before the storm, that was it.

Chapter Four

▼

Super Bowl LIV was played in Burlington, Vermont at the Equal Rights Dome, a state-of-the-art facility with seating for over ninety thousand spectators. The first mezzanine featured a shopping mall with retail establishments selling products that were exclusively fair-trade and made from materials that were biodegradable or recycled. In fact, much of the stadium itself shared these characteristics. For example, next to the main scoreboard was a peace sign, over fifty feet in diameter, made from compacted eyeglass frames.

There was a requirement that at least eighty percent of stadium employees belong to one of the following groups: gay or transgendered individuals, the severely disabled, former illegal immigrants, Native Americans, or ex-felons. The eighty-percent rule extended to all visiting contractors, including television crews. Thus the network commentators had to be reshuffled to suit the occasion. The competing football teams, however, were permitted to retain their usual composition.

We played against the Hawaii Sun Monarchs. When that franchise was established in 2014, the Hawaii state legislature passed a law mandating that all players be of East Asian or Pacific Island descent. Controversy erupted in 2017 when the Sun Monarchs drafted star quarterback Roger Smith from Ohio State University. Smith was only one-half East Asian/Pacific Islander. Under heavy pressure from the public, the law was amended to allow this single exception.

During the last couple of days before the game, my thoughts and those of my teammates turned entirely to football. Mahinta Zagumbi had been withdrawn from view, and Azala was absent from the scene. The press was concentrating exclusively on the football-related aspects of the contest. Even the U.N. resolution calling for the abolition of all-male professional sports teams, passed the day before the game, generated little interest.

We practiced hard—very hard. There was no excess emotional space in which to foment a hostile action of any sort. Thelonius spoke incessantly of how he was going to shut down the Hawaii wide receivers, and flatten the quarterback Smith with a safety blitz.

Contact with Ashley was scant. She had come to Burlington well before the game, but we could not meet, being that all players were restricted to quarters. We did speak a couple of times on the phone, however. She was looking forward to the game, and cheered me on with enthusiasm. The ticket I had given her was for a seat on the forty yard line, about fifteen rows up from the field. She would have Thelonius's sister and her husband on one side, Rebecca Gonzales on the other. I made arrangements for a bodyguard to be seated alongside them.

A few hours before the game, I informed the stadium security personnel that a terrorist attack was likely to occur. I urged them to keep an eye on Azala and his entourage. The security people looked at me like I was crazy, and refused to consider the possibility that the guest of honor, a man invited by the president herself, would be involved in illegal activity. They assured me that security at the facility was hermetic, and that every single person would be checked with sophisticated detection equipment before entering the stadium.

I will never forget Coach Petersen's pep talk in the locker room just before the game. He poured his heart out. He said he loved us like his own children, and would still love us whatever the outcome of the game. The players were more attentive than ever. I caught a glimpse of big Hubbard wiping away a tear. The coach informed us that he would be announcing his retirement a few days later; this was his last hurrah. Each of us had an open invitation to come see him at any time in the future, just for a friendly visit if we so desired, but also to share our toughest personal problems.

The team burst onto the field, awash in adrenalin. After completing our warm-up exercises, we withdrew to the sidelines. I scanned the stands and found Ashley. She blew kisses in my direction, and I returned the gesture. The ceremony of the coin toss was conducted at midfield with great solemnity; among the VIPs present were the NFL commissioner, the mayor of Burlington, and the governor of Vermont. We won the toss and elected to receive the opening kickoff. The Coyotes assembled around Coach Petersen for the full team huddle. I was near the edge and couldn't hear most of his words, what with the deafening roar of ninety thousand excited people. The huddle broke, we cheered wildly, and our receiving team took the field.

Thelonius was back deep to receive the kick from Hang Chen, the placekicker for the Hawaii Sun Monarchs. Chen was considered to be one of the best kickers in the league. He certainly proved it on this occasion, booting one to the back of our end zone. But rather than take the touchback, Thelonius decided to run it out. The man was on fire. Carefully navigating his way behind the excellent blocking, he broke two tackles and was in the clear, with only Hang Chen between him and the goal line. I winced as Thelonius dispatched the kicker onto his rear with a merciless straight-arm, and raced the remaining thirty-five yards for the touchdown. The New Mexico bench erupted into a frenzy. In the midst of it, I saw Coach Petersen applauding, but with a calm face. He knew all too well that such a surprise breakthrough at the outset of the game could have deleterious effects, leading to overconfidence and impaired concentration. But there was soon to be an event that returned everyone to a more sober state of mind.

I was about to march onto the field for the extra point when Coach Gramercy grabbed my arm. "We're sending Mahinta Zagumbi on for this one," he said. "We only have to do it once, so let's get it over with." I nodded and ran to the huddle. Mahinta was already there. A bizarre silence overtook the men, in the presence of the alien. Normally, Steve Gonzales would be there to lead us, but in this case I stepped into that role, and announced the snap count. We broke the huddle and entered our formation. As I measured my steps back from the spot of the kick, I noticed that Mahinta was shaking. It was too late to do anything. She tried to bark the count but was off beat. The ball was snapped at the wrong moment and she bobbled it. I halted in mid stride. Mahinta picked up the ball and ran toward the sideline. A second later, she was buried under a pile of Hawaii jerseys.

The officials cleared the pile, revealing a small, motionless body at the bottom. The players gestured toward the bench for help. The medical team raced over. A hush descended upon the crowd.

The injury timeout took a full fifteen minutes. More and more equipment and personnel found their way onto the field until the area around the ten yard line looked like an emergency room. Finally, Mahinta was put in a body brace. An ambulance drove onto the field. She was loaded in and taken to the hospital. I watched all this with a sinking heart.

I trotted back to the Coyote side of the field for our kickoff. It wasn't one of my best, a wobbler that was scooped up by one of the upbacks at the twenty and returned to around the forty. The Sun Monarchs went to work. Our defense held them to mostly short gains, but they managed to eke out a couple of first downs, arriving at our thirty-two yard line. That was as far as they got before sending out Hang Chen to boot a field goal. He succeeded, and the score became 6-3, in our favor.

The rest of the half consisted of long, grueling drives, or as one of my former coaches used to say, "three yards and a cloud of dust." There were no turnovers and no drama. At the half, we were up 16-13.

My curiosity at what would transpire during halftime was at a fever pitch. After a couple of minutes in the locker room, I feigned leg cramps, and asked Coach Gramercy whether I could return to the sidelines and practice kicking into the net. This would allow my leg to be loose and ready for the second half. (What I have described actually does happen once or twice per season.) He agreed, and I half-ran, half-fake-limped back to the field. I grabbed a tee and a ball, and began exercising.

Meanwhile, the stadium grounds crew was wheeling a stage onto the gridiron. The backdrop displayed the seal of the United Nations. Dozens of balloons were in place. There were no chairs, only a lone podium. I surveyed the rest of the stadium for flags; the only visible ones were those of the United States and the state of Vermont. The main scoreboard displayed a still image of a smiling President Malpomme.

A number of somber-looking people, Azala among them, ascended the stairs at the edge of the stage and arranged themselves in a line, side-by-side. Azala took his place behind the podium. A battalion of photographers crowded into the space in front of the stage. The stadium public address system blasted an announcement: *"Ladies and gentlemen, we are proud to present the members of UNSAINE, the United Nations Special Advisory Institute on National Expropriation. Delivering a message will be the UNSAINE chairman, the Honorable Dr. Joseph Hoomty Azala."* There was light applause.

Azala, with a solemn air, removed a piece of paper from the inside pocket of his jacket, unfolded it, and placed it on the podium. He put on a pair of wire-rimmed glasses and adjusted the height of the microphone. "Dear friends," he began. "It is an honor to be addressing in person this important event. The Super Bowl is the very incarnation of American and capitalist domination of…" His lips continued to move, but the sound had been shut off. He carried on for several moments before one of his associates approached and whispered the bad tidings in his ear.

Another announcement was heard from the loudspeakers: *"Our apologies, ladies and gentlemen, we are experiencing technical difficulties. Please stand by."* Technicians raced onto the stage and examined the podium and microphone from every conceivable angle. Azala, shaking his head and muttering under his breath, stepped back to allow them space to work. After a minute or so of this embarrassing silence, the balloons began to pop. At first, there were several seconds in between pops, but then the rate increased until it sounded like popcorn in the oven. More technicians arrived. The photographers wildly snapped their shutters. Azala was livid, screaming at everyone, hands gesturing in the air.

The surprises had not yet ceased. The scoreboard image of the president suddenly went blank. Meanwhile, the technicians signaled to Azala to resume his speech. He approached the microphone, straightened his tie, coughed, and began to speak. But instead of his voice, the occupants of the stadium heard a rendition of the national anthem at ear-splitting volume. Total confusion ensued. Technicians, photographers, and security personnel ran up, down, and around the stage like agitated ants. Most of the crowd stood up in acknowledgment of the anthem. Azala motioned to his UNSAINE colleagues to follow him off the stage. They left the field in a huff. The stage was hastily removed by the grounds crew.

I continued kicking into the net until my teammates trotted onto the field. I found Steve, and then Thelonius, and recounted all that had transpired in their absence. They listened in utter disbelief. I asked whether they had heard anything about Mahinta. The answer was negative.

Minutes later, I took the field for the opening kickoff of the second half. Fired up from Azala's demise, I booted it out of the end zone. That was the last play in which the momentum was on our side. From then on, it was downhill. Hawaii dominated both offensively and defensively. They could do nothing wrong; we could do nothing right. I kicked a field goal for our only score in the second half. We lost the game 38-19.

During the flight back to Albuquerque on our chartered jet, the players were silent and dejected. Our defeat overshadowed all else. The halftime fiasco was as far from my mind as the plane was from the ground. The overall gloom was compounded when Hank Hannibal stood at the front of the cabin to make an announcement.

"We just heard from the doctors that Mahinta Zagumbi is…well… not doing so good. They're airlifting her right now to New York to try some special surgery, but in all probability, she'll be paralyzed for the rest of her life. The hope now is to at least give her the ability to speak and move her hands." He stopped, evidently choked up. "That's it. I just wanted to let you know."

What a horrible fate, I thought, for that lovely woman. I glanced at Thelonius next to me, and at Steve across the aisle. Both of them were staring out the window with sad, motionless faces.

I was notified by the steward that someone was calling me, could I please come to the front service area at once. I jumped up, my heart racing. As I made my way forward, my thoughts ran to my family in London, and the possible machinations of Azala and his men. At the service area a flight attendant was holding a telephone, which she promptly passed to me.

"Yes?" I said.

"Hi Jayesh, this is Tom Hubert from Cable5."

"Oh, hi Tom," I said, relieved that my family was not the subject of the call.

"You remember that I'm a good friend of Sam Kapulski?"

"Yes, of course."

"I'm in Phoenix at the moment. Can I hop over to see you this evening in Albuquerque? It's important. It's about Sam."

"Is he okay?" I asked.

"Physically, yes, but he has some problems that I'd like to tell you about. Oh, and bring Steve Gonzales if you can."

"Yes, certainly. I'll see if Steve can make it."

"Good," said Tom. "I'll meet you at the Eagle One Hotel, say around ten o'clock?"

"Okay…By the way, could I bring someone else from the team?"

"Sure, if you think he can be trusted."

"He can."

We ended the call, and I returned to my seat. I told Steve that I was going to see Tom, and asked whether he could attend the meeting. He apologized, saying that he had to return home to his wife and young child. I then asked Thelonius, who immediately agreed to accompany me.

After landing in Albuquerque, we found our cars and drove separately to the Eagle One Hotel. We met up in the lobby, and took the elevator to the rooftop bar. Tom Hubert was already waiting for us in a booth, adjacent to the one in which Steve and I had sat with Sam Kapulski. We joined Tom and ordered drinks.

Tom Hubert was a flamboyant character, always ready with a good joke. He was in his mid forties, skinny, with shortish blond hair that stood straight up in clumps, giving his head a spiky appearance. Like Sam, he was one of the few journalists I knew that had his integrity absolutely intact. One could speak freely in an interview because Tom would never twist words or take a statement out of context. He also guarded confidentiality at all times.

"I assume you guys know about the halftime circus in Vermont," he said.

"Yes, we know," I moaned. "I happened to be on the field. Saw the whole bloody mess."

"Well, let me tell you about a couple of things you *didn't* see. First off, in the middle of the fourth quarter, while you guys were busting your butts out on the field, security discovered a bomb in one of the men's rooms. A big one. They just managed to diffuse it."

"Wow," exclaimed Thelonius.

"And that's not all," said Tom. "The disruptions you saw, Jayesh, during halftime—the sound system going haywire, the national anthem blasting away, the balloons popping, the scoreboard shutting off—guess where that came from?"

I shrugged my shoulders.

"Sam Kapulski. He was there in the stadium, disguised as one of those crazy fans with all the war paint. The story about the forced vacation, that was all rubbish, as you British would say. Sam was busy planning the operation. I don't know how he pulled it off, but he did. Unfortunately, sitting in the basement fiddling with all those wires, he blew his cover. Security was onto him in a heartbeat."

"Incredible," I said.

"Is he in jail?" asked Thelonius, nervously adjusting his rings.

"Yes," said Tom, "but not any old jail. Nosiree. At first, they just held him in some room. Meanwhile, our friend Hoomty-Doomty Azala somehow got wind of it, and made a few calls. Then the secretary-general of the U.N. called President Malpomme, who was also, shall we say, quite annoyed by Sam's little policy initiative. After all, he wrecked her presentation as well. Anyway, the whole thing became an international incident." Tom paused to sip his cocktail.

"And we thought Sam had withdrawn from the battlefield," I said.

"That's exactly what he wanted everyone to think," said Tom. "And it worked. But there'll be a price to pay."

"And what's that?" I asked.

"At this very moment they're flying him to Paris, where he'll be turned over to the jurisdiction of the World Tribunal for Peace and Justice. I spoke to some media people there, and the word on the grapevine is that Sam will be charged with a crime under the provisions of the Havana Treaty of 2016. Probably racism with intent to defame the peoples of the Third World."

"Oh no," I said. "He could get life imprisonment, like that guy…I forget his name…"

"Arnburgen, former manager of the Zurich airport, who refused to allow a U.N. plane to land there."

"Why did he do that?" asked Thelonius.

"Because," said Tom, "the plane was carrying the terrorists who blew up the American aircraft carrier last summer. They were on their way to a rock concert, part of that worldwide 'Save the Militants' campaign."

We sat in silence for a moment, pondering the unfortunate news.

"Well," said Tom, "that's about all I can tell you."

"What are you going to do?" asked Thelonius.

"I don't know. Maybe go to a funeral parlor and arrange for the formal burial of American sports. We'll invite Azala to give the eulogy."

Thelonius and I chuckled.

"Seriously, though, I really don't know," said Tom. "I have an appointment in Chicago in a few hours. Then…" He paused for a moment. "Then it's anybody's guess."

The meeting broke up a few minutes later. Tom returned to the airport. Thelonius and I parted with a firm handshake and a promise to get together the following day to discuss our next move.

That night I slept soundly, but woke up late the next morning feeling groggy. After dressing, having some coffee, and otherwise pulling myself together, I noticed on my phone that there was a message from Ashley. I returned her call. She was still in Vermont, about to board a plane for New Mexico. We agreed to get together that evening or the next. She was very sweet, lauding the team's accomplishments despite the defeat. She advised me not to take it to heart; it was a good effort and we'd be back next season for another try. In any case, she had been very excited to see me play.

I called Tom. He had left Chicago at the crack of dawn and was on his way to New York to get the scoop on Mahinta Zagumbi and see some people about Sam's imprisonment. He shared some more information about the case. I asked him to keep me updated on all developments.

The doorbell rang. It was Thelonius. I opened the door and greeted him. We headed to the living room. He was dressed in his casual attire: football jersey, sweatpants, and old sneakers.

"Hey, Blackstone," he said with a big smile. "How does it feel to be starting the off-season?"

"Pretty good," I said. I went to the kitchen to pour some coffee, and he joined me for a stand-up conversation, leaning on the marble countertop.

"Jayesh, my man, how do you feel about not making the Pro Bowl this year?"

"Actually, I'm relieved. The season's over, so let it be over. Anyway, they need to give someone else a chance. What about you?"

"Just what you said, that's how I feel too."

"Listen, Thelonius, I think I need to go to London, right away."

"Why?" he asked, pouring some cream into his cup.

"I just have to see that everything is okay there. Check out the security arrangements, you know, all that. And then go to Paris to try and see Sam. I think I might leave tonight."

He nodded, sipping his coffee.

"What are your plans, Thelonius?"

"Don't know. Probably take a vacation somewhere warm. Maybe go to the Virgin Islands and see if I can find one."

I chuckled after a slight delay, absorbed as I was in my thoughts. "By the way, I spoke to Tom Hubert this morning. He's on his way to New York, to check on Mahinta."

"He's a good guy."

"Yes, he is," I said, downing some coffee. "Do you think we should tell Steve about these developments with Tom?"

"No, leave him out of it. He's got too much pressure at home and from all his local-yokel connections."

"I guess you're right…Oh, no," I said, holding my forehead.

"What?"

"I forgot about Ashley. What am I going to do? She's flying back right now."

Thelonius put his arm around my shoulder and gave me a little shake. "Come on, my man. Snap out of it. Life is good. You're rich, you're healthy, the season is finished, and you have a hot babe coming over. Stop talking like the world is coming to an end."

I smiled. "Sorry. You know, your advice is quite solid. But I still need to take care of all that business. I want to talk to Sam. He saved us from having to do anything. He took the hit."

"I know," said Thelonius, now with a serious face. "Maybe I can take my warm vacation in Europe somewhere, and then end up in Paris."

"We'll end up there together, then."

He wandered into the open space between the living room and the foyer, and started kicking imaginary field goals. "You know, Jayesh, I've never been to Paris."

"Really? Oh, it's a beautiful city, magnificent."

"That's what everyone says…Hey, why don't you take Ashley with you?"

"I don't know," I said. "This trip might get too political."

"So what? She's all fired up about the Super Bowl. My sister said that Ashley went berserk when you came on the field."

"That may not be enough. She might waffle at some point. Maybe she thinks Sam should be sent to prison, for all I know."

"I doubt that."

"I hope you're right."

Before Thelonius went home, we agreed to keep each other apprised of our whereabouts. Our intent was to organize a rendezvous in Paris within a fortnight.

As soon as he left the house, I made arrangements for travel to Europe. At the last minute I abandoned my plan to go directly to London. After having devoted some thought to the matter, it seemed that it would be unwise to interfere with the security arrangements that had been put in place by my brother-in-law. No, I said to myself, the priority was Paris. I felt that there was an important task waiting for me, that I needed to help Sam. This sentiment was not derived from some altruistic impulse, or from guilt. Rather, I believed that I *could* help him, that in some strange way I might hold the key to his release.

I booked two flights for the following morning: one from Albuquerque to Houston, and the other from Houston to Paris. There was a four-hour layover in between, so I called my parents and asked them to meet me at the airport. They suggested lunch at a restaurant not too far away.

Ashley arrived in the late afternoon. She stepped through the door and flung her arms around my neck. It was wonderful to hold her tight against me. After we settled down, I gave her the details of my trip. I asked whether she would be interested in joining me for a time, all expenses paid, once I took care of business. She was thrilled, and rewarded me with another hug.

We were soon discussing the Super Bowl. Ashley wanted to know whether I was depressed at the outcome.

"No," I said, with a melancholy smile. "We gave it our best shot, and Hawaii was heavily favored to win. We're a young franchise, this is just the beginning. Next year will be big."

"You were great out there," she said.

"Why, thank you. So you enjoyed the game, then?"

"Oh, *yes*. It's so different when you see it live. You all look so cute in your uniforms. And I love when the team celebrates, and the fans join in. It's exciting."

I smiled, pleased that Ashley was drawn to my world, if only in this preliminary way. It could lead to progress on other fronts, I figured.

I proposed a festive dinner, and Ashley accepted my idea without hesitation. First I took an hour or so to pack my suitcase and make a few calls. We then got in the Salzburger and headed downtown to the Tickled Rib, a steakhouse generally considered to be Albuquerque's finest restaurant. We had a marvelous time, though interrupted more than once by Coyote fans who wanted to say hello and offer their condolences for our defeat at the hands of the Hawaii Sun Monarchs.

When we returned to my house, I felt on top of the world. I could not get enough of Ashley. At this point in the story, there is no need to further describe our physical relations. Suffice it to say that we had reached a high level of intimacy, with no politics, no artificiality, and no agendas. I was very comfortable and relaxed with her. My only wish was that it would continue indefinitely.

The trip to Paris passed without incident. As planned, I stopped off in Houston to see my parents. My mother was still quite distraught over the death of her father, though not nearly as much as when I had seen her at the funeral in London. I did not mention the underlying reason for my trip, portraying it as simply a personal, post-season vacation. I described to them the Azala affair and my motivation for insisting that they hire bodyguards. After having seen what transpired at the Super Bowl, they understood much better the stakes involved.

After all those years in the NFL, my parents had finally become reconciled to the fact that I was a professional football player. In their eyes, it was the equivalent of performing in the circus. They had urged me to pursue a career in business, or at the very least, in one of the more prestigious professions, such as medicine or a cutting-edge branch of science. My father had paved the way. He was raised in Boston by a family with roots deep in the New England elite, some branches "going back to the Mayflower," as they like to say. He studied business at Princeton, law at Yale, and took his first position with a respected Wall Street firm. Utilizing family connections, he was introduced to people in oil and gas exploration. This led to a position with a top company in Houston, in whose employ he remained ever since.

I partially caved in to the pressure to follow in his footsteps by attending Yale. But I insisted on my preferred area, liberal arts. That was the compromise I worked out with myself: Yale yes, business no. My parents reluctantly accepted my decision, deluding themselves that I would follow the desired path when it came time for graduate studies. Of course it never happened. I kicked field goals for the Yale football team, and then jumped at the chance to play in the pros. It was just the exit from drudgery I had been dreaming of.

My mother would have been happy were I to select virtually any respectable profession, but not sports. For her, the issue was less prestige and more having a "normal" and sedentary life, with a wife, children, and community. Her own family was anything but standard. It was replete with spiritual guides, artists, and other unorthodox personalities. The life she found with my father, with its dignified calm and sense of order, was her escape hatch. Although she would never admit it, I believe she feared that I would return to the unsettled ways of her ancestors in India.

After a model childhood, when I could do nothing wrong and was always adored, there were some tense years between myself and my parents. The tension never went overboard, but things were strained nonetheless. Over the previous three years or so, the two of them had softened. According to my sister Julie, it was because they yearned for the golden days of my childhood. As late middle-age approached, they felt it was time to open their hearts and let the past be the past. And that suited me just fine.

Arriving in Paris, I took a taxi from the airport to my favorite little hotel, the Rostand, located next to my favorite spot in the city, the Jardin du Luxembourg. The hotel was housed in an old five-story building on the Rue de Médicis, facing the gardens on the northeast side, near the Odéon theater. Over the years I had enjoyed several stays there, and numerous relaxing strolls through the gardens.

I checked in, receiving the key to the suite on the top floor. The room was modest by American standards. Amenities included a large double bed, a couch, a desk, and a bathtub. The salon area overlooked the Jardin de Luxembourg.

It was late, and I was exhausted from the trip and the jet lag. Less than half an hour after checking in, I was fast asleep.

I woke up the next morning at around half past nine. After a delicious croissant and café au lait in the hotel's tiny but cozy dining room, I set out to explore the Jardin du Luxembourg. The February air was rather cold; fortunately, I had brought warm shoes, gloves, a hat, and a sheepskin coat that I received as a birthday gift from Steve and Rebecca Gonzales. My first destination was the Médici fountain, a secluded little oasis. I confess that I was somewhat perplexed by the work of art in the middle of the pool: a giant sculpture of a fully-deployed condom, fashioned out of brass and plastic. On the other side of the water was a tour guide with his flock. He was reciting, in impeccable English, the interminable curriculum vitae of the artist.

I continued my walk, stopping to observe several of the fine classical statues that had inhabited the gardens for centuries. When I passed alongside the Senate building, I noticed that the windows on one side had been replaced by stained-glass panels depicting scenes from the great epics of Africa, Asia, Oceania, and the pre-Columbian Americas.

After my walk, I called the offices of the World Tribunal for Peace and Justice, using a special number given to me by Tom Hubert. I asked for an appointment to visit Sam. It might be possible, said the man on the other end of the line. Come in the next day at nine o'clock in the morning, and they'll see what they can do.

Early that afternoon, as I was finishing my lunch, I received a call from Thelonius. It turned out that he had left Albuquerque just an hour after my own departure. He was in Tunisia, staying at a five-star hotel on the beach. He shared with me a rack of complaints: bad service, veiled women, and hostility of the natives toward people "with skin darker than theirs." He mentioned several times that Paris would be so much more interesting. I warned him that it would be much colder, and that the women would also be covered up, if only for protection against the elements. He said he'd take his chances. We agreed that he would fly to Paris on the next plane. Meanwhile, I needed to reserve a room for him at my hotel.

I fulfilled my task without delay. I then went for another walk around the neighborhood, wandering the quaint and narrow streets of the *Quartier Latin*. After dinner, as I was returning to the hotel, Thelonius called. He was in a taxi, on the way into Paris from the airport. We met up a short while later in the lobby of the hotel, where I supervised the check-in procedure.

After getting settled, we took a walk over to the Boulevard Saint-Michel to buy him a winter coat and hat. He had arrived from Tunisia with only a sweater and light jacket to protect him against the cold. After finishing our shopping, we went to a café on Place Edmond Rostand. At the top of the street facing us, Rue Soufflot, loomed the domed silhouette of the Panthéon.

"Deux cafés, s'il vous plaît," I said to the waiter, a kind-looking older gentleman. "Avec une carafe d'eau."

"Oui, monsieur," he replied in a formal tone, bowing slightly before turning away.

Thelonius smiled his wide smile, full of large, glistening teeth. "Jayesh, you speak a pretty mean Frog. At the hotel, too, you rattled off a few good ones."

"Nah, it's just tourist lingo. If I had to talk about anything other than food, lodging, or hours of operation, I'd be lost, believe me."

"So when can we find out about Sam?"

"I set up an appointment for tomorrow morning at nine o'clock."

"Great!"

"However," I cautioned, "it's only an appointment with the people at the World Tribunal of Peace and Justice, with no promises about seeing Sam. I don't know how the whole procedure will work exactly."

The waiter arrived with our coffee and water. Thelonius, with a knitted brow, looked down at his demitasse of espresso. He loaded in some sugar and slugged it down like a shot of whiskey. "Wow, that's strong stuff," he said.

"I think it's meant to be sipped slowly."

"By who, a mouse?"

"Or a desperate elephant. As I was saying, I don't know how fast we can get to see Sam, and under what conditions. Tom gave me the number of a hot-shot lawyer here, in case we run into difficulty. Sam is being held indefinitely, pending the next session of the Tribunal."

"When is that?"

"I don't know, we need to inquire."

"What about the arraignment?"

"There is no arraignment. According to Tom, it's suspended for people arrested on charges of racism."

"Racism?" said Thelonius, rolling his eyes. "Sam Kapulski, a racist? He might be the only one who ever interviewed me without saying a word about race."

"I know, he was the same with me. I never had to worry about explaining the whole India saga."

"I bet explaining that saga annoys the hell out of you."

"Yes, it does, actually. I don't mind discussing childhood, family, high school, growing up, all that. I understand that it spices things up, and satisfies the curiosity of the audience. But when it becomes the centerpiece, with all sorts of assumptions, then it bothers me."

Thelonius began fiddling with his largest ring. "The last guy who did a story on me, all he wanted to know is how much I resent the white power structure in football for exploiting black people. I told him that I make more money than everyone I ever knew before college put together. If that's exploiting, well hell, let's exploit every black person in America."

"Indeed," I said, finishing off my coffee. I paid the bill. We put on our coats and headed out. Fortunately, the hotel was only half a block away.

"Are you sorry you left Tunisia?" I asked, as a gust of freezing wind licked our faces.

"I hate cold weather," said Thelonius, grasping the collar of his coat.

We happily entered the warm lobby of the Hotel Rostand. The cramped, slow elevator brought us to our floor. We said goodnight, agreeing to meet in the dining room at eight o'clock the next morning. I entered my room, and was soon placing a call to Ashley.

She was quite pleased to hear from me, and immediately wanted to know when she could come to Paris. I almost told her to hop on the next plane, but thought of Sam and the grim responsibility that awaited me the following day. I asked Ashley to be patient, promising that I would be free very soon.

In the morning I felt refreshed, more in tune with the local clock. Thelonius and I had our breakfast downstairs, and then took a taxi to École Militaire, site of the World Tribunal of Peace and Justice.

École Militaire was built in the eighteenth century as a military academy. Among its many graduates was Napoleon. It was donated to the U.N. in 2015 by the people of France in order to house the Tribunal. The original structure was left largely intact to serve as a reminder, as the plaque at the main entrance states, that "houses of war can be transformed into houses of peace." The new tenants erected a round steel and glass building in the center of the compound to hold the Tribunal's actual chambers. Some of the former stables had been renovated and converted to detention blocks. It was there that Sam was being held.

The entrance hall of École Militaire featured a life-sized bronze sculpture of an Algerian patriot sprawled on the ground, with a pole driven through his chest. At the top of the pole was a French flag. One of the man's hands was gripping the wound while the other was clutching a book, *The Wretched of the Earth*. The high ceiling above was capped with a dome of frosted glass upon which was embossed the seal of the United Nations. We walked around the sculpture and approached a reception desk that was finished in a luxurious pink and brown marble. A sweet-looking young woman of Asian extraction was there to greet us. I explained the purpose of our visit. In a calm and professional manner, she called the appropriate offices, made copies of our passports, gave us visitors' badges, and summoned an escort.

The escort was a U.N. soldier with a sky-blue beret and an impressive submachine gun. He acknowledged our presence with a cold nod, turned on his heels, and began moving into the building. We followed close behind, without exchanging a word. We exited the building toward the rear, crossed the central courtyard, skirted the Tribunal chamber, and entered one of the detention blocks. The soldier brought us into a nondescript waiting room with raw fluorescent lighting, on the far side of which was a small window. The window slid open with a screech, and the man behind it motioned for us to step forward. We filled out some papers and again showed our passports. We were led by the soldier into a corridor, from which we soon entered a small room. There were several chairs facing a thick glass divider. On the other side of the divider was Sam. He was seated, flanked by two guards standing several feet to the rear.

It was a great shock to see this eminent personality being guarded as if he were a serial killer. The image was harrowing, and it became deeply etched in my memory.

Thelonius and I took our seats and stared at the prisoner, silently, waiting for him to make the first move. "Gentlemen," he said finally, with a subdued smile, "this is very, very kind of you."

"Tell us what to do, Sam," I said. "We're here to help you."

"And get you out of this stinking rat-hole," added Thelonius.

"We can provide whatever you need," I continued. "Lawyers, media, phone calls, money, you name it."

Sam's eyes were moist. "Thank you so much, both of you. I am very moved. But I'm not sure what you can really do, other than what you've done; that is, give me moral support. I already have a first-class attorney from Brussels, a specialist in international law. Tom Hubert is in Paris, he arrived yesterday. He interviewed me, and then composed a feature-length article about my case. It was rejected by all the major media, including the stations and newspapers that run Tom's material on a regular basis. He may have put his career in jeopardy just by writing a nice word about me.

"According to Tom, the State Department is making every effort to help convict me—on the personal order of President Malpomme herself. Can you believe that? The president herself." Sam looked up at us with sad eyes, and put his hand flat against his heart, as if reciting the Pledge of Allegiance. "I'm just a sportscaster, that's all. I don't want to be a political icon. Okay, I ruined their show, but I didn't hurt anybody."

"Don't apologize," said Thelonius. "You took the hit for us. We, the players, should have been out there doing something, but we were too worried about our own glory. You saved the day."

"He's right," I said. "Listen, Sam, we'll get in touch with Tom, so that we can coordinate our efforts."

Sam nodded, again with his subdued smile. He rose from his chair. "Thanks so much."

We also stood up. "Do you need anything?" I asked.

"Thank you, but I have everything I need." He turned and exited the room, guards in tow. Thelonius and I also departed. The soldier accompanied us back to the reception room, and from there across the courtyard to the main building. We turned in our badges, and soon found ourselves on the cold pavement of Avenue de la Motte Picquet. The Eiffel Tower was looming in the distance, at the other end of the Champ de Mars.

We decided to head for a café to regroup and consider our options. On the way we came upon a kiosk, where I picked up a copy of the daily *Le Monde*. We entered the adjacent café, a fancy-looking establishment with plush velour upholstery and art deco fixtures.

"Look at this," I said to Thelonius after we were seated.

"That's Sam!" he exclaimed, pointing to the photo on the front page of the newspaper.

"Indeed it is. The caption says *Raciste américain incarcéré au Tribunal Mondial de P&J*. An American racist locked up at the World Tribunal of Peace and Justice." I scanned the rest of the article. "They say Sam is dangerous, a threat to peace, and involved in some kind of plot, but I don't exactly understand it."

There was a youngish man at the next table, well-dressed, tapping away at his laptop computer. I leaned toward him. "Excusez-moi, monsieur."

"Oui?" he replied, with a deadpan expression.

"Parlez-vous anglais?"

"Oui, un peu."

"Could you translate this sentence for us?"

I placed the newspaper on his table and pointed to the phrase in question. He examined it for a long moment. "I think it says, Mr. Kapulski is also believed to…eh…to be the one who put the bomb in the stadium, which he planned to use for exploding the…how do you say it…what you have in a theater to hold the actors."

"The stage?" I offered.

"Yes, the stage. He planned to use the bomb to explode the stage, where the U.N. officers were doing their speaking." The young man passed the paper back to me, and resumed his typing as if nothing had happened.

"Merci, monsieur," I said.

"Nice," said Thelonius. "On top of everything, they're framing him."

"It's starting to look rather grim. Perhaps we should call Tom and see what he's up to."

"Good idea."

I pulled out my cell phone and called Tom. He did not answer, so I left a message.

"I'm getting hungry," said Thelonius. "What's that guy eating over there?"

I glanced in the direction he was pointing. "Mussels and french fries."

"Looks good. Hey, do they call them french fries here?"

"No, just fries, *des frites*." We summoned the waiter. Thelonius ordered the mussels, and I took a simple broiled chicken filet. Thelonius stepped out of the café to go to the kiosk, and returned with an English-language newspaper. While he perused its pages, I struggled with *Le Monde*, understanding at least the main idea of the articles. We read quietly until the food arrived, and then ate with gusto.

Thelonius paid the bill. "What do you want to do now?" he asked.

"How about something recreational? At least until Tom calls."

"Okay. Like what?"

"The Eiffel Tower," I suggested. "It must be about a five-minute walk from here, wouldn't you say?"

"Sounds about right. Let's go."

We put on our coats and headed out. We crossed Avenue Bosquet, walked the short distance to the Champ de Mars, and turned right toward the Eiffel Tower. The weather was cold but clear, with a very light wind. We walked quickly. Thelonius was thrilled to see the famous monument up close. We decided to take the elevator to the observation deck at the top. There was a line to get in, so we were obliged to wait for several minutes. Before we could reach the ticket booth, Thelonius began to feel ill. At first it was just a matter of discomfort, but soon it was clear that something more severe had set in. We headed for the street to find a taxi. On the way, Thelonius passed behind some bushes so that he could vomit in relative solitude.

At the hotel, I accompanied him to his room. The concierge summoned a doctor, who diagnosed the ailment as "light food poisoning." There was no treatment other than rest and bland food. Thelonius fell asleep, so I watched TV on low volume.

It occurred to me that I should return to the World Tribunal of Peace and Justice, not to see Sam, but to talk to the people there. Perhaps there was some deal that could be made. Or I could gather useful information. In any case, I was accomplishing nothing sitting in the hotel.

When Thelonius awoke from his nap, I shared my thoughts with him. He encouraged me to go, saying that he was content to rest and watch TV, and could call downstairs to order food or anything else he needed. I promised not to be long, and left the hotel.

Chapter Five

▼

My plans were soon frustrated. The lovely young woman at the front desk of the World Tribunal of Peace and Justice suddenly became less lovely. My request to speak to an official from the Tribunal was highly irregular, she said. This was not McDonald's, in which you just stroll in like you own the place and order whatever you want. I needed to apply in writing to the person with whom I wished to speak. I tried several lines of argument, but to no avail. Her stubbornness could not be bent. Then I tried calling the number I had used earlier to arrange the visit with Sam. Again, the response was negative.

I briefly considered offering a bribe to one of the employees. After all, most of them came from cultures where such an act would be a daily, humdrum affair. I rejected the idea as too risky. I considered contacting Sam's attorney, but thought it would be prudent to wait until I had the chance to discuss the matter with Tom. I wanted to avoid duplication of efforts, which easily could produce some embarrassing situations.

I decided to return to the Hotel Rostand. Turning to head for the exit of the lobby, I literally bumped into Joseph Hoomty Azala. He was accompanied by a very large man in a loose-fitting black suit. We looked at each other for a moment before Azala, with an ambiguous smile, patted me on the upper arm. "Jayesh, good to see you. You are here because of Sam Kapulski?"

"Yes," I said, displaying no emotion.

"Good, good. Sorry about your loss in the Super Bowl."

"Thanks, it's okay," I replied, amazed that this conversation was actually taking place.

"Listen, I have some time before my next meeting. Could I invite you to dinner? There's a little place down the street that I like. We'll walk there together."

I hesitated, remaining silent.

"You will be my guest," he added, with a warm smile which this time seemed genuine. "We will take our time and enjoy ourselves."

My first inclination was to remove myself with all possible haste. Then again, I thought, this could be an opportunity. Perhaps a deal was in the offing. Azala might be pouring on the charm because he had something on his mind, something that ultimately could help Sam. In any case, he might let slip some information that could be of use.

"Okay," I said. We began moving toward the street. I glanced over my shoulder at the offensive lineman who was following just behind us.

"That's my bodyguard," said Azala. "Pay no attention to him, he won't disturb us."

We walked to a restaurant off Rue Cler, a few blocks from the Tribunal. Along the way I was treated to a lecture about the architecture in the area. Azala seemed quite knowledgeable as he pointed out representative samples of several styles and periods.

We entered the restaurant, which had Pakistani written all over it; in the name, the decor, the staff, even the smell, which reminded me of similar establishments I had known in London. Azala took me aside as the three of us waited in the vestibule. "You don't mind that I am taking you here?" he whispered. "We can leave if you want. I know that you are Indian."

"It doesn't bother me," I said.

"Excellent. As you probably have surmised, I am Indian too. But in this era of global struggle, all of us Third World people must stick together. If we continue to quarrel, it will only play into the hands of the white man. And the white man doesn't care who is Indian and who is Pakistani. We are all inferior in his eyes."

The maître d' signaled for us to follow. Azala spoke with him continuously; evidently, they were well acquainted. We were brought to a room at the far end of the restaurant. Azala and I sat in a booth while the bodyguard parked himself at a table nearby. The waiter arrived.

Azala, with my approval, ordered for both of us his "usual" complete dinner.

"I like you, Jayesh," said Azala. His voice was calm, and he seemed more relaxed than at our meeting in London. "You are a *real* person, loyal and thoughtful. You let yourself explore the options, but when you make a decision, you stick to it."

"Thank you," I said, feeling a bit more relaxed myself. Azala reminded me ever so slightly of my grandfather. Not the character, mind you, and not even the face, rather an undefinable aura that surrounded them both.

Azala placed his palms together. "Jayesh, I would like to explain a couple of things to you."

"Go ahead."

"First, we never intended to harm anyone, neither your relatives nor the audience at the Super Bowl. Please forgive me. I had to say what I said to convince you that we were serious."

I nodded, but felt a bit less charmed than I had been a minute earlier. "What about the bomb in the men's room at the stadium?"

"The bomb? What bomb?"

"The one found by security. You had nothing to do with it?"

"Oh, Jayesh, no, of course not. There is a time for war, I admit, but not at a sporting event. It's like being in somebody's home."

I glanced downward, reluctant to reveal my skepticism.

"You know, Jayesh, I think there is one thing we can agree on right now, and that is the subject of your American women. They are corrupting society with their behavior. We have great fears in my country that it will spread. This is very dangerous. In Asia, as in most of the world, the women are busy with their real obligations; that is, taking care of their families. Look what is happening to the Super Bowl. A woman playing in your greatest game? You can't be too happy about that."

"No, I'm not," I said, newly fascinated by the man across the table.

The food began to arrive. We ate quietly for several minutes, speaking only to compliment the chef. At a certain point I needed a break, so I placed my cutlery on the plate and leaned back. Azala, looking satiated, did the same.

"Tell me," I said, "if my American women repel you, why are you cooperating so closely with our chief woman, President Malpomme?"

Azala began rubbing his thumb against the handle of his fork. "Because she supports us on almost every issue. One has to be realistic, n'est-ce pas?

"Yes, I suppose."

"She will be replaced, like all your presidents."

I wanted to say that this was considered by many to be a positive feature of the American political system, but Azala had uttered the words with such scorn that I backed off.

"Jayesh, there is going to be an important reception at the White House in late March…"

"The one for disadvantaged Asians in sports and entertainment?"

"You know about it?"

"I was invited."

"I'll be there too, representing UNSAINE."

I pictured the scene, which I figured would be a replay of the botched halftime extravaganza at the Super Bowl, but this time without the technical malfunctions.

"It's important that we Asians show solidarity," said Azala. "This is an excellent occasion for doing so. When the White House gives its stamp of approval, well, this is a great moment for us. If you could say a few words there, Jayesh, it would be quite valuable. You know how important sports heroes are in America."

I didn't at that time (or at any other time, for that matter) consider myself a "sports hero." Nor an Asian, and especially not a disadvantaged one, but I said none of this to Azala. There was some positive energy hovering around the table, and I was reluctant to spoil it. I very much wanted to turn it to my advantage—or, more accurately, to Sam's advantage.

"You know, Mr. Azala, there is something compelling about your arguments. I don't think I would be opposed to saying a few words at the White House event."

Azala's face lit up. "That is wonderful…"

"However," I said, holding up my hand, "I cannot make any disparaging remarks about the Super Bowl, or against my teammates, my friends. That I cannot do."

"I understand, Jayesh," said Azala, with the more genuine of his smiles. "And I would not ask you to do that."

"Thank you. Let us say that I would not speak *against* things, but rather in their favor. Urge the public and the government to help poor people in Asia, for example."

"Yes, yes…This is an excellent start."

I caught a glimpse of the bodyguard. He was sipping a cup of tea while staring, expressionless, at a point in space above my head.

"I am so pleased at this news, Jayesh," said Azala, leaning forward. He was looking at me with the same expression I had seen occasionally on my grandfather's face whenever I did something that was especially endearing to him.

I summoned all my emotional strength for the statement that I was about to make. I needed to exploit my advantage, and do it precisely at this opportune moment.

"Mr. Azala, there is something else I need to tell you."

"Yes…"

"If indeed at the White House reception I say something to help the people of Asia, in a manner you would endorse, might it be possible to forgive a certain person who disrupted what should have been a fine moment for you?"

Azala's face adopted a neutral look. "Let me think about it," he said, slowly drawing out the words. "I respect your motives and your loyalty. But, as you can imagine, the matter is complex."

"Of course. We can discuss it further at a later time. And by the way, it would be a good idea not to mention this to anyone. If someone close to me finds out, my situation would become awkward."

"I understand."

Azala paid the bill, and we headed for the street. He said he would be in Paris for another week or so, and invited me to dine with him and some associates at his hotel suite. I accepted the invitation, and was told that I would be contacted very soon. After walking a couple of blocks, we parted on Avenue Bosquet. I hailed a cab while Azala and his bodyguard continued on foot back to the Tribunal.

In the taxi, I considered withdrawing the guards that were protecting my family in London and Houston. I rejected the idea, however, thinking it more prudent to wait until my next meeting with Azala. Who knows what might transpire in the interim.

I arrived at the hotel. After dropping off my coat in my room, I went to visit my ailing companion. Thelonius was propped up in his bed, watching an English-language news channel on TV. He looked well. I pulled over a chair and sat down. I noticed an empty pizza box on the floor next to the bed.

"Is that a special type of pizza for people with food poisoning?" I asked.

"You got it," said Thelonius, with a chuckle. "Prescribed by the doctor himself."

"That's my kind of doctor."

"So, my man, how did it go?" he said, turning off the TV.

"Rather odd. I wasn't able to see anyone at the Tribunal. They say I have to apply in writing."

"They think they're hot stuff."

"Yes, they do. By the way, I bumped into our friend Azala. He took me to dinner."

"You're joking, right?"

"No," I said, "it really happened. The whole thing was very interesting. Azala was quite friendly. It turns out I may be able to make a deal with him. We discussed it in general terms. I would say something he likes at the White House reception for disadvantaged Asians, and in exchange, Sam is released."

"Wow…"

"It's a long shot, Thelonius. He said he has to think about it. We're meeting again in a few days."

My phone rang. It was Tom Hubert. I put him on speaker.

"Hey guys, how are you liking gay Paree?"

"Not bad," I said, "but Thelonius is perhaps a bit less enthusiastic."

"I had some food poisoning," said Thelonius. "But I'm okay now."

"That's good," said Tom. "Listen, you two. Tomorrow at noon I'm holding a press conference in the courtyard of the Louvre, next to the glass pyramid. I'll be talking about Sam. Why don't you come by, and then afterwards we'll go out for lunch."

I looked at Thelonius, who was nodding his approval. "Fine," I said. "We'll see you tomorrow at noon."

"Oh, and by the way," added Tom, "you have regards from Steve Gonzales."

"Thank you."

"I'm guessing he's too embarrassed to call you right now."

"Probably true."

The next morning, Thelonius felt much better. We had breakfast at the hotel and headed out early to the Louvre, taking advantage of the occasion to visit one of the world's great museums. Fortunately, there were few people and no lines. We decided to go see the Mona Lisa. Thelonius of course had never seen it, and I had done so only once, as a young boy. We bought our tickets and entered the museum.

The Louvre had devised a most curious method of display. The Mona Lisa was one of twenty illustrious works that were spread out in as many rooms. In each chamber, the work itself was shown alongside older pieces of art, from non-Western countries, which the artist had copied to make the famous masterpiece. Alongside the Mona Lisa, for example, was a bronze bust from fourteenth-century Thailand that bore a striking resemblance to the subject matter of the painting. A video presentation explained how Da Vinci and his Chinese servant laboriously transferred the image of the woman from the bust to the canvas via an intricate procedure that included various molds, chemicals, and tracing. Similar stories were recounted in the case of the other nineteen presumed original masterpieces.

This unique cultural experience was followed by Tom's "press conference." In reality, it consisted of Tom and his cameraman standing in the freezing Louvre courtyard, with the glass pyramid in the background. He told us later that not a single journalist had responded to his invitation, which was sent to the entire international press corps. Meanwhile, no one else had bothered to interview Sam. Several articles and news spots had appeared in Europe, and even one or two in the U.S., but they were based exclusively on UNSAINE press releases and interviews with U.N. and State Department officials. Tom's own Cable5 made do with a two-paragraph blurb they picked up from one of the wire services. He had been sure that this story would be a great scoop, since it featured an exclusive interview with Sam, described by Tom as "the dean of American sportscasters, now languishing in a U.N.

prison cell, awaiting trial for racism." It was not clear what he would do with the completed video clip and transcript.

I scanned the surrounding environment, taking in the view of the Concorde obelisk at the far end of the Tuileries gardens, with the Arc de Triomphe looming in the distance. I noticed that Thelonius was shuffling back and forth to keep his feet warm. "Hey Tom," he said, as soon as the sportscaster had paused.

Tom looked our way with a little frown.

"Hey, my man, who are you talking to?" He motioned with outstretched hand to the nonexistent audience.

Tom's shoulders sagged and his arms went limp, causing the microphone to point at the ground. The cameraman stepped away from the camera.

"You know what, Thelonius?" said Tom.

"What?"

"I have no good answer to your question."

"Do you want to interview me?" I said, thinking that it might raise Tom's spirits, but then realized that I had just made a pathetic situation even more pathetic.

Thelonius patted the top of my head. "Jayesh, I think your brain might be frozen." The three of us laughed.

"Hey, you guys," said Tom, "let's get the hell out of here." He turned to the cameraman. "Pierre, you can go. Do the usual edits and send it to me for a final review." The cameraman nodded, folded camp with astonishing rapidity, and disappeared into the pedestrian traffic.

"So where are we going?" asked Thelonius. "Wherever it is, let's get there quickly. I can't stand this cold anymore."

"I know a nice café on the other side of the Louvre," I said. "We can go there just to warm up."

The others agreed, and we set off. We walked through the passage cut into the museum on its Rue de Rivoli side, and headed for the Place du Palais Royal. The café was situated across the square, between the Comédie Française and the Conseil d'État.

We took our seats and ordered hot chocolates, seeking an antidote to the chill that had descended into our fingers and toes. Enveloped in warm air, we became lethargic. Thelonius faded into his thoughts. Tom looked dejected, the picture amplified by the position of his tie, which he had absent-mindedly loosened and skewed to one side.

An eclectic crowd was gathered in the café. A family of loud Italians had spread maps of all sorts across the surface of their table, and were now arguing about their next move. In a dimly-lit corner booth, a middle-aged homosexual couple were engaged in tender kisses and embraces. At the booth adjoining theirs was an older woman with a doleful face and a greasy scarf, sipping her espresso while staring out the window. At the other end of the room, near the bar, two thirty-something women in business suits sat behind a laptop, chirping away like canaries.

We sipped our hot chocolates, our hands wrapped around the warm mugs. Thelonius turned to Tom. "Life sucks, huh?" he said in a playful tone, reaching over and patting the dejected sportscaster on the shoulder.

Tom displayed a pout.

"You know what, Mr. Hubert," said Thelonius, now leaning back and folding his arms. "You need a good night on the town. Eat some snails, some frog's legs, and some moldy cheese. Go watch some cancan girls, drink expensive wine, get to know one of the girls a little better, and forget your troubles."

"What about us?" I asked. "Don't we get to eat moldy cheese, and all that?"

"Nah," said Thelonius. "We're the chaperones. Maybe we'll get some scraps, if Tom lets us."

We all shared a good laugh, and returned to our hot chocolates. I caught sight of the two male lovers, whose tongues were dancing across each other's lips.

Thelonius removed his largest ring and began fiddling with it. "Guys, what are we going to do about Sam?" he asked, leaning forward and lowering his voice, as if in a huddle. I sighed, feeling rather clueless, and looked with anticipation at Tom. His eyes darted between Thelonius and myself, but he said nothing.

A man entered the café and took a seat at the table next to ours, even though numerous vacant spots were available. He bore a striking resemblance to my cousin Robert, from the Indian side of the family. The man, who looked about forty, was of slight build, and wore an oversized beige trench coat. There was a distinct nervousness in his manner, the body movement being somewhat jerky.

I glanced at my companions, who were eyeing the stranger with a mix of suspicion and curiosity. An uneasy silence descended upon us. The waiter took the man's order, a simple coffee.

Our new neighbor's hand was shaking as he rummaged through his coat pockets, failing to find the object for which, apparently, he was searching. He scratched the inside of his ear rather violently, and then, without looking up, said: "I can help you."

The three of us looked at each other with stunned faces. "Are you talking to us?" said Thelonius.

The man stood up and clumsily re-arranged his chair so that it was facing us, banging it several times against the edge of the table. He retook his seat. "Yes," was the reply. He was now looking directly at us with his nervous eyes.

"With whom do we have the pleasure of speaking?" asked Tom, with an expression of amusement.

"My name is Naveen. I am from Sundar Prabhat, the same country as a man we all know, Joseph Hoomty Azala." He spoke with a refined tone, in a classic English of the Indian subcontinent. He seemed calmer now, his hands clasped together in his lap. "I can help you because we are all confronting the same person."

"We're *confronting* someone?" said Thelonius, with a note of distrust in his voice.

"Sorry, a poor choice of words. Let us say that you want to free Mr. Kapulski from his imprisonment at UNSAINE, while I and my colleagues would like to free Sundar Prabhat from the clutches of a tyrant."

"Where the hell is Sundar Prabhat, anyway?" said Thelonius.

"It's a very small country that used to be part of India," said Tom. "It became independent a few years ago."

"Who are these colleagues of yours?" I inquired.

"I cannot mention any names at the moment," said Naveen.

"If you tell us," said Tom, laughing, "you'll have to kill us."

Naveen pursed his lips. "I am trying to be serious with you. But maybe you're not so serious about helping your friend."

"Just kidding, just kidding," said Tom, his smirk still in place. "All right, so what exactly are you proposing?"

"I am proposing that Mr. Jayesh Blackstone visit my country."

"Just Mr. Blackstone?" asked Thelonius.

"Yes," said Naveen. "Just him."

"What about us?" said Tom.

"Just Mr. Blackstone."

"Why?"

"Those are the instructions from my colleagues."

"And what would you have me do there?" I asked.

"Meet with a very special man."

"Who shall of course remain nameless," said Tom.

"Yes," replied Naveen.

"This is crazy," said Thelonius. "You expect Jayesh to follow you all the way to this Sundar Prabhat place, just because you have a *special man* who wants to speak to him?"

"Okay then, never mind," said Naveen, flashing a piercing glance in my direction. Our eyes met briefly, but long enough to convey a certain type of intensity that I had not seen in many years. In fact, I had nearly forgotten what it was, yet it all came back to me in that moment. It was very Indian, unmistakably so. I had seen it on some of my relatives, including my grandfather. This signal was all I needed to proceed with confidence.

"I'll go," I said.

"Are you nuts?" said Thelonius.

"Maybe."

"He's not serious," said Tom, with a pained expression. "Jayesh, we have to talk about this. You don't have to give the man an answer this very second."

Naveen rummaged through his coat pockets, this time extracting a small manila envelope, which he opened. He removed an old-fashioned plane ticket, which he placed under my nose. "There," he said. "A sign that we are serious. One round-trip, first-class ticket to our capital city, Shubh Nagar. The flight leaves just after midnight from Charles de Gaulle airport." Naveen again reached into the envelope, producing what looked like an oversized business card. "You will have a car, and a driver, waiting at the airport. The card is a voucher for up to a week's stay, all meals included, at the Progress Hotel. It's the best hotel in the city. *Now* what do you say, gentlemen?"

I slowly and deliberately gathered the items from the table, placed them back in the envelope and, under the astonished gaze of my companions, zipped it all into the inside pocket of my coat.

"I'm going," I said, solemnly. "I believe that I can help Sam."

"If anything happens to him," said Thelonius, pointing an accusatory finger at Naveen, "I'll come looking for you."

"Me dear sir," said Naveen, "you and I, and my colleagues, share the same goal. We can help you, you can help us. Together we can accomplish more than you can imagine. Of this I am certain." He stood up. "I will leave you now. You may or may not see me again on this trip. Have a good flight, Mr. Blackstone. As I said, the driver will be waiting for you at the airport. He will take you to the hotel and stay with you until my people arrive. They will not waste any time because there is no time to lose. Good luck." He turned and left the café.

Thelonius and Tom spent the next half hour trying to dissuade me from implementing my admittedly rash decision. I tried my best to explain the intuitive feeling that Naveen was trustworthy. They said I was being childish and naïve. When it became apparent that I would not renege, they suggested sending a bodyguard or two, surreptitiously if need be. This appeal I rejected as well.

In retrospect, I believe that another factor was at work, pushing me onward to Sundar Prabhat. Something had awakened my long-dormant connection to Indian people and culture. It began with Azala, but was particularly strong in the case of Naveen. Why it should occur then, under such conditions, is still a mystery to me. Not that an awakening of this variety can ever be rationally explained, mind you.

Tom, Thelonius, and I took a taxi from the café to an excellent restaurant on the Ile St. Louis. The fine French cuisine buoyed our spirits. Lingering over the coffee and *digestifs*, Tom and Thelonius laid out a strategy for the upcoming week: help Sam by day, cruise the city by night. Thelonius insisted on moving Tom and himself (at his own expense) into one of the most upscale hotels in Paris. At that point, it occurred to me that it may have been just as well that I was leaving for a few days. The manner of entertainment they both fancied would not have been to my liking. I do not mean to imply that there was anything objectionable in their plans. It simply would not have amused me, as the French say.

Thelonius and I returned to the Hotel Rostand. It was already evening. I packed for the trip while Thelonius did the same for his hotel upgrade. Few words were exchanged, although he looked at me several times with a frown, shaking his head to emphasize his disapproval.

We parted in front of the hotel, each man taking his own taxi. Thelonius gave me a hug. It was so genuine and his worry about me so palpable that it brought me close to tears.

The flight to Sundar Prabhat was nerve-racking. It was not the fault of the airline; we departed on time, the staff were courteous and efficient, and the flight itself was smooth. The problem was my emotional state. I was confused and apprehensive. What would I find in Sundar Prabhat? Clones of my grandfather, or something much less pleasant?

I was not able to sleep a wink on this nine-hour overnight voyage. The plane touched down just before noon, local time. I dragged myself through the airport, my brain immersed in a thick haze. My eyes glazed over as I watched the luggage revolve around the carousel. I quickly became focused, however, when the man at passport control asked me probing questions about my origins, my profession, and the nature of my trip. After emerging from the customs area, I quickly spotted my appointed driver. He was a large, somber-looking man, courteous yet aloof. He took my suitcase and escorted me to the car, which was parked in a nearby garage.

Once we left the ultra-modern airport, the scenery changed drastically. The city of Shubh Nagar was a depressing sight. The air was hot, humid, and fetid. Poverty was everywhere. Whenever the car stopped, we were surrounded by children, begging for a coin or scrap of food. The driver cautioned me against opening the window, saying it could be quite dangerous. Most of the children were innocent enough, but there could be others lurking among them, ready to cause trouble. So I remained in my secure bubble, my heart aching from the spectacle before me. The anguish was compounded by the resemblance between some of the children and my cousins, as I remembered them from childhood.

The streets, the sidewalks (such as they were), and the buildings were in a state of advanced deterioration. There was no discernible pattern to the architecture. Tin shacks, mud and brick huts, and Soviet-style concrete blockhouses were smack against each other.

All of this changed, however, when we reached the area close to the Progress Hotel. It was an enclave of wealth and serenity. The hotel itself was as magnificent as the slums were squalid. I had the sensation of wandering onto a movie set constructed for a film about Burma in the 1920s. We passed through a majestic iron gate flanked by squatting lions made of beige-colored stone. A crescent-shaped driveway cut a path through a lush garden to bring us to the main building, which had a magnificent white façade in the grandest colonial style. Porters were present in abundance. They would not allow me to lift a finger. My driver informed me that he would park the car and meet me at the front desk, and off he went.

I followed the porter into the lobby. It was a splendid scene. Well-heeled gentlemen and ladies were coming and going at their ease. In the center of the space was a fountain, spewing its water into a pool filled with sparkling tropical fish. On my right, large earthenware pots, holding a wide variety of exotic plants, formed a demarcation between the lobby and the bar. The same pattern repeated itself on my left, but in this case the semi-secluded area contained an elegant restaurant. Those fortunate enough to dine there were treated to beautiful china, finely-carved crystal, and gold-plated cutlery. Ceiling fans kept them cool while a battalion of waiters catered to their every need.

The check-in procedure was smooth and painless. As I was signing the registry, my driver returned. He exchanged a few phrases with the clerk. The porter led us to a wing of the hotel adjacent to the lobby. We climbed a flight of stairs to the second floor. The room, or rather the suite, was no less impressive than the earlier scenes. It contained sumptuous rugs, vases, and fabrics decorated in classic Indian motifs. The porter opened the windows and shutters, letting in the abundant light. With great pride, he showed me the balcony, which overlooked bountiful gardens. At the back end of the gardens, about thirty yards away, was a high stone wall topped with barbed wire.

I tipped the porter, who responded with a bow before leaving. The driver informed me that in addition to being a chauffeur, he was also my temporary bodyguard. He would be waiting in the hallway, just outside the door, and I should holler, quite literally, if there were any problem.

My original plan was to make some phone calls and take a bath, but the five-minute rest on the bed turned into a three-hour nap. I awoke in a foggy state, but anxious to rise and organize myself, which is what I proceeded to do. The phone rang at precisely the moment I had finished washing and dressing. It seemed that Naveen's statement proved to be correct, that his colleagues would waste no time.

"Hello," I said, answering the phone as I leaned back in a Victorian wingchair.

"Mr. Blackstone," said the voice on the other end, sounding quite like Naveen's fine colonial English, only with more bass. "My name is Raghavendra Hunter. How was your trip?"

"It was fine, thank you."

"Good. Let me know if there is anything you need. In any case, I am pleased that you have come to Sundar Prabhat. We have many things to discuss. Could I join you for dinner at the hotel, say, in an hour from now?"

"Certainly," I said.

The meeting was set. I was about to dine with Raghavendra Hunter, Naveen's "special man," about whom I knew nothing, in an impoverished city, to discuss the fate of a man imprisoned on another continent thousands of miles away.

I called Thelonius, letting him know that I had arrived safely. Then I considered calling Ashley, but desisted at the last moment. I missed her, and would have liked to hear her voice. But explaining the fact that I was in Sundar Prabhat would be a complex task, and it might worry her needlessly. Better, I thought, to wait until we meet in Paris, at which time I could explain everything that had transpired since I left New Mexico. I was hoping that in very short order, I would conclude my business in Sundar Prabhat, fly back to Paris, make the deal with Azala, and then rendezvous with Ashley.

About five minutes before my scheduled meeting with Raghavendra Hunter, the driver knocked at my door. He informed me that Hunter was arriving. I was escorted downstairs to the lobby. After a few moments, I saw a man walking toward us. "That's him," said the driver, who promptly disappeared from the scene.

"Nice to meet you, finally," said Hunter, shaking my hand.

"Pleasure," I said, smiling as I viewed the *special man*. He looked a bit like myself, but about twenty years older. The skin tone and face seemed quite Indian, yet the body was tall and lanky, like a certain strain of Englishman. He wore a flowing white gown and simple leather sandals.

"Perhaps we can take a little stroll around the block, before eating."

"That would be delightful," I said, eager to see some of the local sights. We headed for the front door. A blast of hot, humid air awaited us on the other side. We began to follow the driveway. A black Mercedes was parked a few yards ahead. As we passed it, Hunter raised his arm to attract the driver's attention, then motioned toward the gate. The driver nodded, and pulled slowly out of his spot. "That's my bodyguard," said Hunter. "He'll be following us."

I glanced over my shoulder, apparently with a concerned look.

"Don't worry. We're in Freeville, probably the only safe neighborhood in Shubh Nagar. Most of the embassies are here, as are the residences of anybody who is anybody. I bet there are more bodyguards, security devices, and firearms per square foot than any other spot on the planet. But we still can't be too careful."

We passed through the gate of the Progress Hotel and began our walk along the street. There were few pedestrians and no shops. The numerous trees exuded coolness and a fresh, pleasant scent. Most of the buildings were located within walled, gated enclaves, many having surveillance cameras and armed guards in sentry posts. All the while, Hunter's bodyguard was creeping along in the Mercedes, just behind us.

"Can I call you Jayesh?"

"Yes, please do."

"You know, Jayesh," he said, slowing the pace, "we have a lot of similarity in our backgrounds. My parents are like yours. I have an Indian mother and a British father. I was born in Sundar Prabhat. But I spent the greater part of my childhood in England. It was during the summers, mostly, that I found myself here. I speak English much better than I do the local dialect. Eventually, I received my PhD in economics from the University of Edinburgh, and then found a post at Oxford. I was all set, or so I thought."

"What happened?" I asked.

"When Sundar Prabhat became independent from India in 2015, the new government asked me to come here, to help place the economy on a solid footing."

"And did you?"

"Yes," said Hunter, emphatically. "It was actually a minor miracle. Before our independence there was a bloody insurgency and terrible corruption. The place was a mess. I think the Indian government was pleased to wash its hands of us. Anyway, we liberalized business rules and cleared out most of the corruption. But all that changed in late 2018, following the coup d'état, led, as you probably know, by Benzona and his men."

I remained silent, barely aware of the existence of the man's country, let alone its politics or history.

"A shakeup occurred, as dramatic as the one in 2015, but in the opposite direction. We became inundated with bureaucracy and bureaucrats. Suddenly, there were U.N. projects everywhere, along with hostility to Westerners. You know the drill. The People this, the People that, while the *real* people slide into ever-deeper misery and dependence."

"That's a shame," I said.

"Indeed it is. And it's also a shame that Joseph Hoomty Azala was involved. His family is very powerful here, and close to the Benzonas. They made sure old Joey got a comfortable little job, which was ambassador to France. He gravitated toward the U.N. crowd, definitely his natural habitat, and then UNSAINE scooped him up. Now *that's* a match made in heaven."

"I'm sure what you say is true," I said. "But when I met Azala, he seemed to be very enthusiastic about the rising power of the Asian countries."

Hunter laughed. "Oh, is that how he seemed? He dreams of power, all right, but only his own. And where is our savior now? Here in Sundar Prabhat, doing the hard work of developing the country? Or is it rather dining in fancy restaurants in New York and Paris? His approach is quite different, Jayesh. One could say that he has made some real contributions—if you count support for every petty dictator in the world, and condemning America in the middle of the Super Bowl."

We passed the British embassy. It was fortified to the hilt, looking like it could withstand a nuclear attack.

"What we need," continued Hunter, "is to work *with* the West, not against it. This is what we had been doing. Businesses were created, and I convinced some important expatriates to come home. We began to clean up the city. But alas, Jayesh, this is the Third World. Nothing is stable, and everything can be reversed from one moment to the next."

We turned the corner onto a wide boulevard. I could see the hotel in the distance. "That's all very interesting," I said, "and I admire your commitment. But surely you didn't fly me down here to educate me about your country."

Hunter stopped walking and smiled. "I will explain everything, but not here on the street. What I propose is that we go to my house. We can relax and have a serious talk, and of course some dinner. What do you say?"

"That would be fine," I said, brimming with curiosity.

Hunter signaled his driver to approach. We got in the car and sped away. After reaching the end of the boulevard, about four long blocks from the hotel, the scenery changed rapidly. Aside from a few tolerable streets just outside the Freeville quarter, the dive into poverty was abrupt. As in my trip from the airport, the avenues were teeming with people. Beggars were everywhere. While we were stopped in traffic, I saw the police drag a man from a doorway, whack him with a club, and throw him into a waiting van. Neither Hunter nor the driver paid any attention, leading me to the conclusion that this was a common event in Sundar Prabhat.

We emerged from the dense urban space into a more airy suburb. Much of the backdrop was the same, only spread out. We crossed a bridge over a canal, on the other side of which the land use was primarily agricultural. Soon we turned onto a side road and passed what looked like an armed checkpoint, though with civilians, not soldiers, holding the weapons. We followed a winding road, coming to a stretch that looked like Freeville: High stone walls with barbed wire, interspersed with gates. The difference was that here, the gates were not manned, though I did see surveillance cameras. At one point we stopped to allow a group of well-dressed children to board a school bus. Moments later, we turned and passed through one of the gates.

The compound resembled a smaller version of the hotel. A crescent-shaped driveway cut through lush vegetation, and even the façade was quite similar. There was only one porter, in this case the butler, an aging African man in a spotless white suit. He opened the car door and greeted us. Hunter escorted me into the house.

An unexpected sight met my eyes: A massive quantity of antiques and works of art, most of it continental or English. There were paintings, statues, clocks, cabinets, floor lamps, and chandeliers, as well as shelves holding knick-knacks of every description. Hunter, with a wise and subdued smile, allowed me a minute to survey the objects. He then led me to a patio overlooking the rear yard. The area contained beautiful manicured gardens, small fountains, some statues, and a modest swimming pool. I sat in a large stone armchair (with comfortable cushions) whose back rose up into the head of a Hindu deity.

Hunter motioned for me to be seated, and then took his own place in another stone armchair that faced mine at a ninety-degree angle. The deity carved into the top of his chair seemed in a better mood than the one behind my head. It was an odd sensation to have a god breathing down my neck, as it were.

"How are you doing?" he asked.

"Fine, thank you. By the way, you have a beautiful home."

"Thanks. You know, Jayesh, I have been doing some genealogical research over the last few months, turning up some interesting facts about my mother's family, things I never knew." Hunter slid forward in his seat. "Tell me something, isn't your own mother's family from the Sundar Prabhat region?"

"Some of it, yes, but you have to go back a few generations."

"Hmm…I see. Do you have any relatives here?"

"Probably, but they would have to be quite distant. In any case, I don't know of any."

"I know of one," said Hunter, his lips quivering from a repressed grin.

"Really? Who is it?"

"Me!" he exclaimed, a smile bursting across his face. "Your mother's father and my mother's mother were first cousins. I'll show you the charts sometime. Welcome to the family."

"Thanks," I said, amazed by the revelation.

The maid brought us tea on a serving trolley. Hunter expounded on his family tree and how it intersected with mine. He seemed very eager to attach himself to me, emotionally as well as intellectually. At that moment, he was succeeding handsomely. To say that I was charmed by the visit to Sundar Prabhat would be an understatement. I had almost forgotten about Paris, Sam, Thelonius, and Tom, not to mention Albuquerque, Ashley, and the Super Bowl. I had to remind myself that I was in the country for a specific purpose.

As if reading my mind, Hunter put his teacup down. "Perhaps, Jayesh, I should have saved the happy part of the conversation for last, but I just couldn't resist. Anyway, let us proceed to our somewhat unsavory business."

"Go ahead," I said.

"Jayesh, what did you think of Azala's little demonstration at the Super Bowl?"

"Pretty shocking," I said.

"Yes, shocking is the word. It could have been a lot worse if your friend Sam Kapulski had not been successful in disconnecting the sound system."

I straightened my back at the sound of Sam's name.

"It was all done, Azala's intended program that is, with the full backing of President Malpomme. In fact, they tell me it was her personal intervention that overcame the resistance of people in the football league. How is it that your president allies herself with such disagreeable types?"

"I really don't know," I said. "I suppose she agrees with Azala's message."

Hunter pressed his fingertips together and gazed into the distance, deep in thought. I waited for what was figuring to be a significant statement. "You know, Jayesh, it is ironic that President Malpomme is such an enthusiastic supporter of Azala. Because at this very moment, he is plotting *to assassinate her*."

I must have had a look of extreme bewilderment on my face, judging by Hunter's nervous laugh. "Sorry to have to break it to you so suddenly," he said. "But it is a fact. It will take place at the White House reception next month."

"The one for disadvantaged Asians in sports and entertainment?"

"Yes."

"That's impossible!"

"Is it? You don't think they have open access to the White House? They can come and go as they please. Setting up and executing the operation would be no more difficult than using an infantry platoon to rob the grocery store down the street. In any case, the plan is to hire a devout Christian to be the assassin, and then blame the atrocity on Christian fundamentalists. Actually, the plan is brilliant."

"How do you know all this?" I asked, unwilling to accept the enormity of the affair.

"We have our sources," said Hunter, calmly sipping his tea. "The only missing piece of the puzzle is the aftermath. We haven't been able to ascertain Azala's intentions; what exactly he wants to put in motion by means of this deed."

We sat in silence for several moments, as the news enveloped me like a billow of London fog.

"We've got to stop him before this goes any further," I declared.

"That is nearly impossible, and the reason is simple. The popularity and prestige of UNSAINE is so great that they have become unreachable. No one would believe us, and even if someone did, and publicized the plot, he would be instantly discredited. He would be accused of undermining UNSAINE, an act known in the international legal community as *racism*. And you know what that means—such a brave soul would, in short order, find himself in a jail cell down the hall from Sam Kapulski."

"I see your point."

"We have to be clever about it," said Hunter. "We must foil them on the spot, right there in the White House, finding a way to link Azala to the event. And it must all be done in full view of the TV cameras, with millions watching. Afterwards, it will be a relatively simple matter to free Mr. Kapulski."

I leaned forward and held my head in my hands, trying to digest the incredible stream of data that had just flooded my brain.

Chapter Six

▼

When I lifted my head, Hunter was standing, facing the house. I looked in the same direction, and saw a young woman just a few feet away. It was a striking image. She had long, silky black hair, and her large, dark eyes had just a hint of an almond shape. Her mouth was small, with delicate lips like the petals of a flower that is just beginning to bloom. She was a fine example of the Indian subcontinent's understated yet intense sensuality.

An awkward moment passed as the three of us remained motionless.

"Jayesh," said Hunter, "this is Indira."

"Hello," I said, rising from my seat.

"Indira, this is Jayesh Blackstone, the distant relative from America that I was talking about. He's a football player, American football that is. And he's quite famous."

"Nice to meet you, Mr. Blackstone," said Indira, in a soft voice as sweet as the mouth from which it came. We stared at each other for a moment, until a look of bashfulness crept over her features.

"We adopted Indira years ago when I was at Oxford. Her parents were good friends of mine, academics visiting from New Delhi. They were killed in a car accident." Hunter looked as if he might have something else to say, but then turned to Indira. "I hope you are still planning to join Jayesh and me for dinner?"

"Yes, of course. That would please me very much."

Hunter led the way to the dining room, Indira trailing just behind. The manner in which she walked fascinated me, being quite unlike anything I was accustomed to. There was a subtle undulating movement that emphasized her femininity without being in any way crass or provocative.

The dining room, like the hall I had seen upon arrival, was loaded with antiques and decorative objects. Along one of the walls, across from where I sat, was an ornate chest of drawers made from teak. On top of the chest was a massive green and white ceramic vase. Strange yet fascinating animal figures were depicted on its surface, and it distracted me throughout the meal.

We ate like royalty. The cook brought out a procession of delicacies, each platter outdoing the previous one. The meal revived long-dormant memories of similar cuisine I had enjoyed at the homes of my aunts and uncles in London.

"In case you're wondering why I am alone," said Hunter, "it's because my dear wife passed away two years ago."

"I'm very sorry," I said. "It must have been a difficult time for you."

"Yes, it was. She was killed by terrorists during the long days of violence that surrounded the coup d'état of 2018. She happened to be at a social gathering at the home of a government official who was targeted for assassination. The terrorists—under direct orders from Benzona himself—wiped out the whole building with a car bomb."

I stopped eating at hearing this disturbing story.

"Eat up, Jayesh," said Hunter, his deep voice booming more than usual. "We must go on living. I hope to remarry some day. Indira is helping me, aren't you my dear?"

Indira lowered her head.

Hunter laughed. "I always seem to embarrass you, Indira. But there's no reason to take it that way. You see, Jayesh, she is assisting me in the matchmaking department. We started about three or four months ago, isn't that right?"

Indira raised her head and let slip an angelic smile.

"We've had a couple of close ones, actually. Like that widow from Hyderabad. She was rather...well...do you speak any Hindi, Jayesh?"

"No, I'm afraid not."

"Never mind, then. This whole matchmaking business is complicated here, much more than in America, I am sure. In addition to attraction and general compatibility, we need to precisely line up social status, sectarian loyalties, pedigree, and wealth. Luckily, I am not obliged to face such a daunting task alone. I must convey my appreciation to my beloved Indira, for her patience and persistence. It is time for me to return the favor. Her own marriage is overdue."

We continued our feast, which ended with delicious sweets and relaxing tea. The subject of Azala and the alleged assassination attempt on President Malpomme was not broached. Hunter forged ahead on the personal track, drawing me into the family circle. Looking back, I am astonished that a man of his standing would divulge so much private information so quickly.

After the meal and some additional conversation in the sitting room, Hunter escorted me back to the car. We agreed that we would get together within twenty-four hours to discuss strategy. We parted with a feeling of great fraternity.

Hunter's driver returned me to the Progress Hotel. Stepping into the lobby, I decided to visit the bar. I was in need of some time to decompress; to digest the impressions and emotions I had experienced at the Hunter residence. I passed through the row of exotic plants that separated the core of the lobby from the bar area. The plants seemed to filter the greater part of the noise emanating from the constant comings and goings. The wall behind the bar was packed with every imaginable variety of high-end alcoholic beverage. The only patrons to be seen were two dejected-looking men in business suits. My eye was drawn to the unusual counter, made from an exotic hardwood, possibly macassar ebony, with rich maroon tones. It had a wavy shape, like a whip that had been snapped and then frozen so that the curves remained in place. I sat down at the far end, ordered a beer, and was soon taking my first refreshing sip.

A man parked himself at my left side. He wore sandals, baggy linen pants, and a gray short-sleeved T-shirt upon which was printed the name of an obscure American university. His hair was blond, but a silvery, aging blond. The face, bloodshot and leathery, showed signs of a difficult life. One could tell from the way he carried his frame that he had been muscular in his prime, though most of the bulk had disappeared.

"Hello sir," said the bartender, wiping his hands on a towel. "The usual?"

"Yeah, Patel, thanks," said my neighbor, lighting a non-filtered cigarette that he gripped between his thumb and index finger. The bartender served him a gin and tonic. He promptly guzzled about half of it before turning his attention to me. "What are you, English, American?"

"A little of both."

"What brings you to this miserable hell-hole?" he said, with a voice made coarse from what I surmised were decades of smoking and drinking. His lips, teeth, and fingertips were a tawny yellow. The accent was American, vaguely Midwestern.

"I'm visiting some relatives," I said.

The pout that came over his face expressed his disapproval of my answer. We sat quietly for several moments.

"Wait a second," he said, pointing the cigarette at me as he spoke. "Weren't you that field-goal kicker in the Super Bowl?"

"Yes," I said, smiling. "I'm Jayesh Blackstone."

"Nice to meet you," he said, shaking my hand. "Randy Bingham's the name. We don't get too many people like you down here. Hey, didn't you break some kind of record?"

"Yes, most consecutive field goals."

"That's right," said Bingham, taking a drag from his cigarette that was too big even for him, causing a fit of coughing. "Yeah, I remember seeing an interview with you in some pregame show. They said you were from London, the saint-something neighborhood, what was it..."

"St. John's Wood."

"That's it. The interviewer called you 'the kicker of St. John's Wood'. Well, here's to the kicker." He raised his glass in my direction, and then swallowed the remaining liquid.

"And what do you do here?" I inquired, as the bartender replaced the empty glass of gin with a full one.

Bingham stretched his arms, releasing an impressive yawn in the process. "Sorry, it's just that in this damn climate I need to stretch all the time. What do I do, is that what you asked? Well my official job is tour guide, but the real thing I do is take care of the Americans here."

"Take care of them?"

"Yeah, that's right. Iron out problems, you know, that kind of thing. I've been here almost twenty years, yup, since the turn of the century." He handed me his business card.

"Thank you," I said, placing the card in my wallet.

"Give me a call when you need me. Everyone does, sooner or later." He slapped a bunch of coins on the counter and left the bar.

I finished my beer and paid the bartender. The other two patrons, the dejected businessmen, were still nursing their drinks. I was about to leave when my cell phone rang. It was Ashley. We exchanged greetings, and I assured her that everything was going well.

"Are you all right, Jayesh?" she asked.

"Yes, of course. Why?"

"I don't know…you sound a little nervous."

"Oh," I said, laughing even more nervously, fearful that I would spout something about Indira. "Don't worry, Ashley. I had to take a little side trip, to help Sam. How are you doing, anyway?"

"Not so good," she said. "I really wanted to come see you in Paris. Can we still do that?"

"Yes, but I can't say when. This whole story has taken on a life of its own; who knows what will happen next. Some very big things are going on, but I can't discuss it on the phone. I'm sorry about all this. I'll be with you as soon as I can."

"Can I come see you there?"

"No," I replied, a tad too forcefully.

"Why, are you afraid that I won't be able to take it? Is it because I'm a girl? There are women spies, you know, who do all kinds of dangerous things. I can handle it."

She probably could, I thought. "It's not possible, I'm afraid. Let me do what I need to do, Ashley. Soon this whole thing will be behind us and we can get on with our lives."

"I miss you."

"I miss you, too, Ashley. Don't worry, we'll be together very soon."

The conversation ended and I returned to my room. I was pleased to discover that the bed was large and quite comfortable. It did not take long before I settled into a deep sleep.

In the morning, I received a phone call from Hunter. We needed to discuss our strategy in more detail, he said, but it would be a shame if I left Sundar Prabhat without having seen anything other than the hotel, his house, and the uninspiring route between the two. Would I be interested in visiting the National Game Park, located just a twenty-minute drive from the city? We could have our discussion there, but if not, there would be plenty of time to retreat to the quiet oasis of his private garden. I agreed, not realizing that this seemingly innocuous plan would have profound consequences for the future of our collaboration.

After breakfast, I went to the main entrance of the hotel to wait for my ride. A few minutes later, Hunter pulled up in a shiny new SUV. I climbed into the back seat. Indira was sitting there quietly, following my movements with her eyes. She was wearing a denim skirt and an embroidered, multicolored blouse, both very becoming to her figure. I felt speechless in her presence. Fortunately, Hunter narrated the journey continuously. This relieved me of the need to make conversation.

The comparison with Ashley soon came to mind. It must be conceded that in purely physical terms, Ashley was the superior of the two. Yet with Indira, the attraction was an intriguing mystery. It had a deeper origin. Something buried in the more remote layers of my soul was connecting with the essence of this enchanting woman. It seemed at the time that if I spent years with Ashley, I could never feel the bond I had developed after only hours with Indira.

It required a great effort to even partially concentrate on Hunter's guided tour. My eyes frequently wandered toward the interior of the car, at which time I would catch myself and quickly look out the window. At one point, however, I could not withstand the temptation and allowed my head to keep going until I was looking directly at her. She had made the same movement at the same time. Our eyes locked for several seconds.

"Jayesh...Jayesh..." said Hunter, raising his voice and turning almost all the way around to capture my attention.

"Yes, sorry about that," I mumbled, feeling rather silly.

"Look over there," he said, pointing excitedly. "The great temple of Sundar Prabhat."

Despite the distraction inside the car, the temple held my undivided attention for as long as it was in view. It was a magnificent structure, built from a white stone that resembled ivory. A multitude of forms—animal, human, and divine—were carved into its walls, which angled inward as they rose to a height of about twenty stories.

"We'll visit the temple on another outing," said Hunter. "I suppose, though, we could go there now instead of the game park, if you like."

"No, thank you," I said, "I prefer your plan the way it was." I was not quite in the mood for a weighty historical and religious monument.

The National Game Park was a less impressive sight. The road was overgrown with vegetation, and there was scattered debris, including the burnt-out shell of a truck. After driving for over ten minutes, the only wildlife we had seen was a small, mangy-looking monkey.

As we reached a broad clearing, Hunter instructed the driver to pull over. "We can get out here for a moment," he said. "Don't worry, if any wild beasts wander into the area, we'll see them before they come within a hundred yards, at the very least."

No sooner did we exit the vehicle than Hunter pointed to a spot on the horizon. It was a small herd of elephants. Hunter had some binoculars, which he passed along to me. I watched the herd for a couple of minutes.

"The park is rundown, I admit," said Hunter. "But at least we have some quality animals here."

His cell phone rang. He excused himself and stepped away a few paces. I could not distinguish the words, but he rattled off several sentences in an emphatic, urgent tone. He then closed the phone and returned to us. "I have a bit of a situation in Shubh Nagar," he said, looking to the side and holding his forehead. "Nothing critical, just a little business crisis. I have to go back." He signaled to the driver to get in the car. The driver obeyed, and Indira and I followed. Moments later, we sped away.

"Sorry about this," said Hunter, almost banging his head on the roof as we hit a large bump in the road. "But listen—we'll be passing the aviary on the way out of the park. I could drop the two of you off. There's security guards; it's a safe place. Indira could be the tour guide.

I'll send the driver back to fetch you in an hour from now. What do you say, Jayesh?"

"Sure, if Indira doesn't…"

"I would love to go," said Indira, looking at me with her tender eyes.

Minutes later, we stopped in front of the aviary. Indira and I got out of the vehicle and watched it pull away with all haste.

The aviary compound was surrounded by a stone wall, about eight feet high. The wall was interrupted by the 'welcome center', a nondescript concrete building of three stories. The ground floor resembled the entrance to a cave, being poorly lit under its low ceiling. The sight was not inviting.

After passing the turnstiles and the security post, we entered an area that looked entirely different. There were clean footpaths, well-maintained gardens, and ornate stone benches. Further into the interior were vast spaces enclosed with thin wire mesh. This is where the birds of the aviary resided.

"What kinds of birds would you like to see?" asked Indira. "We have many varieties."

"I really don't know," I replied, still at a loss for words. "You decide, you're in charge."

"Okay," she said, smiling. She turned onto one of the footpaths. "This is a nice, meandering little lane, and it brings us to the parrots."

"That's good," I said. An exhibit of stuffed turkeys would have suited me just fine.

"How long are you staying in Sundar Prabhat?" she asked.

"Oh…uh…I'm not sure. I have some business to finish up with Mr. Hunter, which shouldn't take too long. But I might stay on. It seems nice here."

"Many things are."

"And perhaps some are not," I ventured.

Indira sighed. "Yes, you deciphered my thoughts. We live a good life, but it is stifling. We are always surrounded by guards and chauffeurs and servants. We are prisoners in a gilded cage."

"I can see that. Are you planning to stay here?"

"I don't know," she said. "Look over there, it's the giant blue parrot. They say it's the largest one in the world."

"Well, it is quite impressive," I said, viewing the colorful feathered creature, about the size of a small eagle. It surveyed us, began to squawk, and flew off to a higher perch.

We resumed walking. Indira had a melancholy air about her, and the look in her eye was resolute, almost stoic. "My life is here. I don't know where else I would go. Back to England, perhaps. I still have some friends there." She came to a halt at a bench facing a particularly lush enclosure. We took a seat and watched a flurry of activity behind the mesh, as a group of birds chased each other to and fro. "How does it feel here for you?" she asked. "Do you have any sense of home?"

"Well, I do have a certain emotional bond. It's hard to say to what extent. I see a lot of people who look like they could be relatives of mine. And when Mr. Hunter revealed that he and I are related, that had an effect. But it's still a long way from feeling at home. I'm connected, that much is clear."

We were interrupted by an announcement over the loudspeaker informing visitors that the aviary would be closing early that day, in just fifteen minutes.

I looked at my watch. "You know what, we're late. We were supposed to have been waiting outside already."

We began walking quickly toward the exit.

"It seems that life is like that," said Indira. "Just when you steal a moment of comfort, a speck of happiness, it is disrupted."

"I know what you mean," I said. "That reminds me of something my grandfather once told me. Our physical reality, the surrounding environment, is always in flux, and outside of our control. We should not be surprised when we see this happening. If something remains constant, or at least appears to be stable—*that* is a circumstance that should surprise us, for now we have found the exception. Instead of pining for illusions of stability, we must accept the flux, and find stability within our own soul."

"Your grandfather was a very wise man."

We passed through the turnstiles and came to the edge of the parking lot. There was no sign of anyone. We waited patiently for several minutes. I called Hunter, but received his voice mail. I left a message.

"A car should have been here fifteen, maybe twenty minutes ago," I said. "Shall I call a taxi?"

"No," said Indira. "Too dangerous. If the driver doesn't rob us, the people in the streets will."

"Do you know anyone who could come and fetch us?"

"I might." She reached into her handbag and pulled out her phone. Several calls ensued, but no one was reachable.

"So," I said, "what do you do in these situations?"

"I don't know," she said, with a trace of nervousness in her voice. "This simply never happens."

"Don't you think it's odd that there was almost no one in the aviary? And that the parking lot is virtually empty?"

"Yes," she said, "it is odd. Maybe it's because of the early closure."

"Should I call the American embassy?"

"No, they'll tell you to take a taxi. They don't like to get involved."

I noticed an old Lincoln Continental at the far end of the parking lot. Its black glass was disquieting, though there was no sign of any trouble. I could not even be sure whether there was anyone in the car.

A sudden metallic clanking noise behind Indira and me caused us to turn around. A man was locking the gate of the welcome center from the inside.

I opened my wallet and removed the business card that was given to me by Randy Bingham, the American tour guide I had met at the hotel bar. I dialed his number. It rang quite a few times before he answered.

"Yeah?" said Bingham, coughing.

"Mr. Bingham?"

"You got that right."

"Hi, it's Jayesh Blackstone." There was silence on the line. "You remember, the football player, the field-goal kicker."

"Yeah, I know. What can I do for you?"

"I'm stranded at the National Game Park, at the aviary. My ride back to town never showed up, and they closed the place. I was told taking a cab is dangerous."

"So you want me to come get you?"

"That would be superb."

"It'll cost you."

"Uh…okay. How much?"

"Two thousand dollars."

"Two *thousand* dollars?"

"Sorry, pal. Let me level with you, Mr. Blackstone. I know about your connection to Hunter. Coming to get you right now is a risky proposition. I have to bring one of my good armed guards, ex-military type, and pay him too. This ain't a Sunday drive in South Dakota."

"Okay, okay, but please hurry."

"All right. Stay calm, and don't move. I'm on my way."

I closed the phone. We waited quietly for a minute or two. Then, for no apparent reason, the Lincoln Continental's engine started up. It began moving toward us. There was no place to hide. I considered calling the police but rejected the idea, not having nearly enough time. Instead, frozen in place, I watched the car approach. The rear window slid down about a third of the way.

"Mr. Blackstone," said a muffled voice in the back seat.

"Yes…"

"Mr. Azala is not pleased with what you have done."

"What exactly have I done?"

"Don't play games with us, Mr. Blackstone. That woman next to you belongs to the household of Joseph Hoomty Azala's worst enemy."

Another car was racing toward us, from the main road, at high speed. The Lincoln sped away, smashing through the fence at the far edge of the parking lot. It then slowed, and out jumped the man from the back seat, who fled on foot toward the wall of the aviary compound. As the second vehicle crossed the area, a man leaned out the window, holding a grenade launcher. He fired at the Lincoln. There was a deafening explosion and a huge fireball as the missile connected with its target. The man who had been fleeing on foot was thrown violently to the ground. The pursuing car made an abrupt U-turn and disappeared from the scene as rapidly as it had arrived.

At the moment of the explosion Indira had hurled herself at me, and I instinctively grasped her and held her close. Several moments passed, during which time I was transfixed by the spectacle of the burning wreck, which was about two hundred yards away. Apart from that, there was no other sound or movement in the area. Except, that is, for the moans of the man who had been thrown to the ground.

To say that I was stunned would be an understatement. It was one of those rare moments that something truly unbelievable takes place, right in front of your eyes. It was not happening in a novel or a movie, but to me.

I separated myself from Indira but held her by the shoulders. "Do you hear that?" I asked.

"Hear what?" she said, her body trembling.

"The guy who jumped out of the car. He's moaning."

Indira looked in that direction. "Oh yes, I see him." She turned back toward me. "I hope your friend gets here soon."

"Me too. Shouldn't we go help that man? Or try to find someone in the aviary? They probably called the police anyway."

"Not necessarily. People here don't just call the police like they do in England." She looked again in the direction of the burning wreck, and then toward the park entrance. A car was approaching from some distance. "Maybe that's your friend, over there."

"It could be. But shouldn't we try to help that wounded man?"

Indira looked at me, her face filled with frustration. "And then what? Bring him to a hospital? We'll never see the end of it. The police will come, we'll be interrogated. They might send you home on the next plane, but me, I would probably be ransomed back to my stepfather or put on trial for attempted murder."

"Yes, I see your point. But still, this is terrible."

The car Indira had seen from afar now pulled up in front of us. It was a ponderous vehicle, looking like a military jeep that had been elongated and given a supplement of armor. Bingham emerged from the driver's seat. He wore the same outfit as when I had seen him at the bar. A hand-rolled cigarette was dangling from his lips.

"Mr. Blackstone," he said, slapping me on the shoulder. "In a bit of a jam?" He glanced at the burning wreck. "Looks like the natives are restless today. They put on a nice show for you, eh?" He opened the back door of the jeep and motioned for us to get in. Indira climbed inside without delay.

"Wait," I said. "There's a wounded man over there. We have to do something."

Bingham laughed. "What, are you kidding me? I will be leaving this spot in exactly ten seconds, with you or without you. I don't care how much money you pay me." He got into the car.

"Come, Jayesh," said Indira, in a pleading voice. "We must go."

I complied. Bingham put the jeep in gear with a horrendous grinding sound, and took us away from the aviary. The noise from the engine was ear-splitting and the ride was quite rough. I exchanged a glance with Indira, who looked to be in great distress. The man in the front passenger seat, a rather stocky gent with a Southeast Asian look, was wearing army fatigues and an ammunition harness. He was holding an assault rifle, the barrel of which was pointed out the window.

"I assume we're going back to the hotel," said Bingham, hollering in order to be heard over the roar of the engine.

"Yes," I shouted.

Once again I found myself with Indira in the back seat of a car. This time, however, I was not in my sweet little dream world, obsessed by the woman and her charms. Now it was reality's turn. Suddenly, that warm, fuzzy feeling I had for Sundar Prabhat faded like mist in the midday sun. My mind was focused on one thing: leave immediately, and never set foot in this country again.

We followed an altogether different route than the one Hunter had taken to leave the city. It included the worst back alleys of Shubh Nagar. They were even more appalling than what I had seen previously. Eventually, I saw a couple of streets that looked familiar, and then we passed into the Freeville quarter. Bingham pulled over about two blocks from the hotel, and motioned for us to get out of the car. Indira and I did as instructed, and waited on the sidewalk. Bingham exchanged a few words with his security man, and then joined us. The security man moved into the driver's seat and zoomed away.

"Here's what we do," said Bingham. "We walk into the hotel, slowly and calmly. I have just given you a tour of Freeville. If anyone stops us, let me do the talking. Okay?"

"Okay."

"Good. Let's go."

We began our staged leisurely stroll.

"You'll need to pay me right away, Mr. Blackstone. You can get cash from your credit card at the front desk. Then we'll sit at the bar and decide what to do. My fee includes accompanying you for up to twenty-four hours, more than enough time to get you out of the country."

"Good," I said, not seeing any other course of action.

"Will the young lady be traveling with you?"

"No, she's staying here."

Everything seemed normal as we passed through the gate: the gardens, the white façade, the impeccably dressed clientele. I felt self-conscious, as if there were something unusual about my appearance. I reminded myself that although I had undergone a very shocking experience, nothing had touched me physically.

We secured a small table next to the bar, in a little nook recessed into the wall. It was the most private spot available. Bingham ordered his usual gin and tonic, Indira had some mineral water, and I took a beer. I went to the front desk to get some money, returned to the table, and paid Bingham his fee.

"Thanks," he said, pocketing the banknotes.

We sat quietly for several moments.

"Does your fee include escorting me to the airport?" I inquired.

"Yes, of course."

Indira was frowning. "Don't worry," I said to her. "I won't leave until you are back where you're supposed to be." She looked away, evidently displeased.

"Getting out of here is a good idea," said Bingham. "You don't need to get involved with the soap operas in this little hell-hole."

"Do things like this happen all the time?" I inquired.

"Yeah, I'm afraid so," he said, leaning back and running his hand over his face, as if clearing away debris. He lit a cigarette. "Here's what I think happened back there. The guys you saw get bumped off went to the game park to kidnap or execute Miss Indira. They paid the aviary people to close early and get out of the way. But Azala called his men off at the last minute. If you would have gotten killed or injured, Mr. Blackstone, the whole thing would have been a mess, what with the embassy, the press, etc. So the guys in the car were thinking about their next move, and boom…they lingered a bit too long. You witnessed a little settling of accounts. Hunter must have sent his men out to do the job. There's going to be a lot more of that before we see who's in charge."

"What nonsense you are speaking," said Indira, straightening her back. "My stepfather is an economist, a former professor at Oxford."

Bingham laughed through his cigarette. "Professor at Oxford, eh? Listen, honey, nobody in Sundar Prabhat has any power without a few men to do these jobs. Why do you think your ride was late? Because Hunter needed all hands on deck. Azala was probably going after someone, maybe even Hunter himself. As soon as that was over, retaliation followed. It happens as surely as night follows day."

My phone rang. It was Hunter.

"Jayesh? Where are you?"

"We're at the hotel."

"Sorry about that. I had some urgent business to take care of. Obviously you found a ride."

"Yes, I did."

"Could I send my driver to get you? He'll bring you back to the house."

"No, thank you. I'll be leaving Sundar Prabhat very soon."

"Leaving?" said Hunter. "Why? You're not angry, are you?"

"No, it's just that I don't want to witness any more assassinations."

"What do you mean?"

"You don't know what happened over there, at the aviary?"

"No…"

"Indira can tell you about it later. Please forgive me, I'm quite shaken up. You can send the driver for Indira. I need to pack. I'll call you soon. We can meet again, but somewhere else."

"Well, if you change your mind, just let me know."

I apologized one more time before concluding the call. It was all very embarrassing. I felt silly and cowardly, now that I could think a bit more clearly. But the memory returned of the exploding car and the man who was moaning on the ground, and I once again felt resolute in my decision to leave. In any case, my mission was over. I had been informed about the plot to assassinate President Malpomme. Certainly, there needed to be some follow-up, some real strategizing with Hunter. So let him come to the U.S., I thought. If he's still alive, that is. Nothing was certain in this God-forsaken corner of the earth. A man was dying from his wounds and we left him for dead. A beautiful and sensitive young woman could not care less; it was just another day in Sundar Prabhat. I wondered what Ashley would have done. She probably would have run over to help him, consequences be damned.

"Where are you flying to?" asked Bingham.

"Excuse me," interrupted Indira, standing up and slinging her handbag over her shoulder. "Mr. Blackstone, I'm sorry that our excursion had to end like this."

I stood up as well, and shook her outstretched hand. "I wish we could have spent more time together."

"Perhaps on another visit," she said, with a sad smile. "I'll go wait by the porters. You two have business to discuss." She turned and walked away. I retook my seat.

"Well?" said Bingham. "Where do you want to go?"

"Back to Paris," I said, though I had no idea what Thelonius and Tom were doing. Of course, I could summon Ashley at a moment's notice. In fact, I was thinking that it might provide a welcome interlude between the chaos of Sundar Prabhat and other crazy experiences yet to come.

Bingham dialed a number on his phone. He began a conversation with an airline booking agent. Meanwhile, I caught a glimpse of Bingham's Southeast Asian gunner, who was seated at the bar. He was without his rifle, and was now wearing an oversized sports jacket, black slacks, and a baseball cap. I surveyed the other occupants of the bar area and the parts of the lobby that were visible. All looked normal.

Bingham closed his phone. "That's it," he declared. "I've got you booked on the next flight to Paris, leaving in three hours. You can pick up the ticket at the terminal. We can hang out here for a little while, then we'll get your stuff, and you'll be on your way."

"Thank you."

"Nice little babe you had there. Wasn't she worth an assassination attempt?"

I chuckled. "Maybe in another life. Anyhow, I have a girlfriend back home."

"They make good wives, those Indian babes."

"Yes, my father would agree with that statement. Indira is very nice, but something bugs me. I can't quite put my finger on it. At first she looked naïve, then I saw her abandon a dying man with no hesitation. It's complicated, I realize. But no remorse whatsoever? I'm not sure that's a quality I would want in a wife."

"C'mon, cut her some slack," said Bingham, finishing off his drink. "People are gunned down here as often as you change your socks. Hesitate for a second, and you might have a bullet in your skull. Not to mention the fact that the guy you're crying about was probably sent there to kill her."

I remained silent, taken aback by the logic of Bingham's statement.

"It's none of my business, but what the hell is someone like you, big-bucks football star, doing sticking your nose into this mess? Don't tell me it's because Hunter is your grandmother's uncle's cousin, because I won't buy it."

"I thought he could help a friend of mine who is in trouble," I said, calmly.

"Oh, okay," said Bingham, leaning back and taking a long drag from his cigarette. "That's different. But right now I think it's Hunter that could use the help."

We sat quietly for several moments, and then I called Thelonius. He and Tom were busy running from one specialist to another, upgrading Sam's legal representation. I announced my imminent return to Paris, much to the delight of Thelonius. We agreed that I would call him right after my arrival.

I then made an impetuous decision: I called Ashley. A strange sensation came over me as I watched my hand dial the number, as if I knew that it might not be advisable. The impetus was much more than the need for the comfort of a woman in my hour of distress; rather, I felt an urge to return to normal life, to be with people whose behavior, if not always palatable, was at least familiar and reasonably predictable. In any case, the two of us decided that Ashley would fly to Paris as soon as possible, charging the ticket to my credit card. I did not divulge my location, but stated once again that I had been compelled to take a brief side trip, and would tell her everything when we had the opportunity to speak face-to-face.

My initial feeling of consolation soon changed to one of regret. I had business to attend to. Sam was still incarcerated, and there would be meetings with him, with attorneys, and with Thelonius and Tom.

In addition, I needed some time to recover from my disconcerting experience in Sundar Prabhat, and from my brief but intense connection with Indira. How would I explain *that* to Ashley?

I resigned myself to my own impetuosity and got on with the business of leaving the country. Bingham accompanied me as I packed my bags and checked out of the Progress Hotel. His security man joined us for the trip to the airport. I watched the scenery as if I were in a film, it all seemed so unreal.

I felt most uncomfortable on the flight back to Paris. I was relieved to be leaving the "hell-hole," as Bingham referred to Sundar Prabhat. But my nerves were severely rattled. The atrocious events at the aviary ran repeatedly through my head. In addition, my abrupt departure from Hunter and Indira left me frustrated. I felt I was abandoning them to a fate that did not look particularly rosy, and this after they had been so warm and hospitable.

Another thought nagged me: What if the car from which the missile had been fired was not sent by Hunter? Bingham seemed convinced, and his version of the story was plausible. But was that conclusive evidence? Hunter had denied any knowledge of the incident. I could not rule out the possibility that he was telling the truth.

It seemed that my visit with Hunter had probably spoiled any chance for a deal with Azala to secure Sam's release. Granted, it was a long shot, but a longer one still was Hunter's idea of catching Azala or his people in the act of assassinating the president. It appeared to be a far-fetched conspiracy theory, a product of the heated rivalry for the leadership of Sundar Prabhat. Alas, I thought, I had traded a bird in the hand for two in the bush, and may have ended up with nothing to show for my efforts.

Chapter Seven

▼

The plane touched down in Paris at eight o'clock that evening, and I checked into the Hotel Rostand about an hour later. I called Thelonius, making arrangements to meet the following morning. With my remaining strength I took a quick shower, and collapsed into bed.

The next day, shortly after breakfast, Ashley called. She had booked her trip, and would be leaving in several hours. The flight to Paris was scheduled to arrive early the following morning. There was much excitement in her voice, and it was contagious. I yearned to have her with me, to hold her in my arms and forget the entire world.

Thelonius arrived at the hotel. After an effusive greeting, we left for a stroll in the Jardin de Luxembourg. It was a sunny day that would reach a high of fifty degrees Fahrenheit, warm for Paris in mid February. How different everything looked here than in the last city I had visited, Shubh Nagar. Well-dressed, healthy-looking people strolled at their leisure; there was no fear, no specter of death. I did not anticipate seeing any assassinations in this park.

"So how did you like Sunner Harbat?" asked Thelonius.

"Sundar Prabhat, you mean. It was dreadful. It's like being on another planet. The poverty is overwhelming. People are living in the streets."

"I know. I've been to some of those countries. Bad, real bad."

"The place is a testament to human folly," I said. "They had things on the right track a few years ago, according to that 'special man' I went

- 116 -

to see, Raghavendra Hunter. Azala's people came to power and wrecked everything. What a shame, especially considering that India is doing so well. I don't understand why the Indian government allows this to continue, what interest they have in the independence of that pitiful little country. They could send in their army and reabsorb the whole place into India in a matter of hours."

"Did you at least get to see anything interesting?" asked Thelonius.

"Interesting, indeed," I replied, with a chuckle. "I was at this aviary, in front of the entrance, waiting for a ride. It was after hours; the parking lot was empty. I saw a car approaching. To my surprise, it was one of Azala's men. He rolled down the window and warned me about my activities. Meanwhile another car approaches, the Azala car screeches away, the other vehicle gives chase, and then someone fires a missile at the Azala car and blows it sky high."

"You're kidding?" said Thelonius, stopping in his tracks.

"Unfortunately, I'm not."

"Wow. You must have been shaken up, Jayesh."

"Yes, very much," I said. "And I still feel jittery. It was quite frightening. I never saw anything like that before."

"I know how it is. It ain't pretty."

We resumed our walk, remaining in silence for a few moments. My eyes scanned the manicured gardens, coming to rest on the statue of a classical goddess.

"I also met this Indian woman."

"Oh?" said Thelonius, smiling.

"She was Hunter's stepdaughter. Her name is Indira. She was with me when I witnessed the assassination. At the outset I was quite taken with her. Indira is beautiful, it's true, but it was more than that." I stopped walking to gather my thoughts. "Can I ask you a question, Thelonius? I mean a personal question."

"Sure, go ahead," he said, with a look of attentiveness. Thelonius was an excellent listener, a quality in him that I very much appreciated.

"Did you ever feel drawn to another culture from some obscure corner of the world? I'm not talking about a fascination with Eastern philosophy, or some such intellectual awakening, but rather a more personal one. Like a sense that something within you belongs over there. Do you see what I mean?"

"I think so, yes," he said.

"In your travels, did you ever go to Africa? I assume your ancestors are from there."

"Well, they're sure as hell not from Denmark," he said, bursting into laughter. "Sorry, I know you're trying to be serious."

"It's okay. That was a dumb statement."

"Yes, I've been to Africa. Before I left, I thought I would feel the connection you were talking about. And I did, at the beginning. Just being among so many black people, in a black country, had a strong effect on me. But it wore off quickly. By the time the trip was over, the only thing I felt I had in common with those people was ancient history and the color of my skin. Man, was I glad to get back to the good old U. S. of A."

"What about the women?"

"Nice, *real* nice."

"No, I mean was there anything special about them? Ethnically speaking, that is. Did you feel more at home with them? Did you feel something deeper than usual, more spiritual?"

Thelonius looked calm and pensive as he pondered my unusual question. I pictured him decking a wide receiver at top speed. "No, I don't think there was anything deeper," he said, finally.

"Thelonius."

"Yes?"

"I learned something truly shocking from Hunter. If it's true, that is."

"Yeah…"

"He claims that Azala is planning to assassinate President Malpomme."

"Assassinate her?"

"That's right. He is certain they're going to do it at the White House reception for disadvantaged Asians, which as you know I'm supposed to attend at the end of March. They'll set it up to make it look like it was done by a Christian fundamentalist."

Thelonius was shaking his head. "Man, that is crazy. Why would Azala try something like that, anyway? He's tight with the big lady."

"I realize that the whole thing could be a fantasy. But Hunter did sound quite convinced. He suggested that I expose the plot at the event itself, as it unfolds, so that it can't be denied. Otherwise, no one would believe the story. Not the government, and not the media."

"I dunno, Jayesh. Sounds to me like pie in the sky. Look, right now we have to help Sam."

"But this would help Sam, by discrediting Azala."

"That's a very long shot," said Thelonius.

"I know." At that point I decided to forego further discussion of the issue. Thelonius was not at all convinced, and frankly, neither was I. "Speaking of Sam, what's the latest?"

"We switched his lawyer. The new one is from Geneva, and he's supposed to be the biggest hot-shot for anything to do with the U.N. and international organizations. He's doing what lawyers do, filing motions and all that stuff. For us, there's not much to do right now. There'll be a hearing in a couple of days."

I gripped my forehead, overcome by a wave of melancholy.

"Jayesh, my man, what's the matter?"

It took several moments before I could repel that sensation of faintness that occurs when regret has seeped into every bone and sinew. "Oh, God, Thelonius," I moaned. "I've been so stupid."

He looked at me with disbelief in his eyes.

"Here you are in Paris, you and Tom, engaged in furious efforts to help Sam. And what do I do? Chase phantoms, flirt with women, and discover my roots. Deals and plots and intrigue, instead of just buckling down and doing the hard work. Everything you said before I left, about how ridiculous I was being—you were right. Well that's it, it's over. No more spy novels and exotic countries." I ceased my discourse, realizing that I was raising my voice.

Thelonius put his arm around my shoulder and gave me a shake. "C'mon, man. Life is complicated. We're always getting pulled in different directions. Give yourself a break."

I smiled. "Thanks. I appreciate your support."

We continued our walk, leaving the Jardin de Luxembourg on the north side. We followed the Rue de Vaugirard and then Rue Férou, eventually settling down at a café next to the Church of St. Sulpice. The conversation took numerous twists and turns as we discussed football, family, women, and various events from our past. As always, Thelonius offered fascinating perspectives, based on life experiences that were fundamentally different than mine. I enjoyed the interlude immensely.

We left the café and headed for a nearby Italian restaurant that had been recommended by Tom. Just before entering the establishment, we were surrounded by a group of about a dozen American high school students who recognized us. Thelonius was quite gregarious as he talked and joked with them, resulting in some very happy faces. He invited all of them to dine with us. An explosion of glee ensued. It was a pleasure to see Thelonius radiating all of his charm and wit. I, too, had a few things to say, but there was no question that I was playing second fiddle. After the meal, the students thanked us profusely. We all left the restaurant together, and it took us several minutes to convince them that we really had other business to attend to.

Thelonius and I took a taxi to the Ritz Hotel, where Tom and Thelonius were lodged. We found Tom in the cocktail lounge, relaxing in one of the elegant armchairs, reading a newspaper. He was wearing a finely-tailored business suit, and the spikes in his short blond hair were more pronounced than usual. We exchanged warm greetings. After ordering drinks, he asked me about my experiences in Sundar Prabhat. I gave him the condensed version of the story, reticent as I was to reopen my wounds.

"Did anyone run your story about Sam?" I asked, as soon as there was a lull in the conversation.

"Yeah," said Tom, "some local-yokel TV station in Arkansas. Other than that, zero. Zilch. Nada. Rien. Bupkes. If I knew the word in Hindi, I would say that too."

"We need that word, Tom," said Thelonius. "It's for Jayesh, so he doesn't feel anyone's discriminating against him. After all, he's a disadvantaged Asian…"

"…in sports and entertainment," I added.

"Hey, what about Mr. Tom Hubert?" said Thelonius, putting his hand on the broadcaster's shoulder. "He's not a victim of anything. Are you, Tom?"

"No, I'm just a slice of Wonder Bread, related to every last person on the Mayflower. The only ethnic food I remember my parents preparing at home was a martini. I *am* a victim of discrimination, however, in one area."

"And what would that be?" I asked.

"I'm oppressed by idiots."

"You know, I've had that problem, too," I said.

"What's worse is that they're supposed to be intelligent people. Like the management at Cable5. What can you say? The dean of American sportscasters is sitting in a jail cell in Paris. After he prevents the Super Bowl from being turned into a total farce, our own government turns him over to the creeps at UNSAINE. And what do our illustrious producers say? 'It wouldn't interest anyone'. Well, of course it won't interest anyone if they don't even know about it."

"How is Sam holding up?" I inquired.

"Not too bad," said Thelonius.

"Yeah, but it's hard to say," added Tom. "Sam isn't one to display his emotions. He's old-school like that. Doesn't complain, never moans, never feels sorry for himself."

The conversation was interrupted by the arrival of an older woman in a mink stole, bedecked with every manner of jewelry. She was accompanied by a pair of enormous white poodles. The lady took a seat at the adjoining table.

"A woman after my own heart," whispered Tom.

"Speaking of women," I said, "you two should know that Ashley, my girlfriend, will be arriving in Paris tomorrow morning."

"Ooh, la la," said Tom, with a wide grin.

Thelonius was laughing. "I guess Jayesh didn't want to let us have all the fun in gay Paree."

"Just a minute," I said. "My intent is to remain fully involved with Sam's case. Nothing has changed, believe me. I won't let Ashley interfere with that."

"I'm sure it will be fine," said Tom. "Listen, you guys, tomorrow at four o'clock there's a hearing for Sam at the World Tribunal. There isn't really a hell of a lot we can do, but I think we should be in the audience for moral support."

"Absolutely," I said.

"We'll be there," said Thelonius.

"Good. Now if you'll excuse me, I have to make a bunch of calls to the States. I'll see you at the Tribunal tomorrow at four." We shook hands, and Tom left the cocktail lounge.

Thelonius and I lingered for a while, observing the people around us and cracking a few jokes at their expense. We then took a walk to the Opéra Garnier, and from there to the Church of Madeleine. At that point I pleaded fatigue. Thelonius admitted that he was also tired. He decided to head back to the Ritz on foot. We said goodbye, and I hopped in a cab.

By the time I reached my hotel room, I was exhausted. My nerves were still frayed. There had not been adequate time to recover from my ordeal in Sundar Prabhat. Not that the day wasn't relaxing, but I was in need of some solitude. I decided, therefore, to spend a quiet evening alone. I watched a mindless TV program, took a stroll in the neighborhood, ate a light dinner, and read a magazine. I turned in for the night feeling about as mellow as could be expected, given the circumstances.

The reunion with Ashley the following morning was delightful. Her plane arrived at the crack of dawn, and I was waiting at the airport to welcome her. During the taxi ride to the hotel, I updated her on the events of the past couple of days. She did the same, describing the relief she experienced upon receiving the "green light" to come to Paris. She had been on pins and needles for some time, wondering when the phone would ring.

I had expected Ashley to be weary from the long journey, but she was brimming with energy. After a brief rest at the hotel, she insisted that we set out to explore Paris on foot. I happily consented. I told her that I was completely at her disposal until the mid afternoon, at which time I would be attending Sam's hearing.

We left the hotel and headed north on the Boulevard St. Michel, toward the Seine. It was a gorgeous day. The crispness of winter was in the air, but with a coat and some warm shoes, one could stroll in comfort. We walked and walked and walked. Ashley couldn't get enough of the city. The only hitch was that several times she asked me questions about my trip to Sundar Prabhat, and each time I was evasive. I simply did not want to spoil the atmosphere. Those moments of calm were valuable to me, and I wished them to be carefree.

We had lunch at a small restaurant behind the Assemblée Nationale, and then began a leisurely promenade along the river.

"So what really happened in India?" she asked. "Did you get any information that could help Sam Kapulski?"

"Maybe," I said, stopping to watch a *bateau mouche* filled with tourists ply its way down the Seine. "Look at that thing. How could anyone want to pass their time packed like sardines, with a loudspeaker blaring in their ear? It's noisier than a stadium."

"Jayesh, you're avoiding the subject again. Why don't you want to talk about your trip?"

I looked down at Ashley's face. She was clearly vexed by my refusal to divulge any details about the expedition. I stroked her soft cheek with the back of my hand, and kissed her. "Sorry," I said. "Most of it I would rather forget. There are some ugly things going on down there."

"Like what, Jayesh?"

"Like people living in the streets. Like a car being blown up right in front of me."

It took her a few seconds to respond. "That's terrible…Were the people killed?"

"Yes, they're quite dead." I put my arm around her and we continued our promenade, slowly, along the quay. "And then there was the man I went to see, Raghavendra Hunter. He was supposed to help with Sam. Most of our time together was spent socializing. He claims that the two of us are distant cousins. He presented an idea, an indirect way of helping Sam, but it's far-fetched, and could be dangerous. I need to think about it more, and talk to some people back home."

"What's his idea?" asked Ashley.

"I'd rather not discuss it now, at least until I have more information."

"Why—don't you trust me?"

I turned to face her, holding her shoulders. "Listen, Ashley, it's not necessary to discuss every single thing with every single person."

"Is it because I'm a girl?" she said, her voice turning shrill.

I threw my hands up in frustration. "Now don't go starting that again."

"That's it, isn't it? You don't think I can handle it."

"Oh, I'm *sure* you can handle it. Look, these matters are very delicate. It's not certain that you would have the same, how shall I say it, understanding of events that I do."

"What do you mean?"

I glanced for a moment at the Cathedral of Notre Dame, looming in the distance. When I looked again at Ashley, she was standing in an aggressive pose, hands on her hips. "I'll tell you what I mean. There's some heavy politics going on here, and I'm not sure where you line up with all this. You are, after all, writing a dissertation on ways to destroy professional football, and our friend Mr. Azala is also trying to do precisely that, among other things. Now, perhaps all this doesn't have to interfere too much with our relationship, but it also means that I don't need to share with you every single thing I do." I stopped abruptly, aware that I was sounding rather strident.

Ashley was on the brink of tears. She inhaled deeply. "I'm thinking of stopping my dissertation."

"Stopping it?"

"Yes. After being with you, Jayesh, everything seems different. When I worked on my text, and reviewed my source material, it looked strange. Of course, there are still many good ideas in there, so I might turn them into articles." She looked straight at me for a second, and then threw herself into my arms. "I'm so confused, Jayesh," she said, her voice muffled.

"Really?" I replied, aware that I might have stumbled into a turn of good fortune.

"The Super Bowl was…I don't know…it was kind of, well, *fun*. All those people together, there was some serious bonding going on. We really shared the experience. Of course it's still a male macho thing, but the Christian fundamentalist aspect, well you're not part of that, neither is Thelonius, or the other players I met…Maybe it's the management, I have to do more research." She paused for a moment. "And Azala. I *hate* Azala. I read some things he wrote. He thinks America and Europe are deteriorating because women have too much power. He warned the Third World countries to watch out, that it doesn't happen to them. Yuck."

I rewarded her speech with a strong hug, and began stroking her hair.

"Ooh, I like that, Jayesh. You know, you're a nice football player. You're really, really nice."

I gave Ashley a long kiss, in the classic Parisian riverside tradition. We then walked quietly to the main street, and took a taxi to the hotel.

A while later, I had to ask Ashley to excuse me so that I could go to Sam's hearing. If I did not depart at once, I would be late. When I opened the door to leave the room, she embraced me and would not let go. It took several attempts to pry her, gently, from my body. I must admit that I did not make as earnest an effort as possible to free myself.

I rushed to the street and found a cab right away, but arrived at the World Tribunal for Peace and Justice about five minutes late. Thelonius and Tom were waiting in the main lobby. I showed my passport and received my visitor's badge. A soldier led us to the courtroom, located in the modern glass and metal building in the center of the courtyard.

The chamber was rather drab. The walls and furniture were either beige or a dull silvery color, interrupted only by the blue and white flag of the U.N. and the orange and green flag of the Tribunal. Sam and his attorney were seated at the defendant's table. We sat behind them in the visitors' area, but (at Tom's suggestion) three rows back, to allow a small zone of privacy. Sam glanced over his shoulder and waved at us. He was smiling, but barely. He seemed to be taking it well, but there were signs of strain in his face.

The judge, a young woman with Middle Eastern features, gave a brief introductory discourse. She explained that the purpose of the hearing was to set a date for the trial, and to bring up any outstanding issues related to evidence, witnesses, and the like. She then gave the attorney for the prosecution permission to speak.

The UNSAINE prosecutor rose from his seat. "Your honor," he said, speaking with a throaty Dutch accent, "the prosecution is ready to begin the trial without delay. A week from now, as my colleague has proposed, is acceptable to us."

"Good," said the judge. "The trial shall begin one week from today, at ten o'clock in the morning. Counsel, be ready with opening statements."

"Oh, your honor..." said the prosecutor.

"Yes?"

"If it please the court, the prosecution would like to propose a compromise settlement."

"Go ahead," said the judge.

"We are willing to waive the standard prison sentence for the defendant, and instead would accept the following: First, a public apology from the defendant, to be delivered at an UNSAINE press conference in New York. The text will be composed by our staff, and will include an admission of the defendant's racist ideology. Second, a fine of one million dollars, to be paid into the UNSAINE campaign for anti-racist education. Third, a thousand hours of community work, in a location and role that we will determine. Fourth, it will be forbidden for the defendant ever to mention UNSAINE in any broadcast or publication.

"Non-compliance with any of these provisions will subject the defendant to re-arrest and trial for his crimes. If there is agreement now in principle, counsel for the prosecution and for the defense shall meet tomorrow to draw up the formal agreement. That is all, your honor." The prosecutor returned to his seat.

"Very well," said the judge. "Counsel for the defense, would you like a few minutes to consult with your client? Or even a short recess?"

Sam stood up. "I can give you my answer right now."

"Yes…" said the judge.

"You can all go to hell."

The judge pounded the gavel. "Take him away," she shrieked. "Take him away *now!*"

Two soldiers rushed to the defendant's table, handcuffed Sam, and brutally dragged him out of the chamber. Thelonius made a movement in their direction, but Tom's quick hand stopped him cold.

We remained in our places, absolutely stunned. Sam's attorney turned around to face us. He was a tall, well-dressed man, around fifty, with a thick moustache. "That was not good," he said, shaking his head. "We could have negotiated a better deal. It was only their opening position."

"You know," said Thelonius, "I understand Sam. These guys here just want to humiliate him. A thousand hours of community work? Confessing that he's a racist? That's no deal."

The attorney placed his papers in his briefcase and closed it. He looked at Tom. "Let's be in touch later, to see what we can do."

"Okay, thanks," said Tom.

The four of us headed for the main door of the chamber, where we were joined by our military escort. In a matter of minutes we found ourselves on the Avenue de la Motte Piquet, with the Tribunal behind us and the Eiffel Tower looming in the distance. The attorney said goodbye and continued on his way.

"This whole thing stinks," said Thelonius. "It really stinks. And there's not a damn thing we can do about it."

"I know what you mean," I said.

The three of us stood there, absorbing the shock of the previous scene.

"Well, guys," said Tom, "What d'ya say we head over to that bar near the Madeleine church, you know, Thelonius, the one we went to the other day."

"Sure thing," said Thelonius.

"Not me," I said. "I better get back to the hotel."

"Ahh," said Tom. "Something better awaits you."

"Indeed."

We shook hands and parted. I started walking down the avenue, going toward the Boulevard de Grenelle. The image of Sam being dragged away by soldiers kept reappearing in my mind. I felt powerless and frustrated.

Soon I arrived at the Métro, and took the train to Odéon station. From there, it was a short walk to the Hotel Rostand. When I reached my room, Ashley had just run a bath. She promised to be out within half an hour, and recommended that I "chill out" in the meantime. I took off my shoes and reclined on the couch. I called my parents, but there was no answer. The message they would receive on their voice mail was that all was well, and that they need not worry.

The next call was to my sister Julie. The conversation made me exceedingly nervous. She had canceled all the bodyguards that we had put into place before the Super Bowl. The precautions were unnecessary, she claimed, as there had not been the slightest indication that someone was following, watching, or wiretapping any of the family members. I argued my case unsuccessfully and then, in a fit of emotion, declared that I was on my way there to investigate the situation for myself.

I was still pacing around the suite, mumbling to myself, when Ashley emerged from the bathroom. "Jayesh, what's the matter?" she asked.

"I have to go to London."

"Why? What happened?"

"Julie canceled all the security arrangements. Nothing has happened so far, that was her argument. I have a feeling that Prescott was behind this."

Ashley took my hand in hers. "How long will you be there?"

"I can't say. Hopefully just a day or two. It depends how quickly I can convince her of the folly of her ways."

"What about Sam?"

"I don't think there's much I can do right now. Certainly not in the next couple of days. Anyway, not a moment to lose. I'm taking the next train." I removed my suitcase from the armoire, opened it on the bed, and started loading in clothes.

Ashley sat on the bed. There was a childish pout on her face. "What about me?" she said.

I stopped moving, still holding a pair of socks. Yes, what about her, I thought. She has good reason to be upset; I keep pushing her aside as I run from country to country. I tossed the socks into the suitcase and sat beside her on the bed. "Would you mind coming with me to London?" I asked.

She gave me a sudden hug, not letting up for several moments, before disengaging. "Jayesh, I..."

"What is it?"

"Oh, nothing really. I'm just so happy."

Ashley finished her *toilette* and got dressed. By the time she started packing, my suitcase was ready. I sat on the couch and made a quick call to Julie, to inform her that Ashley would be accompanying me. I then called Thelonius. It was embarrassing having to explain to him my latest country-hopping escapade, particularly after my "full involvement with Sam's case" speech earlier in the day.

"We're all in the same boat," said Thelonius.

"What do you mean?"

"Tom will explain. I'm putting the phone on speaker."

"Hi, Jayesh," said Tom.

"Hi."

"We spoke to Sam's lawyer a few minutes ago. He said there's nothing we can do here, and in fact, our presence may hurt his chances at this point. There's little hope for Sam when it comes to the normal judicial channels. We need to go back to the States and try to lobby, try to find people who have influence politically. Thelonius and I are flying to New York very soon. I already have some appointments set up."

"Good luck," I said. "I'll be back in the U.S. as soon as possible."

"Take care," said Tom.

We ended the call. Ashley announced that she was ready. We grabbed our bags, descended to the lobby, checked out, and found a taxi. I instructed the driver to transport us with all possible speed to the Gare du Nord train station.

Even though I had taken it several times, the high-speed TGV train still gave me a thrill. It was Ashley's first time, and she enjoyed the ride. We spent a long time in the café car, standing next to the panoramic window.

"I'm really glad you're taking me with you to London," she said.

"So am I."

"Something has changed in you, Jayesh. You're more…"

"More what?"

"More trusting, more relaxed. Relaxed about our relationship, I mean. You're letting me into your life. Before, you were always separating your world into parts that never met."

I pondered her words for several moments. "You're right," I said. I put my arm around her, and we watched the scenery pass swiftly before our eyes.

We arrived at London's Waterloo station after what seemed like a short journey. During the taxi ride to Julie's house, we passed several interesting monuments, which I of course pointed out to Ashley. More noteworthy, however, was the incredible number of foreigners. During my childhood, there were quite a few, but it was nothing compared to what we saw at that moment. Ashley looked confused as she viewed the masses of people walking in every direction.

By contrast, the street in St. John's Wood that contained the home of Julie and Prescott Barnes had not changed much over the years. It was old, quaint, and well-kept, the kind of scene American tourists imagine when they think of London. The taxi pulled into the short driveway of the relatively modest-looking townhouse. I paid the driver and we exited the cab, baggage in tow. I gave Ashley a kiss to bolster her courage for the initial entrance, perhaps the toughest part of a visit to a new household. Before I could ring the bell, the door opened and a hand waved us in. We banged the luggage several times against the wall and each other as we made our way down the short, narrow hallway and into the vestibule. We rested our bags with a sigh of relief. Julie gave me a hug, and then engaged Ashley in an exchange of warm salutations.

Julie is of medium height and rather slim, with a skin tone just a tad lighter than mine. Her hair had been cut short for the previous five years or so, after a decade of ever-changing hair styles, as she attempted to create the persona of a truly attractive woman. Sadly, there was little chance of success, due to the form of her face: The bridge of her nose was too prominent, and her chin was too large for her mouth, among other shortcomings. As my grandfather once delicately explained to me, interracial unions often produce exquisite offspring, but sometimes a slightly irregular arrangement of features is the result. Julie compensated for her deficiencies, however, by keeping fit, and by radiating warmth, caring, and genuine interest in those around her.

As she conversed with Ashley, I viewed the decor. It was decidedly conservative, a restrained good taste leaning toward the Edwardian: harmonious, calming, and inoffensive. It was more the influence of Prescott, my brother-in-law, though it did correspond with the overall style of the Blackstones.

"Come, come inside," said Julie, ushering us into the main hallway, and from there to the salon. It was a grand space, with a cathedral ceiling. A huge bay window and sliding glass doors provided a full view of the garden. The parquet floors were partially covered with plush Persian rugs. The antique furniture, most of which had been inherited by Prescott, was arranged in a most pleasing manner. Nothing was missing; there was a grandfather clock, mahogany end tables, a large oak desk with a rolling top, an eighteenth-century globe, and a vitrine containing a collection of porcelain figurines. In short, the epitome of classic good taste.

Prescott entered the room, shook my hand firmly, and introduced himself to Ashley. He was about forty-five, balding, and beginning to sprout a pot belly, despite his efforts to keep in shape by swimming and playing cricket. He wore an elegant velour smoking jacket. Prescott was a product of the very bottom of the English upper class. There was some money in his family, some good connections, and a long line of distinguished public servants, but absolutely no trace of noble blood. This annoyed him no end. Periodically, he would employ experts in genealogy in a futile effort to uncover the missing link, as it were.

He displayed a tentative smile as he inspected Ashley. "You did all right for yourself, old boy," he said. "Please, make yourselves comfortable. What would you like to drink? Some brandy? Scotch? I even have some bourbon stashed away somewhere, in case some Americans happen to drop in."

"Maybe they want some tea after their long journey," said Julie.

"Just water for me," I said. "We ate and drank on the train, and a bit too much, I'm afraid."

"Same for me, please," said Ashley.

We took a seat on the couch. "I suppose the kids are asleep," I said.

"Oh, yes, it's rather late," said Julie. "I'll go get your water."

Ashley and I remained with Prescott. He asked us about Paris, but instead of listening to the answer, he began to lecture us about his favorite restaurants there.

Julie returned and served us our water. "Prescott, do they have to hear about that?"

"They don't *have to*, my dear," he replied. "All right then, what would you like to talk about?"

I didn't pay attention to the answer. At that moment I wanted nothing more than to end the conversation and get to sleep. Instead, I settled for an escape to the lavatory. Along the way, something unexpected appeared. As I was walking down the hallway, and passed the sitting room, I stopped cold from what I saw in my peripheral vision. It was a tall heap of something. Entering the room, I felt as if I were hallucinating: In the middle of this elegant old English parlor, surrounded by a distinguished collection of legal tomes and great works of literature, was a five-foot high pile of dirt. The more I looked at it, the greater my disbelief. It was a sandy color, with a smattering of white pebbles. Worms were writhing their way through it. At the top of the heap was a wide yellow candle, which, judging from the globs of melted wax, had burned down a ways before becoming extinguished.

"Julie," I shouted, instinctively, as if warning people of a fire. She ran in, Ashley and Prescott close behind. "What *is* this?" I said, pointing to the object of my wonderment.

"Don't you *know*, my dear fellow?" said Prescott, in his condescending Etonesque sing-song.

"Darling," said Julie, grasping her husband's arm, "I don't think they have Essence Mounds in America yet."

"Oh yes, of course," said Prescott, with a hint of annoyance rather than remorse. "I forgot that the old boy lives amongst the cowboys and the cacti."

Yes, I thought to myself, he does, and luckily there aren't too many snobs like you. I wanted to respond more vociferously, but I restrained myself for Julie's sake.

"What's an Essence Mound?" asked Ashley. "What does it mean?"

"It symbolizes the union of our lives with mother earth," said Prescott. "The earth, from which all life springs, is here brought into focus, introduced into the very bosom of our lives, our own home space. It is a sign-post, a reminder that our lifestyles must be fitted to the earth, and not the other way around."

Ashley scrunched her face. "Yuck…there's worms in there."

I burst out laughing, which was greeted by a scowl from my eminent brother-in-law. Julie giggled, but quickly restrained herself. Without missing a beat, Prescott gently lifted one of the worms and placed it in the palm of his hand. "What better symbol could there be of the dependence of all life on the soil than these innocent little creatures." He began to stroke the worm with the most delicate of caresses. "It's a new concept. We just got our mound last week."

"Well, I'm glad we know all about Essence Mounds," I said, frowning. Julie lowered her eyes, looking embarrassed. I excused myself and left the room, making my way to the lavatory, which was my original destination.

I returned to find the others once again in the salon. Prescott was seated at his desk, reading some documents with an air of gravity. I sat in the vicinity of the ladies, but not too close, to avoid disrupting the chatting that was in progress. They seemed to be hitting it off well.

"Will you two excuse me," I said after a few minutes.

"Sure," said Ashley. "I'll be with you soon."

"Take your time," I said, standing up. "There's no rush. Julie, we'll talk in the morning."

"All right, Jayesh. I'll bring you to your room."

"No, no need for that," I said. "I know where everything is." I kissed her and Ashley goodnight, shook hands with Prescott, and headed for the guest bedroom. By the time Ashley joined me, I was fast asleep.

The next day, I awoke quite early, enabling me to be dressed by six o'clock. Ashley was still asleep. I crept downstairs and made myself some tea. While I sat at the kitchen table, Julie came in. This was no surprise; she had always been an early riser.

"Good morning, Jayesh," she said, giving me a hug. "I'm so pleased that you're here. Of course, it would be nice if it were a normal visit, instead of always being crisis situations and funerals. But I'll take what I can get."

"Thanks. So when does everyone rise in the morning?"

"Oh, not for another hour and a half, at least."

"How about a little walk?" I asked, looking out the window. "The weather seems fair. It'll be like the old days, when we went to the high street together, just the two of us."

"Oh, yes. I remember how excited you were, as a little boy, when mom first gave you permission to go with me."

"Julie, you make it sound like you were an adult at the time. You're only three years older than me, you know."

This last remark caused her to give me a little slap on the top of my head, in jest of course. We cleared away the dishes and headed into the vestibule.

As I was putting on my coat, Julie gave me some gloves and a warm hat. We left the house, heading for the high street. It was cold and wintry, but the air was calm and the sky clear, so we could stroll about in relative comfort. I soaked up the ambience of my old neighborhood. There was just a hint of light from the approaching dawn, enough to create a handsome silhouette from the outline of the buildings across the street.

After hearing a brief update of domestic goings-on, I gave a summary of my stay in Paris and in Sundar Prabhat. I emphasized the tension and conflict between the major players, in order to convey the level of danger to which Julie was exposed. She seemed to understand, so I reiterated my demand for reinstatement of the security arrangements that were originally put in place. Julie agreed that I could renew them, but on condition that Prescott not know, and that the arrangements would not be perceptible. I said I would check whether it were possible to proceed in such a manner.

We reached the high street and slowed our pace, poking our noses here and there among the shops. There was some movement of vehicles and people, mostly of the service variety: street cleaners, window washers, delivery men.

"Don't you ever feel the desire to come live in America?" I said.

"You've asked me that before, Jayesh."

"I'm asking you again."

"Not really. My home is here. My whole life is here—the kids, work, Prescott and his world, my friends, everything. Except you, and mom and dad, but we all manage to see each other."

"And you had grandfather, when he was alive," I added.

"Yes," she sighed. "It's been a great big gap, losing him like that."

"I know. I feel terrible about not having seen him for so long. I hope he forgives me, up there in heaven."

"I'm sure he already has, Jayesh."

We stopped in front of a bookstore and peered into the window.

"Julie…"

"Yes?"

"What about India?"

"What do you mean?" she asked, looking up at me with her soft eyes.

"Well, when you took your last trip there—when was it, in 2015?"

"2014."

"Yes, 2014," I said. "How did you feel? Was there any special connection with the people?"

"No, not particularly. Why do you ask?"

"On this last trip, I felt something very strongly. Just seeing the locals, it reminded me of mom's family. I had a longing to be close to them. There was a woman there, too, a beautiful woman. She had spent some time in England as a child. Her parents, who were professors at Oxford, died in a car accident while she was still young."

We resumed our languorous promenade along the storefronts.

"So," said Julie, "What happened with this woman?"

"Nothing, really," I said. "We had some interesting discussions. But when I saw her in a crisis situation, all I wanted to do was run away. Appearances are one thing, but the real way of life is another."

"Yes, that is true...Well then, what about Ashley? Is it serious?"

"I'm not sure yet."

"What do you mean, you're not sure? Do you love her, Jayesh?"

"I *could* love her."

"Could?" she exclaimed.

"Yes."

"Could, if what?"

"If it turns out we're truly compatible."

"You don't know yet?"

"Not completely. Look, I'm dealing with some strange circumstances right now. Ashley was writing a dissertation whose ideas, if they were implemented, would bury professional football. She had some sympathy for the people who tried to ruin the Super Bowl. On the other hand, her feelings have changed since we've been together. She said she might stop writing the dissertation. It's a mixed bag, and I don't know how it will turn out."

"Can I say what I think?"

"Of course."

"I believe that Ashley loves you. It's very deep. A woman can always tell when she sees it in another woman."

I smiled. "Maybe you're right."

"As for those ideas that you fear, that will work itself out. I would say that Jayesh Blackstone is closer to her heart than a thousand dissertations."

Julie's words seemed prophetic as we arrived at the house. No sooner did we take off our coats and return to the kitchen than Ashley practically flew down the stairs and ran into my arms. It was a giant hug, stunning me with its energy. Julie was nodding all the while, as if to say, "I told you so."

Prescott entered the room, greeting us with a groany voice. He prepared his tea and took a seat at the table, where he began to read the newspaper. The two children, seven year-old Lisa and nine year-old Paul, were soon running around in their pajamas. We all spent a delightful half-hour or so in this portrait of domestic bliss, a sight that warms the heart. Ashley interacted quite nicely with the children, revealing a side of herself the existence of which I had not suspected. She had them laughing and sitting on her lap in no time. Once more I saw Julie in the background giving a matronly nod of approval.

Soon the kids were off to school and Prescott to the City. I asked Julie to put me in contact with the security firm that had provided the bodyguards for the household. I spoke with a representative, and after ten minutes or so managed to work out a reasonably discrete arrangement for the renewal of their services. Julie agreed not to change anything unless she consulted with me first.

Ashley, Julie, and I decided to go out and see the town. Our first stop was the British Museum. After viewing some fascinating exhibits, including a major collection of Islamic artifacts from Saudi Arabia, we had lunch at a quaint little restaurant in the West End. The afternoon was spent in Knightsbridge, mostly shopping for the ladies. All in all it was a wonderful experience. Ashley and Julie hit it off beautifully. They laughed and giggled at every turn. It was also a pleasure to show Ashley some of the sights of London—handpicked to avoid the teeming foreign population of most neighborhoods.

We stayed in London another three days. It could not have been scripted any better. Even the weather was cooperative. Ashley and I spent just the right amount of time with Julie and her family. More often than not we scurried off on our own, going to museums, galleries, fine restaurants, and the theater. I showed her the house in which I grew up, as well as the American School and other points of interest from my childhood. I promised her that after the White House reception, and after the problems with Sam blew over, we would return for an extended vacation that would include other regions of the British Isles.

The visit was a turning point in my relationship with Ashley. We were both much more relaxed with each other, and had time to do the silly things lovers do, without the constant refrain of intrigue and danger. The worries I expressed to Julie faded away as Ashley and I became closer than I had ever thought possible.

CHAPTER EIGHT

▼

The next two weeks in Albuquerque were enjoyable and relaxing. This interlude was made possible by a fortuitous alignment of circumstances.

The day after Ashley and I took the train to London, Tom and Thelonius flew to New York. With Thelonius tagging along, Tom began an intensive, high-level lobbying campaign on behalf of Sam. Much of the time was spent shuttling between New York and Washington. After less than forty-eight hours had passed, Thelonius bailed out, returning to New Mexico. He said that the reason for his withdrawal was that he was "getting in the way." Tom needed complete freedom of movement, and very often the individuals he approached for an audience insisted that the conversation be kept absolutely secret, and that no one else attend.

I called Tom once, just after Ashley and I returned to Albuquerque. He was in Washington, about to meet with a congressman. He was in a hurry, and assured me there was nothing I could do to help at that point.

I decided to take a break: No Tom, no Sam, no Azala, no Hunter, no intrigue and no espionage. It was time for a real vacation. Fortunately, everyone cooperated with my plan. For two weeks, there was no communication from anyone connected with Sam's case or with Sundar Prabhat. Moreover, the White House reception for disadvantaged Asians in sports and entertainment was still about three weeks away.

Thelonius was in a similar frame of mind. He chose to occupy himself with interior decorating in his penthouse apartment, and with his girlfriend, whom I shall describe in due course. Steve Gonzales, ever apologetic about his absence from the anti-Azala efforts, was busy organizing his annual family reunion in Santa Fe. My parents were on a cruise in the South Pacific.

Ashley was with me constantly during those two memorable weeks. On a typical day, we lingered in bed until mid-morning, at which time she prepared my favorite breakfast, fried eggs and french toast. Then we went out for an excursion, returning home in the late afternoon. This was followed by dinner, a movie, a stroll around the compound, and a dip in the Jacuzzi.

We took several hikes in the Sandia Mountains, abutting the city on its eastern flank. It was early spring, and I felt like a young, carefree lover, wandering in the wilderness with my sweetheart. I could not have asked for more.

As for Ashley's acceptance of my world, it seemed irreproachable. The emotional energy she had expended on her former obsession with male patriarchies and conspiracy theories was being converted into an intense affection for her mate. She had nothing but unkind words for Azala, not only for his objectionable articles, but for his Super Bowl antics as well. She declared that the arrest and trial of Sam Kapulski was a sham, based on trumped-up charges. She recalled her Super Bowl experience with great enthusiasm, and frequently asked questions about my career, the other players, and the sport in general. The subject of women in professional football never came up.

It was during one of our jaunts in the mountains, about ten days after our return from Europe, that Ashley made an important announcement. It was early evening, and we were heading down the slope, on our way back to the car. We paused to take in a magnificent sunset. A cool, comfortable breeze was blowing.

"Jayesh…"

"Yes?"

"I made a decision."

"Oh?"

"I'm stopping my dissertation. And I've withdrawn from the doctoral program. I asked for a one-year leave of absence."

"That's quite a change," I said, hardly able to contain my glee.

"Who knows, I might continue with some other subject. I just wanted to let you know. It was killing me, the whole thing. I was wrong, I was really wrong." She put her arm around my waist. We quietly watched the sunset. I said nothing, fearful of spoiling a moment that was simply too good to be true.

On the evening of the following day, Thelonius and his girlfriend came over for dinner. Ashley had volunteered to pilot the entire affair, an effort that included obtaining the food and doing the cooking. The guests arrived at around seven o'clock.

Thelonius looked relaxed and content. His afro was longer and bushier than I had ever seen it. A couple of times over the course of the evening I detected something bordering on a giggle, which was out of character for him. His girlfriend, Sandy, was not the type of woman I would have expected him to be dating. She was tall and svelte, dressed in a lady's business suit. Her body movement and restrained manner reminded me of Lauren Bacall. Sandy was an accomplished entrepreneur, directing one of the city's largest advertising agencies. In her spare time, she was the president of a major charity, and served on the boards of several other civic organizations.

We spent the first half-hour or so chatting in the living room. The women soon became absorbed in their own discussion, and seemed to be getting along quite well. This was due in no small measure to the social talents of Sandy, who was adept at the art of conversation, honing in on the disposition and character of those around her. As this dialogue continued, Thelonius and I moved to the patio, where we updated each other on our activities since returning to Albuquerque.

It was at dinner that the conversation took an interesting turn.

"I spoke to Tom Hubert yesterday," said Thelonius, after swallowing a mouthful of Ashley's delicious beef stroganoff. "We talked about an old friend of yours, Jayesh. A lady friend."

"Oh?" I said, my eyes meeting Ashley's for a split second.

"Yes. Her name is Mahinta Zagumbi." Thelonius burst into laughter, and a rancorous outbreak it was, even for him. "You should've seen the look on your face just now, Jayesh. Oh, man." I must have displayed yet another amusing look, because he started laughing once again.

"So what did Mr. Hubert *say*?" asked Sandy.

"Okay, okay," said Thelonius, settling down. "Tom told me that Miss Zagumbi is feeling much better. They let her out of the hospital."

"Where is she now?" asked Ashley.

"In New York. She had been at Mt. Sinai hospital, where they performed some complicated operation, then the league set her up in an apartment in Manhattan with twenty-four hour nursing staff. They want her to go to the White House reception, your reception, Jayesh. The doctors said it's okay."

"At least she's recovering," said Sandy, taking a sip of wine.

"Yeah, that she is," said Thelonius. "But there's more. She doesn't want to go to the reception, at least not until she speaks to you, Jayesh."

"Really?"

"Yes, sir. According to Tom, Miss Zagumbi said you're the only one who would understand her."

Ashley was smiling. "Jayesh *is* very understanding."

"Yeah, he's understanding," said Thelonius. "Maybe he'll invite some other Miss America winners to practice with him in training camp next season."

"Don't hold your breath," I said.

"Well what's wrong with it, anyway?" said Ashley, in an inquisitive voice, as if asking herself the question.

Thelonius became somber. "What's wrong with it? Oh, nothing. Next time we go to the movie theater, and you ladies are powdering your noses, a few of us guys from the team will come busting in and start putting on makeup. You won't mind, right?"

"That's not the same thing," said Ashley.

"I think it's clear that a woman can hold a football on the ground as well as a man," said Sandy, maintaining her usual calm tone. "That much is clear. But I wonder whether we would still enjoy watching the game to the same degree if a bunch of ladies were fighting it out on the gridiron. I'm not sure we would cheer as strongly for that crushing action, like Thelony when he tackles."

"*Thelony*?" I said.

Thelonius turned his palms upward in a gesture of feigned helplessness. "That's what she calls me. What can I do?"

A pleasant chuckle enveloped the table.

"So, Ashley," continued Sandy, "would you enjoy the game, would it be the same for you, if women were being crushed out there?"

Ashley looked especially pensive before responding. "No, probably not. Now that I've had a chance to see a game, to experience it up close, it seems like the thrill would be ruined."

I marveled at Sandy's smooth direction of the conversation, leading Ashley to uncover her own feelings on the matter. She accomplished in a matter of minutes what I had failed to do over a period of several weeks.

We continued eating. The discussion turned to relationships. Each couple shared several amusing anecdotes from their time together. I learned some interesting facts about Thelonius; for example, that he was involved in the administration of a local adoption agency. In fact, this is where he had first met Sandy.

All in all, it was a pleasant visit. We agreed to get together again at the earliest opportunity. After the guests departed, Ashley told me that she greatly enjoyed the dinner, and that Sandy and Thelonius were both marvelous people. She did express surprise, however, that Sandy could be such an accomplished, independent woman, and at the same time not be concerned with expanding women's rights.

Not long thereafter, the glorious fortnight with Ashley came to an abrupt close. The cause was a phone call from the office of the White House chief of staff, the purpose of which was to confirm my participation at the upcoming reception for disadvantaged Asians in sports and entertainment. The young man at the other end of the line briefed me regarding travel, lodging, and other arrangements. He then gave me an overview of the event. Opening the festivities would be a cocktail reception hosted by the First Man. We would hear a statement from the Secretary of Ethnic Reparations, followed by remarks from the Commissioner of Major League Baseball, the noted Hollywood producer Jeremy Chang, and the ambassador of Bangladesh. Then President Malpomme would give a speech, and, to wrap up the event, distribute awards to the Asian athletes and entertainers. The young man did not mention Mahinta Zagumbi.

I barely had time to adjust to this stark reality when another distressing phone call arrived. This time it was Raghavendra Hunter.

"Jayesh, how are you?" he said, in his deep voice.

"Not bad, thanks," I replied, not at all sure what kind of tone to adopt. "How about you?"

"Good," said Hunter. "I have some news to share with you, but first I would like to apologize once again for the way things went during your trip to Sundar Prabhat. It was most unfortunate."

"I understand. It was nobody's fault. I just hope you and your family are safe and sound."

"Everything worked out okay for the time being. Azala and his men, though, are lording it over us. But let us not continue this particular discussion on the phone."

"Okay," I said. "What news do you have for me?"

"I'm in New York right now. I would very much like to meet with you, say, tomorrow. I have some important matters to discuss. Would it be possible for you to come here?"

"Well, I'm a bit tied up at the moment...is it *very* important?"

"Yes."

"Well...okay, then."

"Good," he replied. "Please be in New York tomorrow morning. Someone will contact you to let you know the time and place of our meeting. Try to tell as few people as possible where you are going and what you are doing."

"All right."

"Thank you, Jayesh. I'll see you soon."

We ended the call. It was a little after ten o'clock in the morning. I was sitting on the couch; Ashley was taking a bath. A knot of frustration was building up inside me, worsened by doubt over the hasty decision I had just made to go to New York. Once again, I would have to leave Ashley, telling her some half-baked story. I would have to watch my movements, be aware of everyone and everything around me. What did I do to deserve this, I thought. I'm just a football player. This is the off-season, for God's sake. I should be on an endless cruise around the world with Ashley. We could be going island-hopping in the South Pacific, meeting up with Thelonius and Sandy in Tahiti for a few days, and then continuing on to Europe, wining and dining for weeks on end...

I straightened myself on the couch, holding the sides of my head. These are serious times, I reminded myself, and they demand serious measures and a serious frame of mind. One does not control the world, as my grandfather used to say. We have freedom to act, but only within the framework presented to us by our circumstances. Our worst experiences can occur during ostensibly happy occasions, and from within unfolding disasters can emerge the most gratifying moments. Yes, I thought, he was right. On my nerve-racking trip to Sundar Prabhat, I enjoyed those precious moments with Hunter and Indira, in the eye of the storm. It was unexpected, outside the realm of rational planning.

Just that second, Ashley was standing in front of me, like an apparition. I must have been deep in my reverie, not aware of my surroundings. She was standing with her arms at her side, totally still, with a placid expression on her face. As if by their own will, my hands extended themselves toward her. She approached slowly, with small steps, until our feet were touching. Her expression remained unchanged. We stared into each other's eyes. My hands found hers, and slowly I brought her down until she was seated on my lap. I held her tight, her face resting on my shoulder.

"What do you think of me, Jayesh?" she said, her voice sending a light vibration into my collarbone.

I began to stroke her hair. "What do you mean?"

"Just what I said," she replied, calmly.

"I think you're a nice, beautiful girl."

"Anything else?"

"Well, you're also very intelligent…Was there some specific area you had in mind?"

Ashley retracted her head so that her face was across from mine, inches away. "Jayesh, how do you *feel* about me?"

I chuckled from embarrassment. "I feel close to you, and I feel like I want to be with you all the time."

Ashley closed her eyes and released a muffled groan. Reopening her eyes, she had the same sad face a five year-old girl would have upon learning that her teddy bear went missing. "Jayesh?"

"Yes, Ashley."

"Do you love me?"

"Yes, I do."

She returned her head to its previous position, but this time with a sigh of satisfaction. We remained in our embrace for quite some time.

It was remarkable, in retrospect, that I answered her question so quickly and decisively. True, my doubts about our compatibility were dissipating rapidly. But still, it all seemed quite sudden. Under these circumstances, breaking the news to Ashley about my departure to New York was all the more painful. I was expecting a harsh scene, and perhaps even recrimination. But nothing of the sort transpired. Ashley was sympathetic, urging me to face my responsibilities and carry them out to the best of my ability. She trusted me to return at the earliest possible moment.

It occurred to me that I should take advantage of the trip to visit Mahinta Zagumbi. I called Tom Hubert to find out the latest news about her, and to get her address and phone number. It turned out that Tom was in New York, and planned to remain there for the next few days. We agreed to stay in touch, and hopefully get together. I called Mahinta and set up a visit for ten o'clock the following morning. I then booked a pre-dawn flight and reserved a room at a hotel in Manhattan, in the west sixties, at which I once had a very pleasant stay.

I enjoy visiting New York, which I did fairly often when I was a college student at Yale. This time, however, I felt that I was there under duress, which made the crowds and the noise seem all the more maddening. I was already nervous by the time the taxi crossed the Triborough Bridge, on the way into the city from La Guardia Airport.

By mid morning I had checked into the hotel. From there I walked to Mahinta's apartment, which was located on Madison Avenue in the seventies. It was a crisp, cool day, overcast but dry. Traffic was moderate and the volume of pedestrians was tolerable. Most of them were doing the characteristic New York City hustle, their legs looking like scissors being rapidly opened and closed.

I arrived at the apartment building in which Mahinta was lodged, presenting myself at the front desk. The doorman complimented me on my "fantastic kicking job" during the football season, and then pointed me to the elevator. On my way there, I noticed that the lobby contained an unsettling mixture of classical elegance and contemporary chic. Shoulder-to-shoulder were the American version of Julie's sumptuous

Edwardian wing chairs, and dehydrated insects in a collage by Hervé Culottier, the celebrated French-Canadian artist.

Less than a minute later, I rang the doorbell of Mahinta's apartment. A member of the nursing staff, a middle-aged woman as dried out as Culottier's insects, answered the door. She muttered a few indistinguishable words before leading me into an interior room of the apartment. The furnishings were bland, but looked to be of a fairly high quality. We entered a room that was a sort of den, with a sofa and a Laz-y-boy recliner. Mahinta was nearly horizontal in the recliner, watching TV on a screen of enormous dimensions. She was wearing a thick robe, and did not look particularly infirm.

"Jayesh!" she exclaimed, propping her upper body on her elbows.

"Hello, Mahinta," I said, reluctant to come too close. "You're looking well."

"Miss Zagumbi *is* well," said the nurse. She adjusted the Laz-y-boy so that its occupant was seated in an upright position, and rotated it so that it faced the sofa. She turned off the TV and left the room. I peeled off my jacket, placed it over one arm of the sofa, and sat down.

"She's right, I am well," said Mahinta, straightening her bangs. "I won't be able to walk for a few weeks, so I have to go around in a wheelchair. They say I have to heal from the operation. But I feel good." She had that sweet and unpretentious smile, just as I remembered it from the practice field. "And how are you doing?"

"Oh, fairly well," I replied. "Taking it easy, you know, enjoying the off-season."

There was an uneasy silence for a few moments.

"Jayesh, I wanted to tell you something."

"Go ahead."

"You already know, I think, that they want me to go to the White House event for the Asians."

"Yes, I'm aware of that."

"Well, I don't want to go."

"Why not?" I asked, in a gentle tone.

"I don't know…the whole thing might have been a mistake. I'm talking about my playing in the Super Bowl. I didn't really want to go. And then I got injured. Now the White House wants me. I'm not disadvantaged anymore."

And she's certainly not Asian, I thought. "I know how you feel," I said.

"Why are *you* going, Jayesh?"

I was taken aback by the query. "If it were up to me, I wouldn't go. But the New Mexico Coyotes want me to attend, the management that is. It's worth a lot to them."

Mahinta had a consoling look on her face, her big sad eyes wide open.

"We can chat together at the event," I added. "You know, keep each other company."

There was a flicker of happiness in those sad eyes. "Thank you, Jayesh. You're very nice, you really are."

"Oh, probably not as nice as all that."

"Are you angry with me, Jayesh?"

"Why on earth would I be angry?"

"Because I played in the Super Bowl. Forced you to, well, you know…"

I smiled. "It's okay, don't worry. It wasn't your idea. If you would have refused, they would have found someone else, maybe someone not nearly as friendly. Then imagine how much I would have suffered. At least our time together was enjoyable."

"That's very sweet of you," she said.

Mahinta and I parted with a promise to be in touch before the White House event. The nurse showed me to the door, and I took the elevator down to the ground floor. I was relieved to have found Mahinta on the road to recovery, and in good spirits. At the Super Bowl, when I saw her taken off the field in an ambulance, I feared that she would be crippled for life.

As I stepped out of the elevator and turned toward the exit, the doorman waved at me. "Mr. Blackstone, I have something for you."

"Oh?" I said, approaching the desk with curiosity.

"You got a message. Here." He extended his knobby hand, which was grasping a folded scrap of yellow notebook paper. I took it from him, unfolded it, and read the message. It was from Hunter, telling me to meet him at eleven o'clock on the steps of the Metropolitan Museum of Art. I stared for a moment at the note, as if some additional message were about to appear. Looking up, I saw the doorman eyeing me. "Thanks," I said, and left.

I glanced at my watch: it was 10:45. Fortunately, the museum was only a few blocks away. I looked up at the sky, which seemed to be scowling at me with its gray clouds. I wondered how Hunter knew that I was in Mahinta's building. Was I being followed all day? Was he acquainted with her? Why didn't he just call me on my cell phone?

In short order I arrived at the edge of the museum steps. It was a monumental space, one I greatly enjoyed. Flapping within the colonnade were impressive banners announcing several exhibitions in progress. One of these was a retrospective of Hervé Culottier's work. The banner, undulating gently in the wind, was bright orange with black lettering, and featured a huge print of a locust. On the ground beneath it, a steady stream of people were entering and leaving the building.

Returning my glance toward the street, I saw Hunter walking up the steps, about twenty-five yards away, oblivious to my presence. He was decked out in urban camouflage: sunglasses, a safari hat, a dark blue parka, sweatpants, and sneakers. He continued his steady march up the stairs. My cell phone rang.

"Yes?"

"Meet in ten minutes," said a voice I did not recognize, "in front of Charles Wilson Peale's portrait of George Washington."

"Okay," I said, but the caller had already disconnected. I made my way into the building, and approached a young lady at the information desk. With a quizzical look, she informed me of the location of the gallery containing the portrait. Meanwhile, I lost track of Hunter.

Minutes later, I entered the gallery. No one else was there. I positioned myself in front of the painting, a life-sized rendering of General Washington leaning against the barrel of a cannon. He seemed relaxed, though his facial expression was pensive.

Hunter entered the room and positioned himself alongside me. He also faced the painting. "Hello, Jayesh," he said, in a soft voice, just louder than a whisper.

"Hello."

"Sorry about all this. A museum is one of the places we can be alone in this city, avoiding surveillance. How are you?"

"All right, I suppose."

"Good. Indira sends her regards. She greatly regrets the circumstances that befell you in Sundar Prabhat. She would have liked to get to know you in a more relaxed atmosphere."

"Yes," I said. "That would have been preferable."

"And you are invited to stay with us whenever you want. But I think you know that already. Now, I have something important to tell you. Am I correct in saying that you are still going to the White House event next week?"

"Yes."

"Good. Our intelligence has informed us that the crime of which we spoke will most definitely be attempted. And we know, more or less, who will attempt it."

I swallowed hard, awaiting the news.

"It will be one of the Asian ambassadors."

"Not a Christian fundamentalist?"

"No. They decided, for whatever reason, to abandon that plan. In any case, they will use a very small device, similar in form to a metal wafer that you slide into your computer. From this device will be propelled something akin to a high-tech version of the old poison dart. There may be a delay between the deed and its effect. Initially, it will cause some discomfort. Then the victim will fall ill, and finally die. By that time, the assassin could be halfway across the world. Then again, they may opt for an immediate result, to increase the shock value."

"Will you have one of your people there?" I asked.

"Yes. I cannot tell you at this time who it will be. But you will be apprised of it shortly before your arrival at the White House."

"Will the deed take place at the reception or at the ceremony?"

"Who can say," said Hunter. "Work with our man, and everything will be fine. A lot is riding on you, Jayesh. In one fell swoop you can ruin Azala, free Sam Kapulski, and save your country from a large dose of mayhem."

I nodded, still reticent to look directly at him. We heard footsteps, and turned our heads to see a security guard wandering into the gallery.

"As you can see," said Hunter, raising his voice, "this painting by Charles Wilson Peale is masterful, just like the one you are considering buying. What do you say, is it a deal?"

"Yes, it is."

"Excellent. My people will ship the painting to you tomorrow."

"Thank you."

The security guard drifted into the next room.

"How can I contact you?" I asked, in a hush.

"Better if you don't. I'll find you again within the next twenty-four hours. Goodbye for now." He turned and left the gallery.

I remained alone with George Washington. After contemplating the painting and its neighbors for several minutes, I wandered into the adjacent room. My stroll soon turned into a full-blown tour. It was a desperately-needed interlude of relaxation. Several times I beat back an urge to pull out my phone and call Tom. It could wait a few minutes, I reasoned. A little break would do me good.

My tour brought me to the European paintings, where I headed for the Pissarros. It was a treat to see several works by my favorite artist. I continued through the galleries, coming to the large collection of paintings by Rembrandt. It was there that I spent the most time. I stood transfixed in front of one of his self-portraits. There was a deep introspection in his gaze. I could feel that he was confronting some troubling issues, and I empathized with his plight.

Despite the fine objects that presented themselves to my eyes, I was not able to rid myself of a nagging anxiety. The conversation with Hunter had shaken me more than I had at first realized. The White House reception was no longer a distant concept. It was imminent, and the gravity of the affair could not be denied. I did, however, still harbor doubts about the assassination theory. It simply lacked any basis in logic. Why would Azala wish to eliminate a president who could hardly be more sympathetic to his cause? It seemed that Hunter, as a result of the heated rivalry with his nemesis, had attributed to him wildly exaggerated powers.

I left the museum and wandered into Central Park. A fair number of people were about, and the weather was tolerable. I circled the reservoir, trying not to get run over by the joggers. I had a passing urge to ask a person, someone I would pick at random, what he thinks about the president being assassinated inside the White House. These and other disconcerting thoughts ran through my mind. I was returned to reality by a family of tourists from Wyoming who wanted my autograph.

I figured that it was time to call Tom. It turned out that he was still in New York, at that moment eating his lunch in a Midtown restaurant. We agreed to meet at the observatory of the Empire State Building in one hour. I returned to Fifth Avenue, and began heading south. I walked briskly for about twenty blocks, and then slowed down. The exercise provided an excellent release of tension.

I stopped at a fast-food restaurant near Herald Square, and ate a hamburger. I picked up a newspaper that someone had left behind. A headline caught my eye: *Bye-Bye to All-Male Sports Teams.* According to the article, Congress was drafting a bill to enforce the recent U.N. resolution to abolish all-male sports teams. Anticipating the inevitable, the commissioners of the NFL, the NBA, the NHL, and Major League Baseball had reached an agreement with lawmakers. Beginning in January 2021, all teams would be required to have ten percent female or transgendered players. This figure would increase each year, reaching the equilibrium mark of fifty percent in 2025. I laughed to myself: I had been distraught by one woman playing in one game for one play.

Needless to say, when I met Tom a few minutes later atop the Empire State Building, this news item was a hot topic of discussion.

"There's nothing we can do about it," he said. "It's a different world. Get used to it."

We were looking out over the western half of Midtown, with the Hudson River and New Jersey in the distance. Visibility was fair but the sky was still overcast. I wondered how many of the millions of people in this human beehive had the slightest interest in the outcome of the controversy.

"How did it happen so suddenly?" I inquired.

Tom chuckled under his breath. "It wasn't so sudden. There were meetings here and meetings there, and it's been going on for quite some time. Sports executives have been swarming over Capitol Hill for the past week. They reached a compromise with lawmakers, who were itching to pass an American version of the U.N. resolution."

"A *compromise*, did you say?"

"Yeah, sounds ridiculous, doesn't it? Congress wanted to make it fifty-fifty male-female within two years. The leagues had to fight tooth and nail to stretch it out over five."

"What are we going to do, Tom?"

"You tell me," he said, with a sour face.

I sighed and leaned forward onto the fence that separated us from the thousand-foot drop to the street. I noticed that a few blocks away, a small building was on fire, and about a dozen emergency vehicles were on the scene.

"By the way, any luck with Sam?"

"No," said Tom, tersely. "Another big zilch. Most of the people I turned to for help thought I was crazy to intervene in the case. A guy I know in the State Department said that the orders were coming from the president herself, and boy was she angry. If that guy or anyone else down there dared to challenge or even question the administration on this, they could kiss their careers goodbye."

It was at that very moment that I decided to boycott the White House reception for disadvantaged Asians. Admittedly, it was an impulsive move. The pressure building up inside me, that boiling resentment, had finally reached an intolerable level. I could take it no more. The New Mexico Coyotes would have to survive without the publicity, and Raghavendra Hunter would have to save the world without me.

"Tom," I said, turning to face him. "I'm not going to that White House reception next week, the one for disadvantaged Asians."

"Good," he said, without hesitation. "What made you do it?"

"I can't take it anymore."

"That's about as solid a reason as I can think of, at this point. Oh, and by the way, Jayesh…"

"Yes?"

"You might want to tell your team about the decision. Better they hear it from you than from the White House."

"You're right, Tom, thanks."

We spent a few more minutes on the observation deck, further lamenting the current state of affairs. After the long ride down in the elevator, we said goodbye. Tom continued to the street while I went into an Irish pub adjoining the lobby. After ordering a beer, I telephoned

Hank Hannibal to inform him of my decision to boycott the White House event.

"Hello," he answered, sounding tired.

"Hi, Hank, it's Jayesh."

"Oh, Jayesh," he said, with more pep in his voice. "I was just going to call you."

"Really?"

"Yeah. Listen, nobody died or anything like that, but I have a piece of bad news. The White House just contacted me. They cancelled your participation in the reception for disadvantaged Asians."

I remained silent, stunned by this strange turn of events.

"I'm sorry, Jayesh. It would have been a great opportunity for you. But don't worry, there will be others."

"That's okay, Hank," I said. "Did they give a reason?"

"They were overbooked, had to cut the squad a bit, if you know what I mean. By the way, what did you want to speak to me about?"

"Oh, nothing, just a little question about the event. But of course it's moot now."

"Yeah," said Hank. "Them's the breaks. Take care, Jayesh."

"Okay, see you," I said, and closed the phone.

I finished my beer and placed some money on the counter. Someone sat down beside me, despite the fact that the bar was sparsely populated. I had to do a double-take: It was Naveen, the same young Indian man that had first told me about Hunter at the café in Paris.

"Hello again, Mr. Blackstone," said Naveen in a hushed voice, without looking at me.

"Hello," I replied, in the same tone.

"I am sorry about the way your trip to Sundar Prabhat turned out."

"It was nobody's fault."

"Mr. Hunter would like to see you."

"So he sent you here to tell me that?" I said, not pleased that once again I was being followed.

"He is waiting for you in a car," said Naveen, handing me a matchbook. An address was scribbled on it. "The car will be parked within one block of that building."

"He's there now?"

"Yes." Naveen stood up, all the while looking straight ahead, toward the rows of liquor bottles along the back wall of the bar. "One day," he said, "I hope we will be able to meet properly, like old friends."

Before I had a chance to respond, he turned and headed for the front door. I waited several moments before leaving the bar myself. I hailed a cab on Thirty-Third Street and gave the driver the address on the matchbook. My whole body was tense. The aftershock of the day's events was now combined with nervous anticipation of the encounter that awaited me at the end of that ride. Hunter's ambitious plans for the White House reception would be disrupted, with his star player, myself, on the bench for the duration of the game.

I stepped out of the cab on a quiet street in Tribeca. The buildings were primarily warehouses. At one end of the block a Mercedes sedan was double-parked, its engine running. I walked over to it. The rear door opened; Hunter was visible inside. He motioned for me to enter. I was greeted with a firm handshake and a warm smile. We pulled away from the curb.

"Thank you for coming, Jayesh," he said.

"It's okay."

"I'm very sorry about all this silly spy stuff. Better to be safe than sorry, though."

"I understand." For some reason, when I was with Hunter in person, my anxiety evaporated.

"We'll just drive around for a while. It'll give us a chance to talk. So, how are you?"

"Not too bad," I said. "There's something I need to tell you."

"Go ahead," said Hunter, with the calm tone of someone accustomed to a steady diet of upheaval.

"I was disinvited from the White House reception."

"I knew that would happen."

"You did?"

"I suspected it. They are aware of your connection with me, with Sam Kapulski, and with Azala. Why should they reward you? That was probably the gist of it."

"Sounds logical," I said.

"Now it's my turn to tell *you* something. Life is becoming very dangerous in Sundar Prabhat. I have decided to move Indira here, to

New York. She is staying in an apartment on the Upper East Side. There are many Indians in the building and in the area. She is among her people."

"What about Azala's men?"

"There's probably one or two lurking around."

The chauffeur turned onto West Street and began driving along the Hudson.

"Tell me something," I said. "Why does Azala have so much power? Why does the Indian government allow the continued independence of Sundar Prabhat?"

Hunter was staring in the direction of the river. After several moments, he turned his face toward me. "It is because of Azala's clout in the United Nations. They say that he will almost certainly be the next secretary-general. It would be inadvisable for the Indian government to step in now."

"I see."

"Jayesh, could I ask you for a favor? It has nothing to do with Azala or Sam Kapulski. It's personal."

"Okay."

"Could you keep an eye on Indira? She has people to take care of her, and bodyguards, and sufficient funds. But all that is cold and businesslike. It would mean a lot if she had contact with you, even if it were limited. You are from America, and someone she can trust. I'm not asking for a huge commitment of time. Just a phone call here and there, and maybe, if you can, a brief visit before you leave New York. If doing so would not compromise your domestic situation, naturally."

"I'll see what I can do," I said.

Hunter thanked me and handed me a card with Indira's phone number. "Where would you like us to drop you off?"

"At Lincoln Center, please."

Hunter relayed my wish to the driver. We continued heading uptown.

"Jayesh…"

"Yes?"

"We're friends, you and I, aren't we?"

"Of course," I replied.

"I hope that someday all the madness will settle down, and we can sit and converse at our ease, with no apprehension in our midst."

"That would be nice."

"We live in interesting times," said Hunter. "Strange things are happening in your country, Jayesh. The whole Azala affair, the Super Bowl madness, Sam Kapulski being turned over to UNSAINE—all this represents a profound shift in the political landscape. There are many other examples, but I'm sure you are aware of them. Tell me, do you think that President Malpomme will be re-elected in November?"

"Actually, I hadn't thought about it much. One assumes that she will. She's very popular and there doesn't seem to be any significant challenge mounted by the opposition."

"Be careful, Jayesh. Be careful out there."

The driver pulled over in front of Lincoln Center. Hunter and I parted with another firm handshake. After exiting the vehicle, I walked for a while, trying to dissipate the tension in my bones. It only became worse, however, as I pondered the complex web of dilemmas in which I was entwined.

After joining the pedestrian stream, I called Ashley. She was at her apartment in Santa Fe, taking care of a backlog of domestic matters. I reported that all was well, and that I would be back in New Mexico within a day or two, at which time I would describe the trip in detail.

My next call was to Mahinta, to tell her that I had been disinvited to the White House reception. She informed me that the same thing had happened to her.

I thought about Indira, and whether I should contact her. I had not fully committed myself to Hunter, saying only that I would "see what I can do." A phone call, at least, would be in order. But what if she wanted to see me? Would it be disloyal to Ashley, or could it be classified under the rubric of business? I decided to make the call, and see how my instincts guided me.

The lesson to be drawn from the ensuing conversation was that one should never leave things to instinct when dealing with a young, beautiful woman. Indira was extremely pleased to receive my call. She apologized profusely for the incident in Sundar Prabhat. She also made it clear that she was *very* lonely in her new apartment, and had no real friends in the city. I agreed to meet her at noon the following day in the lobby of her building, from where we could walk to an Indian restaurant off Lexington Avenue.

Returning to my hotel, I reassured myself that the upcoming meeting was innocent enough. If necessary, I could say that she was relaying a critical message from Hunter. The more I thought about it, however, the more it seemed that I was bending the truth to satisfy my own curiosity. Perhaps it was a desire to keep Indira on the back burner until such time as I would want to pursue a relationship with her. I resolved to keep the meeting secret, and approach it purely as part of my commitment to Hunter. The contradictions inherent in this strategy were staring me in the face; after all, a few days previously I had told Ashley that I loved her. In retrospect, it is clear that a certain confusion had permeated my consciousness.

The next morning I had breakfast at an old-fashioned New York diner, and then wandered around Midtown. I bought a gift for Ashley, a piece of jewelry, at Saks Fifth Avenue. As the salesman was packaging the item, I called Tom, just to see whether there were any late-breaking developments I should know about. There were indeed: The FBI had just disclosed that the bomb found in the men's room at the Equal Rights Dome during the fourth quarter of the Super Bowl had been planted by an American terrorist. The bomber was a member of the Storm Cloud, the group that blew up the aircraft carrier in the summer of 2019. Azala had been telling the truth when he denied any involvement in the incident.

From the moment I saw Indira in the lobby of her apartment building, it was evident that my decision to meet with her had been ill-advised. She was more beautiful than ever, and looked at me with eyes full of longing. Her gestures were understated but they were unmistakable. Her action was having the desired effect. I was thoroughly enchanted.

We were alone; there was no bodyguard. The walk to the Indian restaurant took less than five minutes. I asked Indira about the circumstances of her departure from Sundar Prabhat. She informed me that the situation had deteriorated sharply since my visit. The assassination we had witnessed outside the aviary was merely the opening salvo in a round of political violence that was spinning out of control.

Stepping inside the restaurant, we were greeted by a distinctive odor, a mixture of food and incense, that was familiar to me from childhood. The staff were formal yet welcoming, and catered to our every need. Indira spoke an Indian dialect with the waiters. I gave her permission to order for me, seeing that she was quite familiar with the various dishes on offer.

"Do you enjoy living in America?" she asked when the waiter had taken leave.

"Yes, very much."

"And you feel more at home here than in England?"

"Absolutely. Maybe if things hadn't changed there so much…no, even then it would be the same. In America, I can define myself. It's quite a luxury. Of course some people don't like that."

"They don't?"

"No. I'm thinking of a few journalists I've run into, who try to turn me into a full-fledged Indian. Not that there's anything wrong with that, naturally."

We both laughed. Some appetizers arrived, and we began to partake.

"What do you like to do in your spare time?" she asked.

"Well, first of all your question is relevant only for the off-season. From August to January, when I'm a football player—that is, occupied with training camp, pre-season, regular season, and possibly post-season games—there is no free time to speak of."

"Okay, the off-season then."

"I like the outdoors, going on hikes, mountain-climbing, that sort of thing. At the beginning of last summer, I went on a two-month trek through Alaska."

"Sounds lovely."

"It was breathtaking. I should mention, though, that urban pursuits—going to a museum, a concert, or a good restaurant—are also to my liking." I paused to bite into a piece of samosa. "How do *you* like America?" I inquired.

"It's my first trip, and I've only been here a few days. It's all very interesting, and more crowded than I expected."

"Well, that's New York. It's different everywhere else. You need to get out and see the country." I regretted the last remark, which could be interpreted as an offer of accompaniment. I turned my attention to the food.

"I would like to travel here," said Indira. "But my first priority is to learn the city, find my way around, and take advantage of the culture."

"I'm sure you'll do just fine."

The main course arrived. The exquisite cuisine occupied us for several minutes. I was fascinated by the way Indira ate. I had noticed it during our previous meal together, at the home of Raghavendra Hunter. She cut a tiny morsel of food, brought it to her mouth with a slow and delicate movement, and quietly chewed it for longer than one would expect.

"Jayesh, did my stepfather ask you to call on me?"

I swallowed my food and took a long sip of water. "Yes, he did... but it's no imposition. I enjoy your company." I wanted to say more, to share my true feelings with her, but was afraid to step into that unpredictable terrain. Indira seemed to sense my reticence, looking at me with her large eyes and subtle smile. I was at a loss for words.

"You have a girlfriend, don't you?" she asked.

"Well...yes. Yes, I do. In New Mexico."

"It's nice to have someone to share your life with."

"It certainly is."

"Especially when you look at life in the same way, have the same sense of humor."

"True."

Indira sighed. "I had someone like that. We were engaged to be married. About a year ago, he was murdered."

"Oh, I'm sorry."

She bowed her head for several moments, and then continued eating. I felt a strong desire to put my arm around her and console her. Instead, I was immobilized, a prisoner of circumstance.

We finished the meal, with more mundane topics providing the subject matter of our discussion. I rushed things a bit, claiming that time was short, and that I needed to get back to my hotel. After paying the bill, I accompanied Indira to her building. When we reached the lobby, she thanked me, shook my hand, and expressed the hope that I would see fit to call on her again soon.

I walked across Central Park to my hotel, once again in need of exercise in order to decompress. Two contradictory regrets coexisted in my mind: First, that I had met with Indira in the first place, knowing full well that there would be awkward and discomfiting ramifications; and second, that having decided to meet with her, I restrained my feelings. The latter regret originated in a nagging presentiment that Indira was my soul mate. This might sound callous and insensitive, given my relationship with Ashley. But it was out there; it could not be ignored.

Part of me wanted to stay in New York and open myself to Indira. But the prospect of doing so frightened me deeply. It would be connecting with a part of myself that was buried, locked away, percolating in my dreams and my childhood memories. It was not supposed to be—or so I thought—my "normal" life, my fully-conscious waking hours, my future.

I checked out of the hotel and flew back to Albuquerque on the next available flight.

Chapter Nine

▼

Everyone remembers where they were that fateful Sunday afternoon in late March 2020 when President Vesica Malpomme delivered her historic "electoral fairness" speech. It is analogous to Americans of a previous generation who could always recall, in great detail, where they were and what they were doing when the news arrived that President Kennedy was shot. In 2020, the cataclysm was *the Speech*, as it came to be known.

What few remember, if they were aware of the fact to begin with, is that the venue for the Speech was the White House reception for disadvantaged Asians in sports and entertainment. Why it was chosen, I have no idea. One would have thought that an address to a joint session of Congress or to a major public rally would have been more fitting. In any case, the days and hours just prior to the event were marked by an unprecedented bombardment of the public mind, with announcements of the Speech appearing on TV, radio, websites, billboards, theater programs, stadium scoreboards, and beer bottles, to name a few. I even remember seeing some skywriting. That Sunday afternoon, virtually all businesses closed for half a day so as not to detain employees or distract potential shoppers from their obligations. There was to be no other programming on any media. It was essential, we were told, that all Americans be ready in front of their television sets. The country was facing a crisis of enormous proportions. We had to understand what it was, and exactly how the government was going to deal with it.

I watched the Speech at the home of Steve Gonzales. He had also invited Thelonius, with the intent that the three of us take advantage of the occasion to catch up on activities of recent weeks, and to ponder our strategy for the future. Steve said that he wanted to "get back in the fray" after his inopportune absence—an absence that had lasted far too long. Ashley, Sandy, and Rebecca, Steve's wife, were also in attendance.

Up where Steve lived, in the mountains bordering Albuquerque, the air was thinner and several degrees colder than in the city. This suited me just fine; I liked the coolness, and the fresh pine scent was invigorating. As Ashley and I stepped out of the car, I breathed in deeply and took in the magnificent view. It never ceased to amaze me how different the air was, so much like the country, even though we were just a stone's throw from town.

Steve emerged from the house to greet us. He was looking well, dressed in blue jeans and a red flannel shirt. We said hello and followed him into the house. Thelonius and Sandy were relaxing on one of the massive brown leather sofas, drinks in hand. We greeted each other, and I introduced Ashley to Rebecca. Rebecca then went to fetch little Mario and brought him into the living room, where he was the center of attention for several minutes.

Steve announced that the football players would like to excuse themselves for a short while to "talk shop." The three of us headed outside. We walked a ways into the woods, stopping at a small clearing. In front of us, to the west, the mountain sloped downward toward the city. Further in the distance was the seemingly endless desert mesa. Behind us were the peaks of the Sandias. To our left was a small ravine, through which a pair of coyotes were trotting, at a distance of about a hundred yards. Steve boasted that the area was rich in wildlife, which included bears, wolves, and bobcats.

We began to update each other on our recent activities. It was not long before the conversation turned to the new rules mandating the end of all-male professional sports teams.

"I'm quitting," said Thelonius. "There's no way I'm going to go along with this—no way. I've had a good career, and I was going to retire in a couple of years anyway."

"You might not have to," said Steve.

"Why is that?"

"I've been speaking to Curtis Mackelhenny from the players' union. They are not happy at all. Discussions are going on right now with management to see if we can roll back the new rules."

"Wait," I said. "What about the legislation in Congress? If the league rescinds its decision, the law will surely be passed."

"If that's the case," said Steve, "we will probably see a players' strike when training camp begins."

"Good," said Thelonius.

"Support for the union's position is very strong," continued Steve. "I know from speaking to players on the Coyotes and other teams. There is no way the coaches can pack the squads with women—unless they fire us all and start over." He picked up a small branch and started snapping off twigs. "And guys, I want you to know that this time you won't have to worry about me drifting away. I had some illusions, but they're gone. I'm going the distance on this one."

I felt reassured by Steve's report. If the players remained united, it seemed, we could not be bullied, even by the government.

"By the way," said Thelonius, "what does Ashley think about all this?"

"She doesn't like it," I replied. "She thinks that women should be involved in professional football, as commentators, trainers, and the like. And women having their own league is okay. But not playing in the NFL. It looks like Sandy's words of wisdom at our dinner together had a positive impact. Of course Ashley has been coming around to my way of thinking for some time, little by little."

"Excellent," said Thelonius. "Steve, you don't have this problem, do you?"

"Not really. Rebecca is bothered by the fact that women are excluded, which she says is not fair. But she admits that it would be physically dangerous to let them play, and it would downgrade the game."

We returned to the house and joined the ladies, who were chatting away in the living room. Steve herded the group into the den, where we settled into our seats in front of the TV screen. Rebecca, assisted by Ashley and Sandy, brought in tortilla chips, salsa, guacamole, and other appetizers. Steve took orders for drinks. The atmosphere was more suited to watching the World Series than a major political discourse.

The program began. Two network commentators, speaking from their studio, spent several minutes predicting the content of the president's remarks. The broadcast then joined President Malpomme in the White House. I had expected a weighty setting, such as the Oval Office, but instead the scene was the hall in which the reception for disadvantaged Asians had taken place. The president was seated in a simple armchair. Behind her, several rows deep, were the athletes and entertainers who were attending the reception.

Here is what she said:

> My fellow Americans, people of all races and cultures, black, brown, red, yellow, and white; ladies, gentlemen, and the transgendered; young and old; natives, newcomers, and descendants of the European imperialists: We have reached a critical moment in the history of our struggling nation.
>
> When you elected me your president in the year two-thousand sixteen, I pledged to you that this administration would eliminate the last traces of sexist domination. I pledged that racism, which saw a resurgence in the years before I took office, would be purged from our society. I pledged that exploitation of the developing countries by the United States would be a thing of the past. I pledged that no schoolchild would ever undergo the humiliation of failing a class. I pledged that all profit stolen from the working man over the course of our history would be returned to its rightful owners.
>
> In all of these pledges, we have succeeded beyond our wildest dreams. America has become a sensitive, caring, decent nation, not a nation of heartless corporations

that steal from the middle class and the poor to pad the pockets of the rich.

However, my fellow Americans, let us not be complacent. The forces of reaction, led by intolerant religious fanatics, are working day and night to roll back the progress we have made. They have infiltrated the government, and right now, as we speak, are plotting to undermine our great democracy.

These dark forces use many weapons, but first and foremost they *steal elections*. It is a well-known fact that over ninety percent of all elections in the history of the United States were stolen. Ninety percent! This is why it has taken so long to change the system. Decades ago, Americans were already in favor of change and progress. But the will of the people was blocked by entrenched interests who held onto power.

Because of the electoral system in this country, inequality has been perpetuated. Those in control made it their goal to exclude women, minorities, and newly-arrived Americans. The result: an old-boy network, a dictatorship of the privileged. Thus our elections contradict the spirit of the Declaration of Independence, which guarantees life, liberty, and happiness to every person in America.

This fraud can no longer be tolerated. To stop it, my administration is establishing a National Electoral Fairness Commission. The Commission, appointed by the president with the advice and consent of the Senate, will supervise federal elections, ensuring that they are conducted in accordance with the most progressive norms of political conduct in the world today.

In addition, I have ordered special measures to be taken on a one-time basis, for this November's election only. It is our hope that the forces of privilege will never again be able to steal an election.

What are these special measures?

First, the National Electoral Fairness Commission will select the candidates. The selection process will respect a fair distribution of race, sex, national origin, sexual orientation, and other relevant characteristics.

Second, the Commission will work closely with the candidates to produce their publicity prior to the election. This will prevent lies from being spread during the campaign.

Third, the elections will be monitored by UNSAINE, the United Nations Special Advisory Institute on National Expropriation. The Institute's past performance around the globe has been excellent, and there is no reason why we should not take advantage of their services. This will help restore confidence in the electoral process.

Fourth, discussions will begin immediately with state and local governments to help them establish their own electoral fairness commissions.

By following these simple procedures, we will make it impossible for another election to be stolen in the United States. Never again will hard-working Americans see their precious votes go to waste, manipulated for the benefit of the old power structure.

Over the next few weeks, you will hear more about the National Electoral Fairness Commission and how it functions. Thank you very much for being with us this afternoon.

There was applause from the athletes and entertainers seated behind the president. An off-stage announcer informed viewers that normal programming would resume. The scene switched to a commercial for men's deodorant.

All of us sat quietly in our places. Steve turned off the TV. No one spoke for at least a minute.

Thelonius broke the ice. "I had a bad feeling about that lady," he said, rising from his seat. "Real, real, bad."

"This is too much," said Steve. "First the women football players, and now this. What will be next?"

"It will never happen," I said, feeling agitated. "Who would enforce such a thing? What about the Supreme Court, the Senate? They won't stand for it. This is America, we have the rule of law here."

"We *had* the rule of law here," said Sandy, speaking in her slow, purposeful manner. "It has been eroded, piece by piece, for many years. But still—I never expected anything like this."

"I'm going outside," said Steve. "I need some air."

"Me, too," said Thelonius. They both disappeared from view. Sandy and Rebecca soon joined them.

I remained seated with Ashley. She was staring at the blank TV screen, with a look of shock on her face. "I don't believe it," she mumbled. "I just don't believe it. This can't be happening. I voted for Vesica. She was all about equal rights, and freedom for everyone."

I nodded, not knowing quite what to say. We got up, moved slowly toward the front door of the house, and joined the others outside. They were dispersed around the yard. The atmosphere was morbid. Steve leaned against the hood of his car. I took the spot alongside him, all the while holding Ashley's hand. A minute later, the entire group was assembled together.

Steve laughed under his breath. "It's amazing that just a little while ago our greatest concern was football."

"Strange how things work out," I said.

"Well, what are we going to do?" said Thelonius rather loudly, moving away from the group and then turning to face us. "So that's it? What are they telling us—sorry, folks, America is closed? Go home and we'll call you if we need you?" He struck a defiant pose, hands on his hips.

We all looked at him, but no one spoke. I presume that the others shared my inability to mentally process the scene we had just witnessed. I felt as frustrated as Thelonius, but was unable to articulate my dismay.

A long silence followed, until Steve offered his thoughts. "Let's all digest this for a little while. I need to think, Thelonius. We have to approach this intelligently, see what other people are doing. That includes people in the government, the media, and the courts. Maybe what Jayesh was saying is true, that it won't come to pass, it won't be accepted. Let's give it a day, and then put our heads together."

Thelonius nodded, but his face expressed a deep skepticism. I glanced at Ashley, and then at Rebecca. They both had a terrible look of apprehension in their eyes. Sandy, on the other hand, seemed cool and collected. She was gazing into the distance, toward the city, apparently deep in thought.

"When is President Malpomme going to give us the details of the plan?" asked Rebecca.

"*President* Malpomme?" said Thelonius. "I don't think she's president anymore. We need to give her a new title."

"You know," said Sandy, "I can speak to some government people, find out whether they're going to do anything. Senator Hutchinson is an old friend of my parents, I'm sure I could reach him. Steve, aren't you related to Congressman Gonzales?"

"He's a distant cousin. But there are some strong connections to him in my family. I can look into it."

"And we can call Tom Hubert," I said, looking at Thelonius. "He's right on top of everything, all the time."

Several additional ideas of the same type were proposed. We all agreed to reconvene in a day or two to report our findings. Sandy took it upon herself to organize another gathering.

And thus my post-Speech life began. It was clear that things would never be the same, even if the president was somehow persuaded or forced to abandon her design to cancel free elections in November. From that day on, the image of President Malpomme in her armchair, with the disadvantaged Asian athletes and entertainers applauding in the background, was etched into my mind.

The next twenty-four hours were spent in furious communication with the world. I spoke to my parents, my sister Julie, Tom Hubert, Coach Petersen, Coach Gramercy, and a number of players from the Coyotes and other teams. A distinct pattern emerged: All of the individuals with whom I spoke were deeply distressed by the Speech. However, all of the people they knew in positions of power had remained passive, offering no challenge to the president. When I asked Coach Petersen what people in the military were thinking, he said he didn't know. The way he formulated his response led me to suspect that he did not wish to confide in me.

On TV and in the local newspaper, the entire affair was discussed as a fait accompli. Commentators argued over the details of the plan, not its merits.

The same group of friends reassembled two days after the Speech, this time at my house. We confirmed in person what we already knew from our phone conversations: a stone wall was blocking our path. We vowed to continue our efforts, though no one seemed to know exactly what those efforts would be.

That evening, the Speech and the political climate it engendered first touched me personally. In fact, it was Ashley who was impacted directly. After the meeting at my house, she had returned to her apartment in Santa Fe, intending to spend the following day there. I received a call from her in the middle of the night, pleading with me to come immediately. Though not entirely coherent, she managed to convey to me that she was in danger, that it could not be discussed on the phone, and that she was too distraught to think of driving all the way to Albuquerque. We set a time to meet at a 24-hour fast-food restaurant on the outskirts of Santa Fe. I left my house as fast as possible. There was no traffic at that hour, so I was able to reach my destination in about forty minutes.

When I embraced her in the parking lot of the restaurant, she was trembling. I calmed her with a hug, and led her inside. We ordered some hot tea and sat in an isolated corner of the dining room.

Ashley began the story. "Just after I got home this evening, a letter was delivered to me by courier. It was from the FBI; a summons to appear immediately at their local office. The subject was my 'involvement with foreign agents'. I thought it was a mistake, so I called the Bureau, only to be told that I had better show up right away. Within twenty minutes, I was seated across the desk from a real live agent, who opened a dossier with my name on it. The first document he removed was an article I had written about Azala in the *Journal of Matriarchal Pride*.

"The agent asked me whether I was the author of the article. I said I was. He wanted to know who paid me to write it. Then he pulled out of his file a photocopy of a bank statement, and asked why there was a deposit of five thousand dollars into my account from a Mr.

Jayesh Blackstone. I told him you had given me a gift to help pay my tuition. Then he got all huffy, and wanted to know about the three thousand dollars I charged to your credit card. I said it was for my trip expenses."

"What nerve!" I interjected.

"So then he gives me this little speech about your time in Sundar Prabhat, where you just happened to meet with people who are plotting to overthrow the government and assassinate Joseph Hoomty Azala. In Paris, he said, and I quote, 'Mr. Blackstone was involved with individuals organizing the defense of one Samuel Kapulski, an American racist on trial for sabotaging the Super Bowl and ruining Mr. Azala's and President Malpomme's appeal to the nation.' He wanted to know if that, too, was a coincidence." Ashley halted her recitation and stared into her cup of tea.

"I don't get it," I said. "Why did the FBI summon *you*? Maybe I'm the real target, and this was just some information-gathering for a future case."

"I really don't know," she replied, shrugging her shoulders. "What's up with this Azala guy, anyway? No one's allowed to criticize him?"

"I guess not. If you do, then apparently you're a racist."

"But that's ridiculous. We're not racists. My article had to do with women, not race, and not even nations."

"It doesn't matter," I said. "Look at Sam. Did his action at the Super Bowl have anything to do with race?"

"I'm scared, Jayesh," said Ashley, reaching across the table to grasp my hand. "The whole world is going crazy."

"I know. So how did it end with the FBI agent?"

"He said they would contact me if they need more information. But Jayesh…"

"Yes?"

"I'm worried about *you*. What will you do if…if they arrest you?"

I smiled and tightened my grip on her hand. "Let's hope that doesn't happen. But if it does, I will tell them everything. As far as I know, there is no law against organizing the defense of an accused man, or paying for a girlfriend's trip, or soliciting the advice of someone in a foreign country—a person who happens to be a relative of mine. Of course, I didn't watch the news this evening, so I don't know whether any new decrees have been promulgated in the last twenty-four hours."

Ashley stood up and came around to my side of the table. I put my arm around her and held her tight. We remained in that position for some time. Then we walked out to the car and drove back to my house in Albuquerque.

Ashley slept for most of the trip. Despite the late hour, I did not feel tired. Thoughts were racing through my mind, among them the status of my relationship with the woman dozing in the front passenger seat. My overall appraisal was very positive. Lately, we had been confronting some daunting problems, and we were doing it as a team. Ashley was supportive of me at every turn. There were no lingering doubts about our compatibility, nor fears that she would be driven by ideology to act against my interests.

Any thought of Indira was far from my consciousness. She had appeared once around that time in a dream, but only as a passing image, without any action or emotion manifesting itself. I wondered what would happen if she suddenly appeared in real life. Such an event, I thought, would not alter my attachment and fidelity to Ashley.

This confidence was partially tested the next morning when I received a call from Raghavendra Hunter. I was relaxing at the kitchen table with a newspaper and a cup of coffee. Ashley was still in bed.

"I am very distressed about recent events in your country," said Hunter. "I tried to drop a hint when we spoke in New York."

"Are you referring to the president's speech?"

"Precisely."

"You knew about it?"

"In general terms, yes. There was all sorts of buzz in diplomatic circles over the past few weeks. In any case, something of the sort had to happen. It's been brewing for a while."

I made a mental note to ask Hunter to explain that thought to me in detail at our next face-to-face meeting.

"However," he continued, "there is something about which I was very wrong. And that is the assassination attempt on the president, which obviously never occurred."

"Mmm…maybe we ought not to discuss this on the phone."

"Why? Because it might be tapped?"

"Yes," I said.

"Don't worry, Jayesh, my phone has been tapped for as long as I can remember. So has yours, for a while now I'm sure. I've learned to relax with it. There is little I can say that they don't already know. Anyway, on this issue, I was trying to protect the president."

"True enough."

"We uncovered a mole in our organization. Someone was trying to set us up for a very embarrassing scene at the White House. Good thing neither of us was in attendance."

"Indeed," I said, wondering what became of the mole.

"There is something else you should know, Jayesh, if you haven't heard it already. It's not good."

"What is it?"

"Sam Kapulski is dead."

My heart sank.

"Jayesh, are you there?"

"Yes…"

"Sorry to have to break it to you."

"No, it's okay. Do you know what happened?"

"Suicide. He reportedly overdosed on some pills, some sort of medicine he was taking."

There was another lengthy silence as I struggled to assimilate the news.

"Jayesh, forgive me but I have to cut this short. Indira sends her regards."

"Thanks," I said. "I hope we shall meet again soon."

"We will, I am sure."

I hung up the phone and sagged into the sofa. I was overcome with grief for Sam, for this man that I really didn't know very well. What I had seen, though, left a deep impression on me. His courage and defiance in the face of such a fundamental miscarriage of justice had raised him to tremendous stature in my eyes.

When Ashley woke up, I shared with her the news about Sam. She took it very hard. She expressed in harsh terms her distaste for Azala, and her frustration that our own government was partially responsible for Sam's death.

I called Thelonius, who reacted with a prolonged rant, complete with threats against "those murderers in Paris." When his wrath had subsided, I asked him to come over to the house so we could discuss things.

My next call was to Steve, who was reading about the story on some European website. He mumbled some words of regret, and then excused himself to take care of a problem with Mario. Tom called me a bit later, apologizing for not having contacted me. His theory was that Sam had taken his own life after hearing about the Speech.

When Thelonius dropped by early that afternoon, he was severely agitated. It was evident from the moment he arrived. I asked Ashley to excuse us so that we could take a little walk around the complex.

It was a pleasant day in the early New Mexico spring, with the temperature in the mid sixties. As we strolled, I tried to calm Thelonius, reminiscing about some of the great plays of the season, including his spectacular kickoff return in the Super Bowl. When it seemed that his emotions were stabilized, I related the story about Ashley's experience at the FBI.

"They're going to go after you next, my friend," said Thelonius.

"Perhaps."

"Jayesh, I don't know what I'm going to do, but I've got to do *something*."

"What did you have in mind?" I asked.

"Some kind of protest…Hey, let's get all the guys together and fly to Washington. Rent a bus, like the one we took to the governor's victory party in Santa Fe. Get out at the White House, or the Capitol, or whatever."

"It does sound like an interesting idea."

"It is," said Thelonius, now smiling. "Maybe we could get the Hawaii Sun Monarchs to join us. Imagine, the two Super Bowl teams together, protesting. Now that would draw some attention."

"I like it. Do you think the guys on the team would go along with it?"

"Who knows, but we have to try."

"Perhaps Coach Petersen could help us organize it. I think that he would sympathize with our aims."

Thelonius stopped walking, his face illuminated from excitement. "That is one good idea, my man. Let's do it. How far is his ranch from Albuquerque?"

"Oh, maybe an hour's drive, not more."

"You want to call him?"

"You prefer that I do?"

"You're better at explaining things," said Thelonius. "And everything sounds more convincing with that English accent of yours."

I chuckled. "No problem."

"We'll get Steve to come with us."

"Absolutely," I said. "But what about Ashley?"

"What about her?"

"Should she come along?"

"No way," said Thelonius. "This is serious business. Let's keep it in the family."

"Okay. I'm afraid to leave her by herself, though."

"I'll get Sandy to come over."

"Yes, that's a good idea, thanks."

Thelonius called Sandy, who said she was busy at the moment, but would join us in the late afternoon. Meanwhile, I called Coach Petersen. The way I presented the matter was that Thelonius and I wanted to visit him immediately, to discuss something urgent. Steve might also be with us. He agreed, and the meeting was set for that evening. I then called Steve, telling him to come over right away, so that we could discuss our plan with him. I was not willing to divulge any details on the phone.

Steve showed up about an hour and a half later. Thelonius presented his idea. Steve was quite enthusiastic, and pledged his full support and involvement. He wanted to start making calls right away, but I insisted that we first speak to Coach Petersen, to hear his advice. It would be a shame to ruin our chances by proceeding with haste.

Sandy arrived a short while after Steve. It must have been around four o'clock. I proposed ordering some food from the excellent Chinese restaurant not too far away. Ashley, however, wanted very much to cook dinner for everyone.

Once again, she demonstrated her culinary talents, preparing some excellent lamb chops. I uncorked a bottle of expensive French wine, a Chateau Lafite 1959. In the midst of the confusion and frustration that was permeating our existence, we celebrated being alive. It was a grand feast.

It was not easy for me to leave Ashley behind when Steve, Thelonius, and I departed for our visit to Coach Petersen. I distinctly remember standing with the other men in the foyer, about to pass through the front door after saying goodbye to the ladies. I looked over my shoulder and saw Ashley smiling and waving to me. It was an image of domestic bliss, of a warm home and a beautiful woman. But now I was going forth to battle, confronting the tide of history. There was no way to know how it would all end, and whether the image I was seeing could ever be transformed into a sustainable reality. Why, I lamented, could I not have met Ashley several years previously? On the other hand, the fact that our relationship developed and blossomed as it did was due in no small measure to the bizarre sequence of events that had occurred over the previous weeks.

Steve drove Thelonius and me to Coach Petersen's ranch. The atmosphere in the car was upbeat. Thelonius expounded at length on his Washington idea, describing a number of possible protest strategies, such as having the two Super Bowl teams, New Mexico and Hawaii, play football on the Capitol steps.

It was dark by the time we arrived. A bumpy dirt road connected the highway with the central compound of the ranch. I was glad we were in Steve's SUV and not in my Salzburger, which could easily sustain damage in such an environment. After driving for about half a mile, we came upon the compound, which contained the main house, the garage, a separate building for the guest quarters, and some sheds.

Coach Petersen was waiting outside. I hardly recognized him, dressed as he was in full-blown Western gear: blue jeans, a wide brass belt buckle, a denim shirt with a bolo necktie, and a beige cowboy hat. His smile was also different, much broader than I had ever seen.

After a warm greeting, he brought us into the house, where we settled into the living room. It was like something out of those interior-decorating magazines you see in the lobby of a doctor's office. The room was immense, two stories high, crowned by a cathedral ceiling that was dotted with skylights. Thick golden-colored wooden beams crossed the space, attached to the frame of the house at the point where the walls joined the roof. The walls were made from stone, with a few rows of logs inlaid for a rustic effect. Several trophy heads were hanging. The largest, a buffalo, graced the arched fireplace, in which a substantial fire was burning. The floor under our feet was paved with beautiful stone tiles. Its inherent coldness was balanced by colorful Navajo rugs.

A young man dressed in cowboy garb came in from another room. Coach Petersen introduced him as Blake, one of the ranch hands. He looked to be in his early twenties, tall and slender, with broad shoulders. He had a grim air about him, as if his mind were fixed unalterably on his duties. He asked us what we would like to drink, and returned shortly thereafter with our beverages.

We spent some time relaxing and conversing with the coach. He had all kinds of questions about our backgrounds, likes and dislikes, future plans, and women. When one of us spoke, he listened intensely, as if it were the most important thing in the world.

"You know, guys," he said after some silence had passed, "let's take a little walk, let me show you the place. You'll have to come back in the daytime, so you get the full effect, but there's still a few things to see." The four of us put on our jackets and left the house.

We walked past the garage, and then another hundred yards or so over a grassy area to the stable. The coach opened the huge sliding door, and we stepped inside. There were rows of stalls on either side of a central walkway. About a half a dozen horses were present. The coach stopped in front of one of them, a sleek black mare, and began stroking its neck.

"Guys, say hello to Peppercorn. Peppercorn, these are some of my boys: Steve, Thelonius, and Jayesh."

We took turns petting the animal and complimenting its good looks.

"So what's on your mind, fellas?" said Petersen.

The three of us looked at each other, uncertain how to proceed.

"Coach," said Steve, straightening his back so that he stood to his full height. "We have come to seek your advice concerning the most effective way to protest the threat to democracy that our country is facing."

"Go ahead."

"Thelonius has an idea which Jayesh and I support," said Steve.

Thelonius cleared his throat. "We want to take the whole team to Washington, rent a bus, and protest what that damn lady's doing to wipe out the elections. There's all kinds of things we could do. Man, if we get Hawaii involved, we can attract a lot of attention."

Coach Petersen sighed, looked down, and ran his fingers repeatedly over his lips. He didn't seem to notice Peppercorn sniffing the back of his neck. "Thelonius," he said finally, "I like your idea. Unfortunately, I cannot help you right now."

"Why not?"

"Because I'm involved in various discussions, and I've got to keep my powder dry. I'm as upset as you are about what's going on. But I'm following a certain strategy."

"Coach," I said, "isn't it possible to try several strategies at once? The more protest, the merrier, no?"

"Not necessarily. Let me use a military analogy. Assume that my forces are in disarray, reeling from the shock of a devastating attack. We're in retreat. Now let's say I have a small, elite unit that is completely intact. Do I want to send that unit into the field at this point? Probably not, unless there were some overriding reason to do so. They could strike a blow at the enemy, but there would be nothing behind them, nothing to follow up with. I'd be better off waiting until the retreat is over and I can regroup my forces. When all units are ready, the commandos can be the spearhead of a broader attack.

"Think of that damn lady, as you put it, Thelonius. When did she make her move? When everything was lined up in her favor: Congress, the courts, the media, industry; in short, anybody who's anybody. This is just the beginning, boys. The election maneuver was the spearhead, the commando raid, designed to strike fear into the heart of the enemy."

"So you're saying that we have to regroup," said Steve.

"Correct. Let me think about this for a few days. Come back and see me again next week, and it is very likely that I will have some news for you. In the meantime, stay put, and see what develops."

He began walking out of the stable, waving us forward. We followed like obedient troops. The crisp desert air seemed colder than before. No one uttered a word until we reached Steve's car.

"Remember," said Coach Petersen, "don't go off half-cocked. The most important thing now is to remain calm. Otherwise, you cannot be effective. Nerves will hamper your reaction time, and make you respond in ways you will later regret."

We thanked the coach and climbed into the SUV. I lowered my window, and he leaned inward. He looked at us, one after the other. "I'm proud of you, boys. I don't think anyone else on the team has the intestinal fortitude to do what you're doing. The same goes for your efforts on behalf of Sam Kapulski."

"You know about that?" said Thelonius.

"Oh, yes. I've been following it from the sidelines. Make no mistake about it, the day of reckoning will come." He looked us over once again, smiled, and stepped back from the car. "Take care."

Steve shifted into gear and pulled away.

Our mood during the trip back to Albuquerque was somewhat less upbeat than it had been prior to our arrival at the ranch. We all agreed, reluctantly, to accept the coach's appeal to wait until the following week before launching any projects. Our disappointment was balanced, however, by the strength and confidence that he radiated. Who would have predicted that Coach Petersen would step in to take control of the situation? I suppose that if I had really thought about it, knowing what I did about him, the possibility might have occurred to me.

My thoughts drifted to Indira. Something about the desert terrain had predisposed me in that direction. Perhaps it was because both the desert and the woman were, for me, outside the boundaries of everyday life. She was like a purple flower on a cactus: soft and beautiful, yet springing from something harsh and unforgiving. Like the flower, she beckoned, luring me into uncharted territory.

How I wished at that moment that I could have spoken with my grandfather. His first piece of advice undoubtedly would have been to meditate, to clear the mind of distractions. I closed my eyes and leaned my head onto the headrest. The effort to focus on nothingness, however, was unsuccessful. Diverse images were marching through my mind: Ashley, Mahinta Zagumbi, the dinner with Azala in Paris, the Essence Mound at my sister Julie's house. It was an incoherent jumble, as if in a dream.

I opened my eyes and viewed the dark desert landscape. What course of action would my grandfather have advised me to pursue? For the women—that is, being torn between Ashley and Indira—he would have counseled "an alliance of the heart and brain." In romance, he always said, the heart must lead; it must provide direction and impetus, taking the bait as it were. But then the brain must step in to survey the situation and weigh the alternative paths of action. I tried to apply this to my predicament, but with no luck. I could not get past the first stage and determine unequivocally what my heart was telling me.

Regarding the political debacle, I knew quite well what his guidance would have been: Go slow. Wait for the forces to align themselves, and act only when the route to success is evident.

My mind wandered to the conversation that morning with Raghavendra Hunter. I was uniquely captivated by him. Ever since the moment that he first introduced himself to me in the lobby of the Progress Hotel, wearing his flowing white gown and speaking a perfect Queen's English, I was practically under his spell. Not that he ever tried to take advantage of it; on the contrary, he wished to give, to help.

When I dared to think about it, I arrived at the conclusion that *Hunter was just like me*, only a generation older and thrust into different circumstances. It was as if I were looking at a parallel life, a second Jayesh who had faced another set of challenges, way stations, and luck. However dissimilar our lives were, I had an uncanny feeling that under the surface, our souls were more than kindred.

I wondered about his parting remark in our last phone conversation, that we would surely meet again soon. Would he ask me to come to New York? Or would he show up at my door, together with Indira, suitcases in hand? Anything was possible with Hunter.

We arrived in Albuquerque. Steve dropped Thelonius and me off at my house. We all agreed to keep in close touch, and then said our goodbyes.

Upon entering the house, we found Ashley and Sandy at the kitchen table, with an empty bottle of wine and two half-full glasses. "So, you've been enjoying yourselves," I said, giving Ashley a kiss.

"Oh yes," she replied, looking at Sandy and giggling. "We're celebrating our good fortune in having met two nice football players."

"No one else I know can say that," said Sandy, her elocution slightly less refined than it had been at dinner. "With the exception, of course, of Rebecca Gonzales."

Thelonius, standing behind Sandy, placed his hands on her shoulders. "How much did you two have to drink?" he asked.

The two women burst into a fit of laughter that seemed to have no end. It proved to be contagious; Thelonius and I became full partners in the raucous release of tension.

We finally settled down and had some tea. I reported on our trip to the Petersen ranch. Sandy mentioned that shortly after our departure, she had finally managed to reach Senator Hutchinson. Not only did the senator refuse to help, he went so far as to deny that any problem existed. He asserted that Sandy's fear about the new election rules was bordering on paranoia.

When Thelonius and Sandy left, Ashley and I went straight to bed. Both of us were exhausted mentally and physically, and wanted nothing more than a good night's sleep.

The next few days provided a bit of a lull. There was no news on the political front. We did not hear from the FBI. No fateful meetings or conversations were reported by anyone in my circle of friends. Ashley and I spent some time catching up on domestic pursuits, such as shopping for summer clothes. We took in a movie and enjoyed a walk through Albuquerque's historic Old Town quarter.

There was no question that something was different in Ashley's demeanor. Change had been occurring for some time, but I am thinking specifically of those days following the Speech and her visit to the FBI. There was a new look in her eye and a new inflection in her voice. Her manner was more deliberate and cautious. She seemed to carefully weigh her choice of words and concentrate more intensely before uttering them.

The lull of which I spoke came to an end one afternoon as Ashley and I returned home from the supermarket. As I opened the door connecting the garage to the house and stepped into the hallway, I had a vague sense that something was awry. The scene that awaited us in the living room was such a shock that we stood frozen in place for several seconds before responding in any way. It looked as if a tornado had swept through the room. It would not have been possible to imagine a more extreme departure from normality: glass shattered, frames splintered, cushions against the wall, rugs turned upside down, a chandelier in the kitchen sink.

We set down the packages of food we had been holding and began to survey the other rooms, each of us going in a different direction. It was soon apparent that the mayhem was general, with everything from toothbrushes to t-shirts far from their original places, and in many cases damaged beyond repair.

As I was closing a dripping faucet in one of the bathrooms, I heard a shriek from Ashley. I ran to look for her, and found her in the study. She was peering behind my overturned desk. I glanced at the same spot. The Pissarro was on the floor, a huge gash cut down the middle of it, splitting the canvas cleanly in two.

I pulled Ashley toward me. We held each other, remaining motionless for several moments. I don't recall the thought process that led up to it, but I phoned Coach Petersen. Here is what he said: "Come out to the ranch as soon as possible. Don't call the police; in fact, don't call anyone until we have a chance to speak. Gather up some clothes and leave. Do it right now."

Within fifteen minutes, Ashley and I were on the road. At the time, I had no way of knowing that I would never again set eyes upon my house.

Chapter Ten

▼

Coach Petersen received Ashley and me with open arms. He gave us the best of the three suites in the guest house. The windows on one side of the second-floor apartment overlooked the compound; on the other side, we had a view of the mesa and the mountains in the distance. The furnishings were of a rustic, pleasant New Mexican style. All in all, our quarters were more than satisfactory.

After giving us some time to unpack and settle in, the coach led us on a walk down to the river that ran through his property. It was about a quarter of a mile from the compound.

Ashley took to him immediately, which pleased me greatly. Most of the conversation during our stroll occurred between the two of them, and it was lively. I was happy to step aside and let the comfort level rise, knowing that there would be plenty of time to discuss the grave matters that faced us.

It was our good fortune to have someone like Coach Petersen close at hand. Tough, sensible, realistic, fair—the perfect manager of a crisis, just as he was the perfect coach. A finely-honed discipline helped ensure that there was never any frivolity, never a word out of place. Funny, during all those years with the New Mexico Coyotes I never once thought of approaching him for advice on a personal matter, even though he made it known to the team that he desired playing such a role. There is a time for everything—and this was the right man at the right time.

When life is calm, in periods that seem "normal," we may find ourselves shunning the company of such people, considering them to be boring and stiff. But in times of distress, their inner essence becomes manifest. We discover that under that rugged, stoic exterior lies a fount of wisdom and humanity.

These thoughts were at the forefront of my mind when Coach Petersen, Ashley, and I rested on the craggy bluff overlooking a bend in the river. A light breeze was blowing and the air temperature was cool yet comfortable. We were facing the sunset, which was in its formative stages. The terrain along the river displayed the rich desert colors of the Southwest, abounding in shades of red and brown. There were miles of mesa in the distance, ending in a mountain range on the horizon. It was breathtaking.

"Did you notice anything unusual in your house," said the coach, "aside from the fact that everything was turned upside down?"

"What do you mean by unusual?" I asked.

"Let's assume that someone came into your house with the intent of creating as much disorder as possible. Was there anything that did not fit in with that scenario? Something peculiar that had been removed, or more time spent in one room than the others, or a type of damage that seemed different than the rest?"

"I'm not sure," I said, reviewing the scene in my mind.

"What about the Pissarro painting?" said Ashley. "It was in Jayesh's study, behind his desk, on the floor."

"Keep going," said Coach Petersen.

"It was slashed with a knife, perfectly, right down the middle."

"What happened to your desk?" he said, looking at me.

"It was turned on its side, but other than that I don't think it was touched."

"Nothing was removed?"

"I don't know, I didn't look that closely. But there were no papers on the floor. No sign that the drawers had been opened."

"Do you have an alarm system?"

"Yes, but they must have disarmed it."

"Do you think it was the FBI?" asked Ashley. "They had called me down to their office a few days ago. They accused me of being involved with foreign agents. There were all kinds of questions about me and Jayesh, and Sam Kapulski, and Azala. It was really weird."

Coach Petersen looked out over the vast terrain. "I don't believe it was the FBI. They don't operate like that. From what you describe, this was pure intimidation. You may receive some kind of follow-up communication very soon, in which the action will be explained. It may be the prelude to some kind of blackmail. 'This is just a taste of what we can do', etcetera. My guess is that the perpetrator is UNSAINE. They are operating almost everywhere now, and doing it with impunity. According to some of my contacts in the military, not only is Washington turning a blind eye, they are hiring UNSAINE as subcontractors to do all kinds of dirty jobs. This provides the government with a screen of deniability."

"What can we do then?" I asked.

"Keep a low profile. Avoid any sort of contact with the authorities. And learn to defend yourself. You weren't in the service, were you, Jayesh?"

"No."

"Any experience with weapons?"

"Not really. Steve Gonzales took me a couple of times to the firing range. He has a pistol that he keeps for home defense."

"I didn't know you were allowed to have one of those," said Ashley.

"Normally you aren't," I said. "But with Steve's family connections—his uncle was formerly attorney-general of New Mexico—they cooked up some reason that he needs it, and they got him the permit. It's very rare, I know."

Coach Petersen stood up. "Let's go home, I'm getting hungry." He chose a different route back to the compound, this time following the edge of the river bed.

"We have a fair amount of weaponry here," he remarked, after we had advanced a few yards. "I'll have Blake take you out tomorrow to get started. You don't want to use a gun if you don't have to. But it is possible that someone will come looking for one or both of you, with the intent to kill. The government would much rather have people like us eliminated by UNSAINE or other operatives rather than having the hassle and publicity of an arrest, trial, investigation, or what have you. Hunting accidents happen around here from time to time. If they try to set you up for one of those, there's no use asking questions or worrying about the consequences."

"I see your point," I said.

"If things get too hot here, there are other places I can send you. But let's wait and see what develops."

"Okay. By the way, coach, you told me on the phone this afternoon not to call anyone until we speak. I was thinking of calling Thelonius and Steve. Would that be all right?"

"Yes."

"What about my phone being tapped?"

"It doesn't really matter. Unless you disappear into the Amazon, the authorities will know where you are. Just don't mention any sensitive plans or dates, things like that."

"What about my house? What should I do?"

"Call an industrial cleaning service. I can recommend one that we use at the practice complex. Tell them there was a burglary. Have them first remove your papers and clothing and hold them for you in storage. They should dispose of everything else; vacuum and repaint. Then you can sell the place. Don't ever go back there."

We arrived at the compound. Coach Petersen suggested that we rest for a while, and then excused himself to go give the cook instructions for dinner. Someone would summon us when the meal was ready by ringing the bell outside the house. Ashley and I followed his advice and went to our suite.

We relaxed quietly for a few minutes. I called Thelonius, and told him what happened at my house, and about our "escape" to the Petersen ranch.

"Yeah," he said, "it sounds like Azala and his boys. Sorry to hear about that, my man. You know, Jayesh, I have a feeling the same thing is going to happen to me or Sandy. I don't know whether we should clear out now, or wait."

"Well, if you two want to come out here, there's plenty of room, and the coach would be delighted to have you."

"I'll talk it over with Sandy and get back to you. Maybe even tonight, but definitely by tomorrow."

"Okay, see you."

I called Steve. He was in the middle of dinner with his parents and some relatives, so he couldn't remain on the phone very long. I had just enough time to tell him my story before he was obliged to return to his guests. He expressed his sympathy, and promised to get back to me soon.

The bell outside the main house began ringing. With difficulty, Ashley and I rose from the bed. Fatigue had set in, but we managed to rally ourselves. We walked over to the main house, hand in hand. I thought to myself that if it weren't so dangerous, this sort of adventure might be to my liking.

Blake answered the door and showed us into the dining room. It was a miniature version of the living room: high ceiling, rustic wooden beams, stone walls inlaid with logs. Some Western paraphernalia adorned the walls. There were two muskets, a fading photograph of an Indian chief, and a map of Texas from the days when it was an independent country.

Coach Petersen joined us. No one else was in attendance. Blake served the meal, the centerpiece of which was a delicious rib eye steak.

"We live in interesting times, boys and girls," said the coach, spreading some butter on his mashed potatoes.

"What do you mean?" I said.

"The president of the United States is making a bid to install herself as dictator. Could any of us have imagined such a thing at a previous point in our lives?"

"No, not me."

"Me neither," said Ashley.

"Jayesh, when you were here with Steve and Thelonius, I said that I needed to talk with some folks I know in the military. Well, I did. And I am happy to report that there are key people who are not going to take this lying down."

"What are they planning to do?" I asked.

"I can't discuss any details, but I can mention in very general terms what they might do. First, they could move against UNSAINE. It would be a relatively easy matter, logistically speaking, to clean them out of the country. In fact, it would probably take less than a week."

"Good," said Ashley. "That would teach Azala a lesson."

Coach Petersen smiled. "Unfortunately, it's not so easy. The problem is that there are elements in the defense establishment that are lined up behind UNSAINE and Mrs. Malpomme. The proper moment must be found. Act too soon, and failure could be the result."

"Right," I said.

"Another course of action would be to…how shall I say it…*lean* on the president to rescind her decision. There are some people in the higher echelons of the Air Force who are still loyal to the Constitution. They are itching to do something. I think a simple strafing of the White House would be quite convincing. Again, this is something none of us would ever have imagined. But these are extraordinary times."

We finished off our steaks. Blake cleared the plates and served dessert and coffee.

"Was there something else?" asked Ashley. "I mean, something else the military might do."

Coach Petersen stopped eating. "Yes," he said softly, looking down at his plate. "But let's hope it doesn't come to *that*."

I exchanged a glance with Ashley. We were both taken aback by the remark, with its ominous overtones.

The conversation turned to more personal matters. The coach inquired about my family and my childhood in London. We then heard some details of his own life, including many things I had never known. For instance, his unusual ethnic composition. Of his grandparents, one was Norwegian, one Apache, one fourth-generation Scottish, and one Jewish, from Russia. His father was a career officer in military intelligence, and as a result the family lived in every corner of the globe.

Our host married in his late twenties, after leaving active duty with the Marines. Shortly after the birth of their daughter, his wife accused him of emotional abuse, and filed for divorce. Not only did the court grant her request, it barred him from seeing his daughter, and saddled him with fees and payments that kept him impoverished for many years. After embarking upon his career as a football coach, he eventually made a substantial salary that dwarfed the payments. But he was not able to see his daughter until she was fifteen, and by that time she thoroughly despised him. He had never since been able to repair the damage to their relationship.

After the meal, Coach Petersen accompanied us to the guest house. He assured us that we could stay as long as we wanted. In fact, he would not let us leave until our next step was clear and well-planned. Ashley and I thanked him for his hospitality, and for sticking his neck out on our behalf. We were lucky indeed to have been sheltered, or rather adopted, at such a vulnerable point in our lives.

We spent the next couple of days acclimating ourselves to ranch life. We went horseback riding, visited the cowsheds, went for another long walk to see the far reaches of the property, and received two lessons in basic shooting, one from Blake and one from the coach. At the ranch's firing range, located a few hundred yards from the compound, we learned to handle and fire a pistol, a shotgun, and a military assault rifle. Ashley, who had no experience in such matters, eagerly absorbed the new material. She was not in the least bit intimidated, and proved to be a fairly good shot.

Around mid afternoon of the second day, just after the weapons lesson with Coach Petersen, Thelonius came to the ranch. I happened to be standing next to the bedroom window, and saw him pull into the compound. Instead of the usual chauffeured limousine, he was driving a relatively simple SUV. I found out later that he had sold the limo and let his driver go, in anticipation of rough times ahead.

I went outside to meet him. He got out of the car and shook my hand. His face had a look of great distress.

"Jayesh, I gotta see the coach. Right now."

"Okay, I think he's in the house."

We hurried inside. A ranch hand I had never seen answered the door and showed us into the living room. A minute later, Coach Petersen arrived and took a seat alongside us.

"What is it, Thelonius?" he said.

"Coach, it's something bad. Sandy was arrested."

"Tell me exactly what happened."

"We were at her house. The doorbell rang. I looked through the peephole and saw two guys in suits, about half a dozen uniformed cops behind them, and a bunch of police cars parked in the street. I opened the door, and the guys in the suits showed me FBI badges. They arrested Sandy on—get this—five counts of *aggravated racism*. If the whole thing wasn't so sick, I'd be laughing."

"Racism, huh? UNSAINE is probably behind it."

"That's their calling card," I added.

"So then what?" asked the coach.

"One of them said they were taking her to FBI headquarters. As soon as they left, I ran to the car and drove over there. But they wouldn't let me see her. I was advised to get a good lawyer."

"Did you?"

"Not yet."

"I'll call Joe Ruggiero, the Coyotes' attorney. He's good and he's connected." Coach Petersen picked up the phone on the end table next to the couch and dialed a number. When he had the attorney on the line, he passed the phone to Thelonius, who repeated his story. It sounded as if Ruggiero had agreed to take the case.

"Thanks, coach," said Thelonius, hanging up. "I was thinking of coming to stay here a while, but now I have to bust Sandy out, if you know what I mean."

"Of course. Take care of that first. Keep me updated at all times."

"Will do. Sorry to cut this short, I have to get back." Thelonius stood up, thanked the coach again, and returned to his car. I followed him there.

"I don't know, Jayesh," he said, removing his keys from his pocket. "It's getting out of hand, this whole business." He opened the door of the SUV, climbed in, and started the engine. "Watch your back, my man."

"I will. You too."

He sped away, leaving a trail of dust behind him. I watched the vehicle recede into the distance. Suddenly I experienced a wave of anger. I felt that my best friends were being stolen from me. In fact, whole pieces of my life were being stolen. Here was Thelonius, a decent human being, watching his own life being torn apart. For what? For whose gratification? What purpose did it serve for a young, intelligent woman to be arrested on charges of "aggravated racism"? I closed my eyes in an impromptu moment of meditation, seeking to calm my nerves.

No sooner did I return to the apartment than I noticed a vehicle approaching from the distance. I ran downstairs, assuming that Thelonius was returning. What I saw, however, was a delivery truck from one of the major shipping services. The driver said he had a package for Jayesh Blackstone. I signed for it. He handed me a flat cardboard sleeve, of the type used for express mail. He returned to his truck and departed.

I inspected the package. The return address was in Manhattan, and the sender's name was not familiar. How would anyone in New York know to reach me at the ranch? Was it some kind of trick? Was I a fool for signing? I walked over to the main house and knocked on the door. Coach Petersen opened it. We stood in the foyer as I explained to him what had just happened. He said it didn't matter that I signed; as he had told me previously, it's no secret that I was staying on the ranch.

I opened the package. It contained a letter from Raghavendra Hunter. Here is what he wrote:

Dear Jayesh,

I hope you are well. In Sundar Prabhat things have taken a turn for the worse. There has been a wave of purges and assassinations, and my property has been seized. I cannot return there.

Unfortunately, things have also become precarious in New York, and I fear for the safety of Indira and myself. UNSAINE agents are everywhere, operating with the full backing of the local authorities.

We have decided to leave this part of the country. We are renting a small recreational vehicle in which we can cook and sleep. Our route is to the west, and we expect to arrive in New Mexico the day after you receive this letter. We will wait for twenty-four hours at the Wise Eagle campground outside of Santa Fe. Please come see us there. I would like to speak with you, and tell you about our plans.

If you do not wish to meet with us, I will understand, and there will be no hard feelings.

Best of luck in any case,
Raghavendra Hunter

I showed the letter to Coach Petersen, who read it without any change in facial expression. "I know about this man, Hunter," he said, handing the letter back to me.

"You do?"

"Yes. He is well known to some of my contacts in the military. They think very highly of him."

"He's a good man," I said, folding the letter and putting it in my pocket.

"Go see him, Jayesh. You can bring him and his daughter here if you want. It's your call."

"Thank you," I said, pausing to collect my thoughts. "I'll have to think about it. You see, I have some other, more personal considerations that might dissuade me from following such a course."

Coach Petersen cracked the subtlest of smiles. "Do these personal considerations have to do with women?"

"Yes."

"It may not be any of my business, Jayesh, but I think that Ashley is a good match for you. I wouldn't treat her too casually. Of course, I haven't seen this other woman."

"I agree, coach. Ashley and I have become very close. She's much different than she was a few weeks ago." I laughed to myself, picturing her sitting up in bed, explaining to me the theory of *alternating reciprocity* in sexual relations.

"What is it?" asked the coach.

"Oh nothing," I said, blushing. "Just thinking of some of the ludicrous conversations we had when we first met. She was writing a dissertation on the contribution of Christian fundamentalism to sexist attitudes in professional sports. That's why she attended the governor's victory party, where I met her. I guess you could say that she was conducting field research."

The coach laughed in his understated manner. "Maybe that's what she thought she was interested in. But under the surface, there were deeper emotions at play. You helped to bring them to the surface. And when that happened, the earlier obsession seemed absurd, even to her. You liberated her, Jayesh. You brought out the real Ashley, the one who wants a strong man alongside her, and with whom she can apply her instincts of caring and devotion."

I looked at the coach with awe, amazed that he had distilled the situation down to such a precise formulation.

"What about Hunter's daughter?" he said. "What's her appeal?"

"She's attractive, for sure, but that's not really it. I suppose that she starts off where Ashley ended up. There was no need to liberate her, as you put it. And she's very wise, nobody's fool."

"I see," said Coach Petersen. "But all that wasn't enough to make you go wild over her."

"No, I suppose not. Yet I was profoundly moved, even to the point of being speechless."

"But you didn't pursue it."

"No."

"Why not?"

"I'm really not sure," I said, glancing down at my feet.

"Sorry, Jayesh, if you'd rather not talk about it…"

"No, I rather do," I said, now looking directly at the coach. "You're helping me to clarify things in my own mind. With Indira—that's her name—with her, something disturbs me, though it's hard to put my finger on it. It's nothing about her personally, mind you. She radiates this feeling of…I wanted to say servitude, but that would be too extreme. Perhaps it's a lack of freedom; a frightening world in which everything is structured and preordained. You're stuck with it, and there's nothing to be done. You can't change your life. It's all very deceptive. I meet this woman, and I'm enchanted by her exotic appeal. But it comes with many strings attached."

"I understand, Jayesh. I've noticed the same thing in my travels to other parts of the world. We all represent our culture to some extent, even if we wish to be unique individuals. You can't escape it—she can't, nobody can. You yourself are a product of England and America, and you always will be. You can interact with other cultures and even understand them to a great extent, but you will never feel completely reconciled."

We were interrupted by the doorbell. Coach Petersen opened the door, and Ashley walked in. She saw me standing there, and stopped abruptly. "Oh, I'm sorry," she said. "Were you two in the middle of something?"

"We're finished," I said, noticing that her complexion looked fresh and vibrant, probably the result of the clean desert air.

"Why don't you two go out for a ride on horseback?" said the coach. "It's a nice day for it."

"Yes, maybe we will," I replied.

"Just let me know when you get back so we can have dinner. But don't feel obligated, if you want to do something else."

"Thanks," I said, opening the door. Ashley and I began walking back to the guest house.

"One other thing," he said from the doorway, when we were about fifty paces distant. "I'm going to send Blake out with you, just to be sure you're safe. He'll trail behind you, so you won't be inconvenienced."

"Okay," I said. Ashley and I returned to our apartment. We spent a few minutes there to change our clothes, and then went to the stable. Blake was saddling the horses. Each of us took our appointed horse by the reins and led him outside. We mounted and began riding toward the river. Blake followed us at a distance of around a hundred yards.

I told Ashley about Sandy's arrest. She stopped her horse and looked at me with a pained face. "What are we going to do, Jayesh?"

"Nothing at the moment. Thelonius is taking care of it, and Coach Petersen just set him up with our team's attorney in Albuquerque. Thelonius is supposed to report to us as soon as anything happens. I'm sure they'll let her out soon, after the arraignment."

"But that's what everyone thought would happen with Sam."

"That was different," I countered. "You can't compare being imprisoned by UNSAINE in Europe with being arrested in New Mexico. We still have due process of law here, as far as I know, though these days it's impossible to be certain."

We continued riding. I knew that I needed to inform Ashley about the communication from Hunter, but each time I was about to say something, words failed me. I was quite frustrated by the time we dismounted at the craggy bluff. I don't know what came over me, but at some point I simply removed Hunter's letter from my pocket and handed it to her.

She read it with a grave expression and passed it back to me. "We have to help them, Jayesh."

"I know...I mean, I agree...thanks, Ashley."

"Jayesh, what's the matter?"

I leaned against my horse. "The problem is Hunter's stepdaughter," I said. "She…she likes me."

Ashley giggled. "That's all? I think a lot of girls like you."

"No, this is different. She *really* likes me, and what's more, Hunter had some ideas about our future together. He never stated it explicitly, but it was clear enough."

"Do you like her, Jayesh?"

"Well…yes, I suppose…she's very sweet. I enjoyed her company. But that's as far as it went. Look, all I'm saying is that having her here could produce some embarrassing situations."

Ashley gave me a quick kiss on the cheek. "I think you're worrying too much. From what you've told me, they sound like lovely people. She won't try anything indiscrete, will she?"

"Oh no, certainly not. She's modest and reserved. Nothing like that would ever happen."

"Good. So we'll go see them at the campground?"

"Okay," I said. "Let's go tomorrow, right after lunch."

We mounted the horses and resumed our ride. I felt badly that I had not disclosed everything to Ashley. I wondered, however, if it were possible. Could I tell her that I was attracted to Indira, and that I had been weighing the advantages and disadvantages of the two of them? And all that coming shortly after my declaration of love to Ashley. The wisest course of action, I figured, would be to avoid further discussion of the issue. I felt secure in my relationship with Ashley. What had happened was in the past; let it wind its way down the memory hole. Anyway, there were bigger fish to fry, starting with giving Hunter and Indira a proper shelter at the ranch and extracting Sandy from her predicament.

We returned to the stable, and from there to our apartment. Someone had left on the coffee table some sandwiches and soft drinks. After taking a shower, we ate the food, and then spent a relaxing evening watching an old movie.

The next morning, I found myself alone with Coach Petersen. He asked me to accompany him to the stable to fix a broken hinge on Peppercorn's stall. We walked to the garage to grab a toolbox, and then continued to our destination. I stood by as the coach removed the old hinge and installed a new one.

"So what's happening with Hunter?" he asked, his speech a bit slurred by the screw he was holding in his mouth.

"Ashley and I are going to that campground, the Wise Eagle, after lunch. It's just outside of Santa Fe. We'll see what Hunter has to say, and perhaps bring him back here."

"Good. You're doing the right thing, Jayesh. But realize that you could be in danger. Yesterday, one of the boys saw a couple of cars lingering around the entrance to the ranch, out by the main highway. It might be a coincidence, but prudence requires that we assume the worst. I want you to be armed, Jayesh. You and Ashley both. Here, take this." He reached into his pocket and removed a revolver, which he handed to me. "You remember the first thing to do when someone gives you a gun, right?"

"Check to make sure it isn't loaded?"

"Correct."

I carried out the task.

"That's the same pistol we fired at the range. I have an identical one at the house, which I'll give to Ashley. Do you feel comfortable with it?"

"Yes."

"Remember," said the coach, "a revolver is one of the easiest weapons to use. Once it's loaded, you just pull the trigger. No magazine, no safety latch, nothing. Take it with you from now on, every time you leave the compound. And carry a handful of bullets too, so you can reload." He rummaged through his tool kit and extracted a small leather holster, which he clipped onto my belt. "Load the pistol," he said, placing some bullets in my hand.

I followed his instructions, and then slid the gun into the holster. "Thanks coach," I said.

We walked back to the house. I went to fetch Ashley, and we joined the coach for a light lunch. After the meal, he presented Ashley with a pistol of her own. We were given several boxes of ammunition. He also gave me a set of keys to a super-sized pickup truck, insisting that we be prepared for anything on our trip to the campground, even for off-road driving.

Coach Petersen accompanied us to the truck. He wished us luck as we climbed in. It felt odd to be so high off the ground. Ashley loaded her revolver and put it in her handbag. I put the extra ammunition in the glove compartment.

It occurred to me at that moment that my life had undergone a veritable revolution. For some time, what with the trip to Paris, London, and Sundar Prabhat, I had been living on the edge. I thought of my genteel childhood in St. John's Wood, how quiet and urbane was my existence. It was another world, another life, now tucked away in the recesses of my memory. What connection did it have with my current reality? All of a sudden, there were guns, pickup trucks, ranch hands, craggy bluffs—what would be next? Would I be dressing like a ranch hand and helping to herd the cattle?

Strange as it seems, this new and different life felt perfectly natural. Everything came to pass with no resistance from within my soul. When one adds to the equation Ashley's new outlook and the excellent rapport with Coach Petersen, it seemed as if the entire turn of events were somehow preordained.

We set off on the dirt road to the main highway. I could see the advantages of driving this sort of vehicle. The bumps and crevices were negotiated by wheels which seemed far away from our elevated cab. I felt like I could storm my way through anything, and that was without even engaging the four-wheel drive.

We made a stop at Ashley's apartment in Santa Fe to pick up some of her belongings. Fortunately, the dwelling was in its natural state. There were no signs of intrusion. She filled a duffel bag and a large knapsack with clothing, cosmetics, documents, and some other items. I loaded the luggage into the bed of the truck, and we continued on our way.

The Wise Eagle campground was a small facility about fifteen miles north of Santa Fe. The spot was quite pretty, a clearing in the woods overlooking a small valley. It was no great surprise that the campground was sparsely populated, being that we were in early April, far from the high season. I purchased a one-day pass and parked in the most isolated corner I could find. We stepped down from the truck and surveyed the scene. In my mind I mapped out a search plan, a route that would be efficient without being too obvious.

Ashley and I began our walk through the Wise Eagle. We tried to appear as nonchalant as possible, holding hands and pointing to all sorts of "interesting" things that we saw along the way. We completed the circuit, with no sign of Hunter and Indira. I looked back at our route, trying to determine whether there could be any nook we missed. There was no way it could have happened. Something was wrong. They were not there.

We waited in the truck for a while, then decided to leave, fearing that we looked suspicious. The drive back to the ranch took about an hour. The weather was unpleasant. High winds were sweeping across the region, as they often do in the spring. All sorts of debris were blowing across the highway: dust, pebbles, plastic bags, tumbleweed, loose twigs. There was a constant howling noise, as well as an occasional splattering sound as particles of dirt hit the side of the vehicle.

When we finally reached the ranch, clouds of dust were swirling this way and that. Fences were clogged with tumbleweed. I was glad to be in the pickup truck and not in my Salzburger, which would have taken quite a beating. I parked fairly close to the guest house, but it seemed a mile away when we had to walk with the wind in our faces.

An hour or so later, just before dinner, Ashley and I were in our little apartment, relaxing and chatting. We heard a car pull into the compound. It was Thelonius's SUV. We went outside to welcome the new arrivals. After a lively exchange of greetings in the gusty wind, we all went into the main house. Coach Petersen brought us straight to the dinner table. The food was not yet ready, but we made do with an aperitif and some appetizers.

"Well, Sandy," said the coach, "why don't you tell us all about your little run-in with the authorities."

"Sure. The whole thing was bizarre. I was not intimidated or abused in any way. The FBI kept me in a small suite that they use for low-security prisoners or people who need to be protected for a short amount of time. I was not questioned, but neither was I informed of the nature of the charges, other than being told it was 'aggravated racism'. The agents were friendly, and not particularly enthusiastic about incarcerating me. They sent out for pizza and ordered a separate pie for me. Thelonius was not allowed in, but my lawyer, Joe Ruggiero—who by the way was excellent—was allowed full access."

"One of the agents did come out to see me," said Thelonius. "He assured me that everything would be over very soon."

"A judge arrived," continued Sandy, "and we all convened in the coffee lounge. An attorney from the DA's office joined us. Over the objections of the prosecutor, the judge set bail at twenty dollars, saying that he would have thrown out the whole case had he the authority to do so."

"Very good," said Coach Petersen. "It seems that there was some resistance to your political persecution. That resistance may not have been formidable enough to squash it altogether, but it's a ray of hope nonetheless."

The dinner began. We were served by one of the ranch hands, whose name I don't recall. Once again, it was a splendid feast, with delicious steaks as the main course. As we ate, I observed Thelonius and Sandy. They seemed very much at ease with each other. It was clear that a strong relationship was being formed. They balanced each other so well, Thelonius being demonstrative, sometimes to the point of being caustic whereas Sandy was restrained and cerebral. I was pleased to see them so happy, and relieved that they had arrived at the ranch safe and sound.

As we sipped our coffee after the meal, Blake abruptly entered the room. His clothing was caked with dust. He reported that a recreational vehicle had entered the south arroyo out near the main highway, and was apparently stranded. Another ranch hand had remained there to observe the scene from a hidden spot. Coach Petersen told Blake, Thelonius, and me to get in the pickup truck; he'd be with us momentarily. We followed Blake into the vehicle, and he started the engine. The coach was there a few seconds later, carrying a shotgun.

Blake moved us rapidly out of the compound, heading down the main dirt road. He turned onto another road that was narrower and bumpier. We soon came to a stop at a dark, flat spot. Everyone got out of the vehicle. Blake led us to the edge of the arroyo, where we met up with the other ranch hand.

The recreational vehicle was below us and about seventy-five yards further up the dry stream bed. It looked like a boat that had run aground. It was leaning to one side, and one of its back wheels was enmeshed in a cluster of small boulders. There were no signs of life.

Coach Petersen switched on a massive flashlight and shined it on the vehicle. The driver's door opened, and out stepped Hunter. He raised his hands in the air, as if surrendering.

"It's me!" I shouted, getting up from my crouched position and leaping into the arroyo. I ran right up to him and shook his hand vigorously. He was dressed in a plain business suit and tie.

"Jayesh," he exclaimed, his face gleaming. "What luck this is!"

"I'm so glad you're okay," I said.

"We are indeed. Sorry about not being at the campground. It's a long story."

"Don't worry about that. The main thing is that you're here. Is Indira okay?"

"Oh yes, just fine."

The passenger door opened and out stepped Indira. She walked around to our side of the vehicle. There were no signs of distress, though she did appear to be quite fatigued. "Hello, Jayesh," she said, extending her hand. I shook her hand and smiled, not knowing what to say.

We were joined by Coach Petersen, Thelonius, and the two ranch hands. I conducted the introductions.

"Tomorrow morning," said the coach, "we'll see about getting your truck out of the arroyo. In the meantime, Mr. Hunter, would you do me the honor of staying with us?"

"You are very kind. But I should tell you that it may not be safe for you to harbor us here."

"I'll take my chances. I heard from a very reliable source that you're a friend of Herb Rhinemuehler, the former U.S. military attaché in South Asia."

"Yes indeed, Herb and I go way back."

"Well, that's as good a calling card as anyone could present around here. C'mon, let's go to the house."

"One second," said Hunter, "we'll just grab our things." He and Indira reentered the recreational vehicle. They emerged a few moments later, with Hunter holding two suitcases. Coach Petersen instructed the ranch hands to carry them, and we all returned to the pickup truck. The coach got into the driver's seat, inviting Hunter and Indira to sit in the front. I sat in the back seat with Thelonius, and the two ranch hands climbed into the flat bed, with the luggage. We drove back to the compound. It was a strange sensation to have all these people, from diverse parts of my life, together in the same cramped quarters. I realized, of course, that upon our entrance into the house, the strangeness might very well be magnified several fold.

We arrived at the compound. Everyone got out of the truck. The coach instructed the ranch hands to bring the luggage up to the "blue suite," an apartment in the attic of the main house. He ushered the guests into the foyer, and from there to the living room. Ashley and Sandy walked in from the dining area. I took a deep breath and braced myself for the ensuing scene. In retrospect, it was silly of me to be so apprehensive. The full round of introductions passed with the highest degree of civility.

I sat at one end of a long sofa, with Ashley at my side. Next to her were Sandy and Thelonius. Across from us, on a smaller couch, sat Hunter and Indira. Coach Petersen pulled up an armchair, so that he was located between the two groups. For several minutes, he and Hunter explored the extent of their mutual acquaintances.

I had the sense that most of the time, Ashley was eyeing Indira. This was confirmed by an occasional glance at Ashley's face. Indira was also conducting a visual investigation of her rival, but in a circumspect manner. Meanwhile, a transformation was occurring in my perception of her. She seemed more plain, more ordinary than before. The exotic aura that had surrounded her in Sundar Prabhat, and even in New York, was not nearly as pronounced.

"Well Jayesh," said Hunter, "you must be wondering why you didn't find us at the campground."

"The question did cross my mind," I said, smiling.

"About a hundred miles outside of Santa Fe, someone began tailing us. When we arrived in town, I drove around for a while, but no luck, our devoted friend still occupied my rearview mirror. I didn't want to risk bringing him to the campground, so I headed this way. After a couple of hours on the back roads, our friend disappeared. At that point, I figured it was safe to spend the night somewhere close to this ranch. I had a general idea where it was located. I pulled off the road as soon as I saw a spot which looked like it could be negotiated by that bulky recreational vehicle. Little did I know that I was on your property, Mr. Petersen. Anyway, when you folks arrived, I thought we were about to be arrested, or perhaps eliminated."

"You're safe now," said the coach. "But your troubles are far from over. When I saw you down in the arroyo, you said it might not be safe for me to harbor you here. Well, Mr. Hunter, let me turn it around for you: It may not be safe for you to be harbored here. The authorities have their eye on every person in this room, to one extent or another. You may have stepped into a hornet's nest. Having said that, you're welcome to take your chances for as long as you want, and join our merry band of rebels."

"Thank you."

"I suppose you are aware of the crisis our country faces at this time."

"Yes, of course," said Hunter, looking grave. "It is most unfortunate. Many of us in the developing countries always looked to America for inspiration, and for help in combating the likes of Azala. We came to assume that it would last forever."

"Most of us assumed that," said Sandy.

"Such is human nature," said Hunter. "We mistake a transitory phenomenon for a permanent one. But the collapse was inevitable."

"Inevitable?" said Thelonius.

"Yes, that is my opinion. You had too much freedom in this country—much too much."

"But we're a free people," said Thelonius, in an adamant tone. "We *must* live that way. That's why this president of ours won't win. We're not going to take it. You'll see."

"Mr. Hunter," said Sandy, "why do you think we had too much freedom?"

"Personal freedom is a good thing, up to a point. And in the Western countries, you passed that point long ago. People became rootless; detached from tradition. They thought of themselves as autonomous entities, each person a little nation, not dependent in any way on the legacy of their ancestors. The result was arrogance of the highest order."

Indira released an enormous yawn that seemed to surprise her, being that she abruptly raised her hand to her mouth after it had opened to its full extent. Hunter took note, and with an amused smile, remarked that the day had been very long. Perhaps all present would excuse them if they were to retire. We said goodnight, and Coach Petersen led the newest guests upstairs to the blue suite.

Ashley leaned over onto my lap, as if going to sleep. I began gently caressing her back. Thelonius, with his powerful arms, pulled Sandy toward him; she rested her head on his shoulder. I glanced at Thelonius, who was displaying one of his patented wide smiles.

"Jayesh, my man," he said. "One day you'll have to tell us again the whole story of your trip to India, or whatever that little place was called…Sindy Porebait?"

Sandy and Ashley giggled, but I kept a straight face. "You mean Sundar Prabhat," I said. "Yes, I would be happy to give you all the details, as much as you care to know."

"Let's take a trip, all four of us," he said. "Someplace really unbelievable. Go wild for a few days. What do you guys think?"

"A few days?" I replied. "How about a few *years*?"

Ashley sprang into a seated position. "That would be great…a beautiful mountaintop somewhere, like Bhutan or the Andes."

"Okay, it's a deal," said Thelonius.

Now it was Sandy who released a long, wide yawn. "That's all for us," said Thelonius. "Time to get some shut-eye." He rose from his seat, and the rest of us followed suit. We walked over to the guest house and said goodnight, each couple retiring to its respective apartment. It had been a long and taxing day, and I was happy to turn in.

The next morning, after breakfast, Hunter pulled me aside and asked whether we could go for a stroll, just the two of us. I grabbed my pistol and we set off. I opted for the usual walk toward the river. The temperature was mild, but the wind was kicking up just a bit too much.

"Jayesh, I have something important to share with you," he said, as soon as we had passed the edge of the compound.

"Go ahead."

"I spent much of the night on the phone. My sources have informed me that I am in great danger. Indira and I must leave the country immediately. Mr. Petersen knows; I had a conversation with him early this morning, while you were asleep. He's lending us an old pickup truck and a rifle. We won't be going far, just to a minor airport less than an hour's drive from here. We'll be taken to Mexico in a small plane. We'll rendezvous with some colleagues in a similar predicament, and then fly to our final destination. Several possibilities are being discussed."

"It's a shame," I said, "that once again, circumstances are getting the better of us. It would have been nice to have you here, to be able to talk about everything…"

"Jayesh," he interrupted, stopping in his tracks and placing his arm on my shoulder. "You didn't wait to hear the rest of what I had to say."

I looked on with anticipation.

"We *will* be able to talk about everything, because you're coming with us."

"What do you mean?"

"Just what I said. Come with us, Jayesh. Get out of this crazy mess. There are only a handful of places in the world that are fit for living— for people like us, that is. America was once a marvelous country, but look what happened. If you stay here, they will hunt you down like a dog."

I looked away, toward the mountains in the distance.

"Jayesh, I don't know how much money you have and I don't want to know. But I must make you aware of the fact that I have managed to accumulate a small fortune in various safe places around the world. Even considering the seizure of my property in Sundar Prabhat, what remains is enough for several people to live quite well, almost indefinitely."

"You are very generous," I said.

"You don't know the half of it," said Hunter. "I also have a daughter, you know."

"Yes," I said, with a smile. "I noticed."

"She is such a good woman, you cannot begin to imagine. She would be loyal to you, unquestionably so. None of this American nonsense, where they do whatever comes into their head. No, not Indira. She will make you feel like a king, Jayesh. Like a king. And I will make sure that you begin your new life in the proper style, wherever we end up.

"Indira loves you, Jayesh. When you left Sundar Prabhat, she was in tears; she was depressed for days on end. Any mention of you and she would start to lament her fate. She told me that you are the perfect man for her, exactly what she has dreamed of, for as long as she can remember."

"I can't do it."

"Why not?" said Hunter, with impatience in his voice.

"I'm an American, my life is here. I am not going to run away. I have roots here, deep roots, and I'll be damned if we let them steal the country from us."

We walked several paces in silence.

"I understand what you are saying, Jayesh. Your motivation is honorable. But it is a lost cause. Believe me. I have seen much turmoil in my day. Save yourself and start a new life. There is no reason to throw everything away."

"I'm sorry, I can't go with you. It is very tempting. After all, one does not receive such an offer every day. But I know in my heart what I must do."

Hunter looked at me intensely, with tears in his eyes. Suddenly, he pulled me toward him and gave me a strong hug. He then took a step back, shaking his head. "Jayesh, it is tragic, it is all tragic. Somehow our destinies do not lie on a converging path. I have tried, I have done my best. But you will go where you will go, and I respect your decision. It is honest, and it is real."

We walked slowly back to the compound. When we found ourselves in front of the main house, he gave me another hug, and without saying a word, turned around and went inside. I stood in place, immobile, watching him slip through the doorway.

I was in the same spot several moments later when Ashley appeared at my side. I put my arm around her and began to walk, in no particular direction. The wind was kicking up, blowing dust into our faces. We ended up next to the stable. Meanwhile, an old pickup truck pulled into the compound. Blake got out, leaving the engine running, and hurried into the house. He reemerged a moment later, holding two suitcases, which he placed in the bed of the truck. He was followed by Hunter, Indira, and Coach Petersen. We watched them bid each other farewell.

"Where are they going?" asked Ashley.

"To a faraway land."

"Don't you want to say goodbye?"

"I already did."

Hunter and Indira climbed into the truck and drove away.

"What are we going to do?" asked Ashley, sounding troubled.

"We're going to wait."

"Wait? For what, Jayesh?"

"For the moment when our next step will be apparent."

"What if…"

"If what?"

"If something happens to you?"

"Nothing will happen to me," I said.

"I'm scared, Jayesh."

"Try not to be scared. My grandfather once said it's like turning out the lights, like bringing darkness upon yourself. He said that to me when I was a child. I was ill, and frightened over what would become of me. 'Jayesh', he said, 'do not be frightened, because fear makes you weak'. And just like that, I felt much better. All of a sudden, the ailment didn't seem as bad. I was still suffering, to be sure, but half of the burden was lifted."

"I wish I could have met your grandfather," said Ashley.

"He would have liked to meet you, too."

One of the ranch hands began ringing the dinner bell, and rather frantically. Ashley and I exchanged a perplexed look. We hurried to the main house, arriving at the same moment as Thelonius and Sandy. We all stepped into the foyer.

Coach Petersen was awaiting us there. He stood in a characteristic pose, one that I knew well from his demeanor on the sidelines during a football game. He adopted it whenever a crucial moment had arrived: back straight, feet apart, arms crossed, face stern and impassible, as if carved out of a slab of granite.

"All right, listen up," he declared. "Things are happening very quickly, and there's no time for explanations. Go back to your rooms. Pack one small travel bag each, and keep it light. Hopefully we will return soon for the rest of our belongings. A helicopter is on its way here to pick us up. *The war has begun, my friends.* Meet me here, just outside, in exactly five minutes. Go!"

The four of us dashed out the door and ran toward the guest house. Ashley and I scurried up the stairs and into our apartment. On the bed I opened her large knapsack and my own carry-on bag, and we went to work. I completed my packing in about two minutes, and saw that Ashley had stopped. She was standing in front of the closet, eyes roving among the various garments. I grabbed a handful of her clothes and threw them into the knapsack. I moved quickly into the bathroom and scooped up some toiletries, which I tossed into my bag. I then zipped up everything, slung the knapsack over my shoulder, picked up the other bag, and, with my free hand, led Ashley down the stairs and out the door.

Our cohorts were already assembled in front of the main house. Coach Petersen and the ranch hands were carrying military field packs, and had ammunition belts around their waists. Each man was holding an assault rifle.

"The helicopter is arriving in a couple of minutes," said the coach. "It will land in the clearing about a hundred yards behind the stable. Let's go." He took the lead, moving ahead in a rapid walk. The two couples trailed just behind, while the combat-ready ranch hands brought up the rear. We crossed the compound and waited alongside the garage. The helicopter could be heard approaching in the distance. The wind had died down a bit, but was still fairly gusty. I wondered how that would affect the landing and subsequent takeoff.

Coach Petersen waved us forward, and we headed toward the stable. Suddenly, there was a burst of gunfire. "Run," he shouted, "run to the stable and get down." We did as he ordered. Upon reaching the stable, we flung ourselves to the ground. I clutched Ashley to my side, and Thelonius did the same with Sandy. I raised my head slightly and saw the ranch hands at the garage, returning fire to the rear. Someone was attacking, apparently, from inside the compound. The rumble of the helicopter was becoming stronger by the second. The horses inside the stable were neighing furiously.

"Listen up," said the coach, crouching alongside us. "I'm going to secure a position off to the side of the landing area. When the helicopter gets to about five feet off the ground, make a run for it. I'll join you at the moment of takeoff. Good luck." He bolted. I crawled to the side of the stable, from where I could get a view of the landing area. The chopper had started its descent. I looked back at the garage, and saw the ranch hands lying dead on the ground. The gunfire continued; bullets were hitting the side of the building, just above me. The chopper was now hovering a few feet off the ground. I signaled the others to move. Thelonius literally hoisted the two women, one in each hand, and pushed them violently toward the landing area. They ran, followed by Thelonius and myself. In my peripheral vision I saw Coach Petersen in a small foxhole, from where he was laying down a steady stream of gunfire to cover us.

Two soldiers leaned out of the rear compartment of the helicopter, grabbed the women, and pulled them in. Thelonius ascended under his own power. I threw my bags inside, and was about to climb aboard when the coach rose from his foxhole, took a bullet, and collapsed.

"Coach!" I shouted, and sprinted in his direction. I hurled myself to the ground alongside him. The gunfire had ceased; I could hear only the whisking sound of the chopper and the howling of the wind. I lifted my head to gauge the damage, and saw that he had been shot in the belly. He was unconscious but breathing. I ripped off the sleeve of my shirt and pressed it onto the wound, but could not stem the flow of blood. Thelonius and one of the soldiers arrived, and they carried the coach away.

The old pickup truck screeched to a halt not twenty feet away. Hunter was leaning out the window. "Jayesh," he yelled, "It's me, Hunter. We never left the ranch. The coast is clear, I took care of those men back there. Come, Jayesh, come with us!" Peeking out from over his shoulder was Indira, her large eyes beckoning.

As I stood up, I became cognizant of my hands, which felt warm and wet. I looked down and saw them drenched with blood. A wave of dizziness washed over me. The weight of my body became heavy, and I dropped to my knees. Hunter and Indira were screaming at me to get in the truck. From the other direction, the same appeal was coming from my companions.

The next thing I knew, Thelonius was lifting me. He placed me on his back and hurried to the chopper. Someone yanked me upward, and laid me out on the floor. Coach Petersen was lying beside me; a soldier was attending to his wounds.

As the helicopter lifted into the air, I thought of rolling my head to the side, to try and see my Indian relative and his daughter one last time. Instead, I closed my eyes, holding Ashley with one hand and grasping the arm of Thelonius with the other. I realized that I was surrounded by my true friends, and could recognize Hunter and Indira for what they were: characters in a fantasy embedded in the recesses of my mind.

Epilogue

▼

I have finished the story that was bursting inside me for so many years. I ended it where I did because the conflicts in my soul were resolved. The choices were made; the path forward was clear.

There is no need for me to recount what transpired over the intervening seven years. There will be many stories about the war, some on an epic scale. It is not I who will write them. Men greater and wiser than I will become the poets of the generation, describing the numerous acts of bravery that were required to retake our country and put an end to the madness. These poets will enshrine forever the heroes in our midst, and compose odes to the millions who perished.

Today, I am too old and too far removed to play in the reconstituted professional football league. No matter. Life looks much different now than it did when my career ended on the gridiron of the 2020 Super Bowl. It is time to move on to other pursuits and other tales.

Jayesh Blackstone
United States of America
August 2027